Jakob's PROMISE

SANDRA WILSON LUND

OAKTARA

WATERFORD, VIRGINIA

Jakob's Promise

Published in the U.S. by:
OakTara Publishers
P.O. Box 8
Waterford, VA 20197

Visit OakTara at
www.oaktara.com

Cover design by Muses9 Design
Cover image man holding baby © iStockphoto/dlinca
Cover image woman © 2010 Jupiterimages Corporation
Author photo © Olan Mills. Used by permission.

ISBN: 978-1-60290-226-8

To Mom K
whose character, courage
and faith continue to amaze me,
and to make me smile.

Katherine Lowe Wilson
April 6, 1918—July 28, 2007

*Blessed are the pure in heart,
for they will see God.*
Matthew 5:8

Acknowledgments

I first want to thank the Lord for hearing my prayers, and for holding my hand, opening doors, and teaching me along the way. Secondly, I want to thank him for giving me my companion, strong support, and dear friend of over 37 years, my husband, Tom.

Answered prayer builds faith, and faith builds hope, and hope does not disappoint. I owe much thanks to my prayer friends and family who have come alongside me through this adventure and others. Our prayers are eternal, they really are, and yes, it sometimes takes an army. In my case, thanks are in order to so many I cannot name them.

To Lon Allan, Chris Cauley, Kathleen Ramos, Michael Phillips, and more, thanks for taking the time and patience at the newspapers to teach me whatever I struggled to learn...and for making it fun.

There are a few poor souls who have helped me read, sort, and change this work from the beginning. My son, Robert, whose advice I was most encouraged by, was first to read this manuscript. Very special thanks to Fran Villano, Marie DeKnikker, Larry Bonsell, Jennifer Neider, and Barbara Ertel, who painstakingly combed through my work for me.

Jan and David Kroll, Nina Hawkins, Karen Grencik, Chrissy Vaichis, Teri Snedaker, Becky Nolan, and Jennifer Neider have encouraged me more than they know. And a special *thanks for encouragement* goes to the Cambridge Rough Writers. Y'all have been a joy to me, and a great help, as well as a lot of fun.

My granddaughter, Naomi Konrady, spent a great chunk of her summer vacation reading for me so that I could hear what needed to be changed. I hope to return the favor in spades one day, because it is her ambition to write, too.

Love is given to man
so that he can challenge fate.
The future depends on love.
AUTHOR UNKNOWN

Prologue

1993

From Debra Brown's Journal

Lately an idea is stirring my soul. I seem to be mulling it over constantly. It is this time of day the obsession is worst because I am alone. Michael is out hunting with Caroline. They have found a common interest, and it is my fault I am not with them. I chose to stay behind, as usual and spend my day with my hands in this clay, which I threw and molded and now have destroyed.

At four o'clock they are just beginning their evening trek, side hilling, watching for stirring sticks that are really antlers, gray brush in the form of a body perhaps. I don't think Caroline really wants to shoot a buck. She just wants to be with her dad and find out what makes him tick, why this hobby draws his attention, something she doesn't ever seem to get enough of. In this, she's a little pig, and I call her that. She laughs at me because so often I tell her, "Eat, you little sparrow! You're gonna blow away over the canyon, and we'll never find you.

I could tell her that when her father hunts, it is the journey, not the goal that consumes his concentration. But maybe she'll figure that out for herself.

But it's not Caroline I'm thinking of today. There is a lump of exhausted clay on the wheel, and I'm discouraged with it. I have the idea it is a child sitting on top of God's shoulders, lifting her hands in praise.

Maybe I'll have more success with it tomorrow. Right now I'll pray for a little while. I pray, too, while I mold clay. I keep my hands busy, so much so that if I don't have a new idea going, I speed to finish an old one so a new one will originate in my brain. But all the time I pray. That is what I did today with the clay, and speeding it destroyed it. All the same, prayers are eternal, it's said. I like to think that's true. I have

i

to laugh. Sure hope that means that statue will be molded somewhere in eternity, because I want to see it. It is so clear in my head. I just can't get it to stick in clay.

Grandpa Herb says I am going about it all wrong. He says, "You can't throw a statue. You throw a pot." I know that. But the spinning is something that has to happen—like the world, you know. It spins. It doesn't slow down. I think of my first daughter when I work on this statue. She's 15 years old now, and I don't know her. Still, the world spins. When will I know her? This idea is what I am trying to work through by forming the statue while the wheel turns. To me she is still an infant, but I have to remember that time is turning. The wheel helps me do that.

Herb says, "Still, why don't you try it frozen? See if it works."

It isn't frozen. Her life is not frozen. Thank God.

But I think, *how does he know? How do I know?* And that's why I want it turning. I am afraid to work on it if it doesn't keep moving. The turning means she is still there, but it also means everything is changing. Her world is as real as my own, but separate. And then I think I will have to put away the clay. I cannot see her, and in my mind she will only spin and spin. But I know I will not stop. It's maddening, but I will not stop. It might be a blur, but I will mold and mold and pray and pray....

One

December 22, 2003
Meg

I got out of my car that December morning at the airport and was
met by a stiff wind, the kind that mocks anything humans wear for
protection. It was a fitting antagonist to my mood that day, so I
defied it to pick me up and carry me away, thank you very much. At
least then I'd have an excuse to lay down the impossible task I was
faced with. Patrick O'Malley, my late husband, would say, "Meg, get it
done." And now Greta, his agent, was telling me, "You've done this,
you know. You've been right there with him, in every trench he dug,
and he dug this one. Get up and fight. I want this done in the O'Malley
style, and you're the only one who can do it."

Right.

When Patrick died, I had to will myself to do the most menial
physical tasks. That hurdle took awhile to conquer, and I was proud
once I managed to get myself out of the house on my own and back out
into the world. But I was not proud of the way I'd ignored God lately,
and I would need his help with this project. Patrick used to say real
love never goes away, no matter how you treat it, so don't be afraid.
Just step out, God will meet you. But as far as my feelings were
concerned right then, God and I were strangers. The only prayer I
could manage was: *I'm sorry. Help!*

With my head in that empty limbo where fear deflates resolve, I
gave my fear to the wind. But instead of carrying me away, it pushed
me inside. I confirmed my reservation at the desk, and then took a seat,
positioning myself in view of the floor-to-ceiling window overlooking
the runway. I could see a wide arc of gray light crowning the western
horizon outside. It looked like a good day to fly, and normally this
would comfort me. Today the opposite was true.

1

Nothing was going normally with the novel Patrick had begun and I was supposed to be finishing. At that point, the project was a partially sorted jigsaw puzzle. The outer edges of plot had been neatly picked out and locked together in a rectangle, but that was all. Every attempt I'd made thus far to make headway into the gaping middle of it had not succeeded. I needed clues outside myself, because at that point not one of my instincts seemed in a particular hurry to conjure a solution to the logjam: no unseen revelation, no airy tap on the shoulder, no inaudible flip-flop in my gut save the gnawing trepidation about facing Greta the next day. At most I had a half hour to look for inspiration if the flight was on time, which it threatened to be. By eight o'clock I should be on my way to San Jose via one of the puddle-jumpers standing by outside.

Looking around, I gauged I was not the only stranger impatient with the accommodations offered at the miniature terminal. It was a compact version of LAX, a luxury RV as opposed to a villa. It would do, I decided. People tend to be more themselves in a small-town venue, and so, good for the watching. I scanned the building to see what I could find.

A lanky, pale-skinned man in his mid-thirties shifted uncomfortably in a vinyl chair beside a mock bistro table near the entry doors and adjacent a coffee shop/newsstand. He looked to be well into his second fill of Columbian and the business section of the *L.A. Times*. A salesman probably, but I would bet not a particularly successful one. Success fits itself as naturally into a suit as a Monet or Van Gogh fits into its frame. This one wore a tolerably well-fit suit, but if I were to turn my head and count to ten, that suit would be all I remembered, save the nervous fidget inside it.

This man most likely was not shifting in his chair because he was uncomfortable, but because he was too comfortable. He'd probably spent his early life launching himself out of such pedestrian terminals and feared the familiarity would draw him back.

It was my practice to liken people to birds when I watched them, and he was a scrub-jay, scavenging on whatever came along and fighting those who got in his way, particularly other jays. There had to be more compelling birds here.

Facing me two aisles away sat a woman in her mid-forties, give or

2

take, clutching a floral canvas carry-on bag. She appeared calm, but out of place. No. It was the rest of these surroundings that seemed out of place to her. I looked closer. She wore a tailored, beige cotton blouse and meticulously creased, though worn, blue jeans. Her small, narrow feet were curiously aristocratic, housed though in plain brown leather sandals. Her toes were painted so that only another woman would know they were, in a muted beige semi-shiny polish. They were perched lightly, side by side on the floor, in repose.

I'd seen this one before, but it was rare. This was a lone dove, waiting.

I followed her glance up to the information board above the gate, and then to her wristwatch. It had a red cloth band, and was the kind of timepiece found in a revolving kiosk while waiting for photos to be printed at the drug store. Finally she took a deep breath, closed her eyes for a second, and then dug inside the bag she held on her lap to retrieve a spiral notebook and pen. She opened the volume as though it were a practiced ceremony and a familiar retreat. It was a curious book, thick, with a pink and black cardboard cover in a stripe-and-slash pattern I remembered from the eighties. It was well faded, though, which I decided was a saving grace. Perhaps, and I am sure this is true; it was the only pattern available at the stand when she bought it, likely a couple of decades ago. This fact alone made me ache to know what filled it to this point.

She turned pages slowly, then set her pen to a blank page well into the end leaves. For a while she wrote, and her poised frame slowly mobilized into a rhythmic, practiced animation over her work. Her right hand hovered above the page, as though waiting for the wind to catch it. She crossed her legs and pushed the vinyl tile floor slightly with her left toe, exactly as if she were pushing off for flight. As likely was her hand's slow, tenuous feel for the perfect match of wing to air, and then her toe pointed upward. Each change of movement called back the scenario, until I imagined her in flight high over her surroundings.

I had to chuckle, out loud, unfortunately. It was a perfect analogy, but so unconscious on the part of my dove, that I imagined angels pointing my attention to the scene. Unfortunately this drew *her* attention and slowed her flight of concentration. It didn't matter. How could she know I was laughing at *her*? In her reverie of thought, I was surprised she could be aware of anything on the ground at all, never mind my thoughtless outburst. Still, I was a little ashamed. Just as unconsciously as I had let go the laugh, I uttered an apology.

I was rewarded by her nod, a flash of dimple that belied a spirit much younger than her obvious age, and the glance of a sea-colored eye, one of a pair wide-set beside laugh lines and over a very slightly uptilted nose. This put me in mind of a lady leprechaun (so much for birds) because the glance was more conspiratorial than indignant or embarrassed. There was not one hint of judgment in her reaction, like most would feel they had a right to in this situation. I noticed no change in her complexion…no blush. No. She was in her own world and realized I was in mine, so she was content to allow me my musings. Within an instant she'd caught another wind in her wing, and I was forgotten.

Behind her the double-glass-paned doors of the terminal parted, and a rush of heavy morning air from outside intruded in a rude flurry, blowing magazine pages adrift at the stand in front of the coffee bar. The lanky man's newspaper skittered onto the floor, and he uttered his annoyance in expletives that sorely berated small airport logistics.

If the tidal gust ruffled my lady leprechaun at all, it was only noticeable by a little ripple to her fine blond bob. She did not seem to notice. The interruption of my intrusion earlier seemed to have sent her into a deeper concentration. She was gliding easily on some warm and familiar current now, above all obstructions. Her legs remained crossed. Neither of her feet touched the floor.

On the path of air, which no one seemed to be unaware of save that one, a woman entered, mid-twenties maybe, pulling a rolling white leather suitcase and shouldering a matching bag. She was dressed in tapered tan slacks and a soft brown leather blazer. She walked easily, comfortably, in expensive pumps, straight to the desk, where she produced a ticket and delivered the rolling case for checking. Then, after deftly poking her paperwork into a side pocket of her shoulder bag, she turned and stared in the direction of the information board, glanced at her watch, which glinted expensively when touched at a

4

certain angle by the overhead lights, and then strode confidently over to find a seat.

I noticed her, of course, but I also noticed I was not alone in the endeavor. Eyes turned all over the airport, as if to say, *this is the true traveler—the way it should be. This is the savvy air traveler. Yes, indeed. We are at the airport. We must be now. Maybe it isn't as small as all that, and other true travelers are stuck in these joints periodically. We'll get through this now. No problem. Watch the lady. She's the ticket.*

Swan.

The scrub-jay finished collecting his newspapers from the floor, refolded them clumsily, and straightened himself as he pushed them under his arm in a rolled bundle. He gave one more sip of attention to his coffee, tossed it into a stainless steel receptacle on his left, and strode to the gate. I could not help watching him, knowing he'd not be able to completely ignore the quintessential traveler sitting near the preoccupied dove. No one had. But he didn't seem to. However, I noted a distinct swagger in his gait, like men produce when they feel themselves to be in control.

The lady traveler noticed this too and grinned. It was an elfin pose of mock appreciation, which was, in the next instant shed in favor of the swan-posture she seemed more accustomed to.

I sensed just under her elegant feathers, the swan's sure movements and easy humor, though, that there was a kind of fear, a cry for help, maybe. If it was not a fear of flying in small airplanes, it was a fear of something, I couldn't tell what. It was in the air so that I could almost smell it, though, and then I jumped because an electric shock like lightning stung my ear. This quickly settled into a slight hum, causing me to shudder. I had almost dismissed this one, this swan, as being too hidden beneath her feathers for watching. Now I was too curious to stop. I carefully stored the scene in my brain and even took out my notebook to scribble some words down that came to mind. Who knew when they would come in handy?

And that was when I knew something was completely askew of common reality. My pen jumped, and then flew, in an attempt to put down words as quickly as they bounded into my head. The stream of them was quite unusual, and they'd barely hit my consciousness before they fled to the page, manifesting themselves in black ink faster than I was in the habit of scribbling. My ear's buzz, the electric current I thought was an anomaly, became a companion. I wondered whether others could see it vibrating as much as I could sense it, so much so that I slapped my ear, and then I got the surprise of my life.

Not that from you, Meg O'Malley! I heard. It was not audible; it was somewhere inside the range of common hearing.

"What did you say?" My word, was I talking out loud? And to my own ear?

No. It's not your ear, and yes, you were speaking when there is no need. This, I heard clearly in soft, infant tones inside my head. Had I finally gone mad?

No. But you must listen, and you must write. I'll explain later. Watch that swan.

I closed my eyes, and took a moment to breathe in, and then out, in and out. *Write, watch the swan, and keep writing.* I concentrated, making myself into a patient following doctor's orders, breathing into a bag to avert hyperventilation. *Watch; breathe in. Write; breathe out. Watch. Write.* My pen flew for a while longer, and then I looked up, relieved that the vibration in my ear had stopped.

I looked up to see the dove, still high in flight over the pages of her journal. She appeared not to notice when the girl sat down near her. It was only when a word was spoken by the younger woman that she looked up. When she did, a smile of recognition and surprise animated her face, changing it remarkably. It jumped from concentration to recognition and invitation. To a stranger, the current of kinship was visible, but there was something more. Though the younger woman did not move closer at first, as you would expect a familiar friend or a relative to do, she seemed to want to, then hesitate, as if not sure she should, until the older woman patted a seat closer to herself, and then she did.

The animation of their conversation grew slowly, from polite head nodding to a lively interaction, until the younger woman looked back up at the board and rose from her chair. The older one followed her cue and stood. From the side, the pair of female travelers appeared in profile like copied silhouettes, the older a shadow to the younger. They moved toward the gate, smiling and nodding to one another, laughing.

While gathering my own things, I noticed my scrub-jay again, standing back at the newspaper rack. When had he returned? He was gawking at the graceful movements of the girl. *Aha, he's forgotten himself,* I thought. But my attention must have communicated itself somehow, because he caught his breath and looked, ashamed, back at his headlines, as though caught ogling a protected species.

I jotted my thoughts down in shorthand for future reference, and then collected my carry-on again to join the passengers boarding the flight to San Jose. I was desperate, drawing hope from my impressions of these two perfect strangers, that this was fresh life. In my experience, a dove is always a good sign that hope is near. By then I'd successfully dismissed the shock of my inner-ear experience as an insane overindulgence in my imagination.

It wasn't until the plane landed in San Jose, the hatch was open, and I had finally completed scribbling my thoughts that I discovered the plane was already cleared of passengers, and the steward was cocking an eyebrow impatiently at me. I needed to go. I stashed my notebook and pen, collected my things, and was about to dash out of the hold when something pink lying on one of the rear seats arrested my attention. I looked around to confirm that no one was left on the plane, then reached down and grabbed the book, not offering the steward an explanation.

I ran off the plane, thinking I might be able to catch the dove in time to return her notebook. It was too late, though. Who knew how long I'd been lost in my thoughts? It must have been awhile, because there were no passengers in sight on the runway, and none on the stairs. To my dubious credit, I had no checked luggage to retrieve, so did not think to look for the women near the baggage claims.

A writer is a curious bird, a parrot that thrives on mimicking whatever she can hear or see. She is voracious for the story, always—

hungry, greedy for it. And she has no morals where this is concerned, none at all. What are morals to the parrot? She will be forgiven whatever she says, because it is only mimicking, after all. Her glory is in the true enunciation of the matter, with intonations not her own at all, clear and discernible as the sound of the original voice. And what she does is accepted simply because she is what she is. She shouts out her words when she is alone; she may have stolen them, but they are her words. She's framed them, after all. The parrot, to her credit, is an avid listener, but a greedy one; she is a word thief.

I sat down at the very back of the nearest restaurant I could find within the San Jose terminal, turned my mug over to indicate I wanted it filled, and opened the outer cover of the pink journal. Within a second or two a waitress made short work of my table, efficiently handing down a bowl of tiny half-and-half bottles at the same time as she filled my cup with black coffee. I stirred in enough cream to soften my cup, and got to reading.

Several refills and a hamburger later, I was sure that my leprechaun, whom I now knew as Debra Brown, would be my muse. I had not been wrong in my hunch, but I was humbled by her reality, and more than a little ashamed at having intruded on her life.

Nevertheless, I had, and it was uncanny how the story of this woman's past fit like a map over my heretofore blank jigsaw's middle, infusing the pieces with discernible features that almost shouted out their place in the picture. I felt a troubling wind, as though the waters had stirred and if I jumped in soon enough, I'd walk away in a sure gait toward finishing my project. Whether by miracle or divine appointment, I'd found the dynamite to blow the wall down that separated my novel people from life. I buried my guilt about reading Debra's personal journal by telling myself that, if all went as I was beginning to feel that it would, I would not be stealing her life; I would be giving it back to her. And with that thought, a familiar warmth came over my heart such as I had not felt in over a year.

I finished reading and gathered my things just in time to catch a shuttle on its way to the Holiday Inn. At times like these, I am not the best of company, and small talk flies over my head as though I were deaf. If I had not been in this state, I would have thoroughly enjoyed a little more bird-watching. Instead, I studied the driver, willing him to move along. His only animation occurred when he leaned his peregrine neck out the window to talk to a cabby. I leaned forward to hear as he chatted about his wife and new baby at home while travelers trundled their belongings inside and shelved them.

A moment later the driver powered up his window and became an automaton at the wheel, stiff and unapproachable. But it was too late. I had his number, knew all about his child and his wife, and that he was real. Good to know the world is still real. So often it doesn't seem so— the larger the crowd grows, the more guarded people become. This is why I was surprised by the gallantry of a young man who stood up and waved me into his seat beside a woman and child, probably his own family, so that I not only did not have to glue my middle-aged self to a pole in transit but got to enjoy the cooing and soft baby antics of a probably three-day-old pink creature in ruffles and bows.

The low hum of the engine bubbled into life, and the doors closed to the outside world with difficulty, like a too-full Ziploc® bag. I was glad to be on my way, anxious to write. Just then my ear grew inexplicably warm, so I thought it must be visibly colored. I shook my head, but it began to vibrate so I could almost hear a hum, like a low electric current. I braced myself to control the urge to jump if the voice returned. But it didn't. It simply drew me out of impatience, and therefore my complacency to my surroundings.

I took another look at the baby.

The young wife caught my gaze and smiled, then interrupted my heretofore self-burrowing thoughts with a comment that confirmed my attention. She said, "She's adopted— just today. We're finally able to take her home." The wonder on the young mother's face was magnetic, and I decided just as prophetic as the book in my head was to Debra Brown's diary.

"What is her name?" I asked.

"I'm not sure. We were instructed to change it, but now it's Ellen. I love 'Ellen,' though. I wish we could keep it."

The new mother did not know I was stealing the looks of her little girl, along with her situation, filing them into my brain beside the facts of Debra's life, which were lining up with urgency. Heavens, I felt like

9

a bloated vulture. Oh, how long would this shuttle last? I needed to get to my keyboard. Still, I could not wrench my eyes from the infant, as if my physicality had been hijacked for use by a less self-absorbed person than I.

My impatience did me no good. The more I willed my thoughts elsewhere, the more my senses honed in on the creature in pink. She was a downy-skinned little promise of femininity, cuddled by dreams emanating from her new mother, who had the good sense of appreciation engendered by a little over thirty years of struggle in the world. The object of her love was a waiting vessel, not nearly as thrilled at the concept of being filled as her love-drenched protector was at the concept of doing the filling. Already the scent of baby powder, liberally applied, had overcome the close-put commuters' stale odor. The flutter of her perfectly formed fingers was imperceptible, matching the hesitant quiver of her lips into what looked like a smile of memories. I wondered what this newly delivered child could possibly recall to make her reflect such humor until another sudden vibration in my ear made me gasp.

The new mother mistook this for awe and beamed. "I know! Isn't it incredible how she seems to have come from a whole other life entirely? That she is formed and made and is her very own self already?"

"I know," I told her. "You can feel the connection, the back-and-forth pulling away from one world into another, like one is familiar and wonderful, so that she really has no fear of the other."

Oh, I prayed, *may this young couple never cause her to fear it.*

I looked up at the father, whose eyes were glued to his adopted offspring, enchanted. *There is such hope in beginnings,* I thought.

And then I shuddered, because as swiftly as I'd been assaulted before into minding the baby in front of me, I was overcome by sorrow through no means I could imagine until I remembered Debra Brown's diary, and that one person's beginning might be another's end.

I felt I had to be alone, and soon.

I got myself out of the shuttle at the Holiday Inn and into the bathroom off the lobby in time to grab a tissue for my tears, then sat down in a stall, relieved there seemed to be no other women inside at the moment. I vented my feelings, which took a good deal of time. When I was finished, I wiped my eyes and blew my nose. Reading about Debra's plight, then seeing the baby on the shuttle had gotten to me, I guessed. But the sudden weeping seemed more than an empathetic episode. It seemed I was sharing a burden too heavy to bear...Debra's burden.

Nonsense.

I collected myself, thinking grief assaulted a person at the most inconvenient times, and that somehow I'd managed to suppress my own feelings of bereavement too long this time. That was all. They would probably never go away, and I'd best get used to them. Hadn't I fallen apart at trifles before? Well then, I shouldn't be surprised.

My meeting with Greta was scheduled for the following morning, which gave me time to settle into my room and get to work. This I did with a vengeance, not wishing to lose a single thought. But I was only two sentences into my typing when I felt a tugging at my ear and heard a familiar but inaudible voice say, *Let me help.*

I couldn't speak. I hadn't the first clue as to where this voice was coming from. I'd heard reasonable people say they'd heard the Lord speak to them at times, but always through someone else confirming what they'd read in Scripture; that sort of thing. Whatever the source, it was calming, much like one would expect if they prayed and received a concrete answer. I decided that maybe I had, and since I was itching to put a few good miles into my story, I sent a thought out, saying: *Surely you can, then. Be my guest.* No sense making more of something than what it was.

Sometime later I was satisfied that enough notes had been written into my outline. In fact, I had slipped easily through scenes that should have stopped me cold. Where the diary's facts were sketchy, my mind was not. It certainly seemed as though the voice knew more of the story than Debra had written down. I saluted the invisible person in gratitude and closed my computer.

Tired and a little hungry, I slipped on my shoes and, as an afterthought, grabbed my address book. According to the last page of the diary, Debra Brown would be back from her Christmas in Hawaii in two weeks, and she lived only a couple of hours from my home. I had a friend in Atascadero who wouldn't mind having a visitor. Charlie was as alone as I was now. It might be nice to be together for the holidays. I found her name on my contact list and pushed in her number, but got a recording: "All circuits are busy. Please hang up and try your call later."

I made my way down to the lobby. By then it was past a logical dinner time, and I did not want to waste time in transit to a restaurant. I found a sandwich vending machine, returned to my room, ate, and got back to my keyboard. By the time I had three chapters roughed out, a fourth had materialized in my head, so I made notes out of the latter, then decided it was time to turn in.

Winding down wasn't easy at that point, so I switched on the television with the remote and surfed for news. Several news stations seemed to be reporting the same thing: something about an earthquake of enough Richter-scale clout to ruffle and jolt Santa Barbara residents…an epicenter off the coast near San Simeon. That was a good distance, I thought. It must have been a big one.

I'd heard earthquakes sometimes acted like a violent game of crack-the-whip, and those on the end of the snapping rope fared the worst, and sometimes those in the middle. Still, one hundred miles or thereabouts was a good distance. This wasn't any 4.0.

The San Luis Obispo airport, where I'd been only that morning, was located in the middle of that rope. Curious, I listened for more details, but I must have caught San Jose's conclusion to the story. The anchor promised to return when more information was available, and then the picture switched to a high-speed chase. Groan.

I went back to surfing and found a Central Coast station where the local news hounds were all over the story. Footage was rolling, apparently from Paso Robles, a small town just about twenty miles north of Atascadero. Plumes of gray dust billowed up in clouds around the helicopter's excited pilot, who said as much before he passed the dialogue back to the ground, just after I was able to glimpse what looked like a city block of carnage below.

Rubbled brick lay on the ground, and jagged walls stood like bent and broken teeth behind them. A small white car had been parked at the curb and was now smashed beneath the weight of a fallen sheet of roofing. As the camera panned slowly over the scene, I saw another vehicle, an SUV or van, I couldn't tell, in the same condition around the corner from the smaller one.

On the ground a woman newscaster identified herself as "Patty Fry, standing in for Chelsea Andressen, who is on vacation." The dust, she said, was fallout from one-hundred-year-old, obviously un-retrofitted, brick buildings, which had housed businesses only an hour earlier.

It couldn't have been live footage, I thought, because it was light out. When did this happen?

Sobbing and what might have been screaming, or maybe straggling sirens, could be heard in background noise behind the newswoman, who was struggling to make herself heard. I was watching a rerun, then, which had probably been aired several times since the morning.

"The quake," Ms. Fry shouted, "occurred just before 11:16 a.m. and was centered off the coast of San Simeon on the San Simeon Fault, which is part of the San Andreas system. It was measured at 6.5 on the Richter scale, and as you can see, Paso Robles seems to have suffered the worst of the damage from this one.

"We are live from downtown Paso Robles, where officials say two women were killed when the landmark 19th Century Paso Robles Clock Tower building collapsed, spewing tons of debris into the street here below, as you can see.

"Police are saying it looks like many buildings in the surrounding blocks of this downtown area have been damaged. In the Templeton area, located only ten miles south of here, some residents are reporting their homes virtually torn apart inside.

"Aftershocks continue to occur, and they are—let me tell you— nerve-shattering when they happen."

Just then another one probably hit, because the camera's focus dove and recovered shakily, as did Ms. Fry's overextended voice. The comparatively safe newsroom took over.

"We are getting reports that many people have been injured, but so far only broken bones and lacerations have been reported," said a calm male voice. "The elderly are being monitored closely in many facilities throughout the county…"

I watched until I had heard it all, I guessed, because Patty Fry identified herself again as standing in for Chelsea Andressen, and the screen offered back up its pictures of rubble and dust on the street. I turned the TV off and reached for my cell phone, thinking that maybe enough time had elapsed to allow a call to go through.

I had been sequestered in my room for hours, and I must have been in the air when the quake occurred, so that I didn't feel it at all. But a 6.5 I would have felt had I been on the ground, even in San Jose. Atascadero certainly must have been affected.

I got through on the first ring. "Hello, Charlie! It's Meg. Are you all right?"

My aged friend took a moment to answer, and her normally throaty voice was thin, even though she was trying to disguise it, I knew. "Oh yes, dear. I'm fine. I felt it, but I'm fine."

"Not so for your neighbors up the road, though. Have you seen the news?"

Dumb question, I thought. But as it turned out, it wasn't. Lines had been down all day there, she said, so she'd heard, but had not seen it. "How does it look?" she asked. "Where are you? Are you home?"

It was typical of Charlie to worry about me when she was right in the middle of a mess. "No, no. I'm in San Jose to see Greta—just for a day. I will be there tomorrow, as soon as I can make it."

I could hear relief clearly in her breathing. Charlie was pretty much alone in the world, with children and grandchildren so far away as to be completely unavailable in this situation.

"The news looked pretty devastating," I told her. "Buildings down in the middle of town, I guess. It's hard to tell much on television, you know."

"Oh yes. They do make a fuss, don't they?"

"How was it at your place, Charlie?"

I heard her take a long deep breath on the other end of the line, probably trying to get a little power back into her voice. She liked to play the role of my mother. "Not significant, I think. It was noisy.

Scary. The floor rippled like it was just skin on water. Couldn't believe what I saw! Some dishes came down; that's all, here anyway." Her voice had gone up two octaves suddenly.

"What's wrong?"

"Oh. Oh my!...another aftershock, that's all." She took another long breath. "They're getting to me. They just do. I can't..."

What was she not saying? I was worried. "It must have been frightening," I said. "I'm sorry—"

But the conversation was cut off, and I was unable to reach her again, finding only that maddening "All circuits are busy" message. Maybe, I thought, Greta could do with a simple phone call and a promise. I needed to get to Charlie as early as I could.

The next morning I called Greta first thing, and she did understand, probably because she had read via email the four chapters I'd roughed out the night before, and was able to tell I was on a roll at last. At least I was able to convince her that I was confident now, however distracted. Anyway, I decided it might do just fine for me to be in Atascadero to collect some more material for a while. It was Debra Brown's home.

I'd written enough by then to know there was more to this story than was written in the diary, and certainly she would want it back.

I'd finally gotten used to the little tickling at my ear soon after I took to my keyboard, and found that the same inspiration that had taken hold of my pen was leading my mind and therefore my fingers to fly faster than their usual speed. What I'd read of Debra's journal fit well into the frame I'd laid out for my novel, frighteningly so.

By the time I'd finished for the night I'd made a friend of the little voice. So much so that I named him Omni, meaning that he seemed to be omniscient, popping up at the most convenient and sometimes inconvenient times as I worked, to put me straight about this, that, or the other thing, and to fill in the blanks wherever they arose. I would not be surprised to find out later that the chapters I wrote that night were not fiction at all.

Two

Fall 2003
Debra

The day she met Chelsea was the day Debra Brown saw herself as she might have been, if she had not once made the hardest decision of her life. The more the girl talked, the more Debra felt like she had often felt as a child at the beach, standing on the shore while a wave broke against her legs, and then receded, eroding her feet's once comfortable, solid perch until she thought she must run or fall.

They met under circumstances Debra would not have chosen. It was one of those times she prayed, *Lord, you know what you're doing. I certainly don't, so I'll have to trust you.* But there she was, bedded down in a homeless shelter until she could get herself back on her feet, a few weeks after the fire that destroyed her livelihood. Her potter's wheel, her kiln, her tools, and even her stock of clay had been inside the cabin when it burned. Her work, some of it, had been stored in the shed, and that had been saved. It would be some time before she could afford to set up shop again. The cabin wasn't hers, it was a rental, and she had no insurance. She had just begun to make a steady living from her pottery. She had even sold a sculpture or two, so she had quit her job at the hospital some months before the fire, then let her nurse's license lapse. Now she was working as an aide at a convalescent home, the first job she could secure. But she had no place to live.

She had been somewhat prepared to meet Chelsea. The night before there had been talk in the shelter's common room of a news crew coming through. She had not watched the news lately, and she rarely paid much attention to it when she did, but there was the girl. The name was unfamiliar, but the face and the mannerisms, even the voice, caused her to stop breathing and watch, hungry for just one more minute, one more word, but the broadcast ended too quickly. For years she had met or seen young girls, and then later, young women, who might be her daughter. But there had always been enough doubt to dismiss the idea as wishful thinking. This time there was none of that.

Tomorrow, she'd thought. *I will meet my daughter tomorrow.*

The next day Chelsea led a camera crew up the stairs to the second-floor landing soon after the doors were opened, and the residents were settling in for the evening at the shelter. Debra was waiting nervously, doing her assigned chore, and praying she could face the situation with grace. She had so many questions. She'd taken time that morning to find out what she could on the internet at the library, plugging in Chelsea's name, then exploring the television station's website. She knew Chelsea was twenty-five years old, had grown up in Louisiana, and held a degree in broadcast news and a master's in journalism. She'd been at the station for a couple of months.

What is she doing across the country from her home, Debra thought, *if not to find me?* She wondered whether Chelsea had tracked her to the shelter, and if so, what did she expect to find? Until now, Debra had managed to temper her humiliation by remembering that even Jesus had been homeless for a while. But this was not the way she'd imagined presenting herself to her adult daughter for the first time. What was God thinking? Sure, she'd come through worse things, and only by trusting him, by holding his hand and putting one foot in front of the other. She could not imagine any good coming out of her first meeting with her daughter taking place in a shelter, but there was nothing too difficult for God. She took a deep breath, stood up, and prepared for what she knew would be a shock. She drew in another long breath and steadied her eyes on the doorway.

Unfamiliar chatter rose from the landing...the news crew. And then Debra heard the girl's voice reciting a monologue. She scanned the room she was sweeping. The two women who occupied cots across from hers were lounging, indifferent to the intrusion of outsiders into their temporary home. She wished she could muster their attitude, but then they weren't about to meet a woman who might resent them or hate them, or worse, reject them out of hand. That was Debra's fear, of course. At the very least, she was not about to make her dignified daughter proud, not in this setting. She hoped, at least, that with cameras rolling, the reunion would not be acknowledged. That much was a comfort. And maybe her assumption that Chelsea had chosen this story because she knew where her birth mother was located was unfounded. At any rate, she braced herself to face whatever would come next.

Nothing could have prepared her for the condescending tone of the young woman's greeting, polished and professional though it was. Debra forced herself to breathe in slowly, determining not to meet this rudeness in kind. She smiled, accepted the microphone, and looked into the camera while Chelsea repeated her question. It seemed she was trying to soften the effect of her words, restating them in a more congenial tone. She asked, "Have you been staying here long?" A little more controlled, a little contrite.

Debra considered the question, realizing Chelsea might already know the answer, but she thought she saw uneasiness and doubt cross the young woman's brow, so she decided to erase it. She said, "I'm Debra Brown, and I've been here a couple of days because I lost my home and my workshop in a fire. We all have our stories. I'm just grateful for a chance to get back on my feet."

The next question shot at her like a bullet, and Debra couldn't decide whether it was the way any reporter would handle a similar interview. She was probably assuming too much; she hoped she was. Maybe this girl had not looked her up at all. Maybe there was another reason for her to move all the way to a small town on the California coast from Louisiana. Anyway, it was easier to answer while thinking this woman did not know who she was. Debra studied the reporter's face for clues, but it was a mask.

Chelsea said, "How does it make you feel to be dependent on the charity of others?"

Again, that unmistakable tone of accusation...or was it condescension? Debra could not decide until a tiny tugging aligned her heart, and she knew. This was pain. And it was so raw that it drowned empathy, belying more resentment than a mere reporter's dogged sense of duty to expose reality would conjure.

Debra stared into the girl's eyes for a moment. They were sea-foam blue and dry. She felt her own fill with moist heat and closed them for a moment.

"Well," she said, making an effort to steady her voice, "we are all dependent at one time or another, aren't we? To answer your question, though, it's humbling. However, until now I hadn't thought to be shamed by it. I'd only been grateful. I'm praying that someday I'll be in a position to give back again."

She hadn't meant for her first conversation with her daughter to be caustic. She'd heard that these situations could be volatile because the child might feel rejected and abandoned after learning she was adopted. She was surprised when Chelsea returned the mike to her after asking yet another question, and even more surprised at the question.

"Are you married, Ms. Brown? I mean, do you have no family to help you?"

Debra gathered her courage, cleared her throat, and choked back her tears. "No. My husband and my daughter died ten years ago in an accident."

Three questions. Only three questions, and Chelsea knew her whole history. She'd given her first daughter up for adoption. She'd married the father of that child, Chelsea's father.

Oh, no, Debra thought, *I've just told this girl that she lost her father and her sister. Or, maybe I haven't.* Maybe Chelsea didn't know Michael's last name, only that it was my last name. But there was slim hope of that if she'd seen her birth certificate. Michael had made sure his name was on it. Why couldn't she have thought of a more delicate answer? A simple no would have done.

Still, the younger woman's face remained taut and professional, her voice clipped. After a polished "Thank you, Ms. Brown," she moved on to explore the other rooms, leaving Debra to wonder whether she would ever see her again, and wishing she could take back every word she'd said. Maybe she could have laughed and made light of the whole conversation.

Just then she felt a twinge, like a little gnat brushing her ear. She turned her head slightly. Something inside her rose, not in defense this time, but in strength. *Don't give up*, she whispered, as if repeating words she'd heard outside herself. *Don't give up.*

Chelsea

"Andressen," Jim Overman all but shouted, almost before he'd slammed the door behind her and pointed her to a seat in front of his desk. "What were you thinking? This isn't Los Angeles, where people are numbers. This is small-town county news. That woman you interviewed was a person. I talked to Paula Frean. Debra Brown has lived here all her life, and she's an artist who's made a good name for herself. Down on her luck, that's all. And that's a position I am tempted to put you in right now."

Chelsea massaged her brow and held her lips tight with her teeth, hoping to hold back the wail rising to her throat. She was mortified. Her eyes were red, swollen, and her hands were shaking. Her boss wasn't saying anything worse than she'd said to herself all the way home in the van, during the icy silence the camera crew dealt her. She managed to choke out, "You're right," before she grabbed a tissue from the box on his desk and handed him her resignation, which she'd written in the van.

He read it and nodded several times while he did. When finished, he said thank you, and that he hoped she would apologize to the woman, that Paula said it was in order.

Then he opened the door for her. On her way out, he said, "John Milton's been teasing me about stealing you for his paper. I think he's serious. Give him a call if you like. Until today you were good, Chelsea. I don't know what happened. Stay with Milton for a while; interviews go through him before they hit print, so I don't think this will worry him. Give it some time. When things blow over, come back. We'll say you're on vacation."

But he wasn't finished. He took her arm. "I actually had planned on giving you better news today. Uh, you won that 'Christmas in Hawaii' thing everyone was talking about last week." He reached back to his desk for an envelope and handed it to her.

She'd lost her job, but she'd won a trip to Hawaii.

Her cell phone rang as soon as she'd collected her things and made it out the door. It was John Milton. Apparently Jim had phoned him as soon as she left his office. She told him, yes, she'd come down to talk to him, right after she made a phone call.

Paula Frean, the shelter's administrator, was understanding; she even invited Chelsa back for breakfast at the facility in the morning. Apparently John had phoned her to say Chelsea might be her new contact for the Community Pages.

Three

Debra

That night Debra opened her journal, an old one she hadn't perused in years because it had been stored in the shed. She wouldn't sleep; it was a night for memories. As she opened the book, time flew backwards twenty-five years, and she was standing in her living room telling her parents she was pregnant. She relived the wave of their disapproval, crashing and receding while they made their plans for her.... Then she allowed the second wave of her memory to pick her up, willing it to carry her away from the too-large room, too-narrow cot, and too-raw memories of the unsettling interview with Chelsea.

It was mid-June, 1978—and the few hours before Michael changed. At least that was what he used to say. He'd so often told the story of their graduation day that when Debra thought of it, she could hear his voice again. Again the fluttery sting, the warmth grew in her ear, and she closed her eyes to concentrate. The whisper grew into a voice, walking her back into a familiar story. With her eyes closed, she could see it all.

Michael

Seagulls materialized in ever-swelling numbers out of nowhere, hovering greedily over the heads of the squared-off, white-robed rows of tittering, hung-over seniors set down in lines of folding metal chairs on the high school football field. As though rehearsed, at Principal Hodgkiss's last welcoming word 425 hands rose above mortar-board perches to offer anchovies in pay for the show the birds would surely perform for the sober onlookers that lined endless climbing rows of bleachers to the south.

Hoots of laughter rose and collected into a roar, which flew up and then settled down to meet grinning faces, raised to gauge the reaction they'd gotten. Michael Brown, director of the show, hoped it would lighten his mother's mood. "Pomp and Circumstance" was the one song that left her weeping every time she heard it. Actually, most any song or movie or bad choice of words had the same effect on her lately. She hadn't smiled since Grandma Hattie had died last year. How he wished his mother would smile again.

That was one thing he loved about his girlfriend, Debra. She looked for things to smile at. She was always on the prowl for jokes. He told his friends that if something was sad, it was for sure she'd be turning it over to see the funny side of it before anyone had a chance to cry. It was hard for her to be around his mom for that reason. It was hard for him, too, especially since he was missing Grandma Hattie as much as anyone. But then, he had Debra.

He turned around to stare at his girl until her eyes met his, and he could read her thoughts. She'd told him this prank would only make *her* parents mad. But now, the flash of her dimple—she had one on the left side of her mouth that tattled on her moods—relieved him. He shrugged to convey his sympathies, no apologies.

Debra squared her body to jump up. She was flanked by Rose Wall on her left, who stood five-eight, four inches taller than she. Dennis Walters, on her right, was six-four. Michael grinned and shook his head. *It's just as well she's surrounded,* he thought. *The Wallaces won't see her. They can go on thinking their little girl is the only one in the class who wouldn't lower herself to such a level.*

If you could count on anything from the Wallaces, it was blind obstinacy where Debra was concerned.

Michael shook himself and looked up just in time to receive a larger-than-life glob of hot, wet guano on his cheek. This wouldn't be the first time his actions had backfired on him. Sure enough, if anyone was to be bombed in this, it would be him. His dejection lasted a second or two before he noticed the caps, tassels, and robes of his classmates had been similarly blessed. Still, right on the face; it figured.

That was an appropriate prelude to the next hour's long tirade about dreams and visions and plans and hopes for the future, delivered by wiser souls. The bird dropping on the face was nothing in contrast to the pounding his ego took with each word spoken. But when he saw Debra walk up to the podium to receive highest honors and an art scholarship, he froze. Her gown was littered with gray and white smears. Her usually smooth blond mane of hair was matted with goo.

She should never have jumped, he thought. He'd wiped the muck off his own face with one of the handy-wipes he'd passed around earlier. But he hadn't thought of Debra's gleaming white-blond hair. It was no comfort to him that half the class was similarly defiled. He let out a deep, nervous sigh and watched as she squared her slim shoulders and quietly stepped back to her seat.

"Hey, Brown! Got any more ideas?" Harvy Bright was elbowing his left rib, hard, raising his sleeve for Michael to appreciate an admirable dome of white and black ooze, still dripping down to the hem of it. Michael noticed that his friend's gesture had transferred the stuff to his own robe, and he felt a little better.

Herb

Herb Jentzen squared his shoulders and straightened his spine, sighing and grasping the arms of his chair in a less beefy grip than he'd used in past years. His legs weren't as sturdy as they used to be, either. In fact, his arms had grown a bit stronger over the past few months since Hattie's death, because of those reluctant legs of his. He wondered whether he'd ever get the strength back in them. Part of him acknowledged that he didn't care. Part of him wanted to—care, that is—and part of him didn't. The part that wanted to was the part that still enjoyed his grandson. Michael was his joy. Hattie and he had only raised one child: Michael's mother, Katherine. And Katherine and Bud had given them Michael. Herb smiled, remembering all the T-ball, baseball, basketball, and football games they'd cheered him on at over the years. That was probably most of what kept him going since Hattie died, too, because he'd continued the practice, knowing she'd expect him to.

"Well!" he bellowed. "Better get up while you still can." He detested silence in his house just about as much as he hated being alone in it. Who cared; no one was there to call him crazy except himself, and he could deal with that.

Regardless of his declining strength, the man made a remarkable presence when he stood. He'd done his time in the military, served what he had to, and had come home. He had not liked it, but it had left its mark nevertheless. When folks first met Herb, they'd invariably ask, "Ex-military?" He stood just that straight and imposing.

Early on he'd taken to replying, "Just call me General."

No one questioned him until Hattie set them straight. She wasn't one to tolerate lies or fibs or falsehoods of any kind, but she did love a good joke. There were still people in the community who called him the General, and that was due to the times Hattie had smiled, nodded, and held her tongue, just for fun.

The doorbell rang, and Herb consulted his watch. If it was the good Reverend Jakob Highland, he was almost an hour early for his weekly visit. But when he opened the door, he was surprised to see Debra.

"Sunshine!" The girl dove into his arms for a hug, clinging to him just a little longer than he was used to. He placed his hands at the sides of her head and lifted her face for a good view. "What is it? I would think you'd be out celebrating. If you're here for the gardening, you did that the other day."

Debra cleared her throat and turned away, as though she was afraid to talk, didn't trust her voice. When she tried to, Herb could not hear anything but a gasp and a swallow. Her shoulders were heaving. He pulled her inside, shut the door, and wrapped his arms around her, wondering what could be wrong.

After a little while he coaxed her to sit down on the couch. She sat up and met his eyes with an effort. It took a long time for her to find her voice, and even then Herb could not ascertain what it was that had her so upset, until she managed to say, "Michael doesn't know."

Living with his Hattie had taught him something about respecting women's emotions, and this child did remind him of Hattie, somehow. Maybe it was the way she'd taken over the garden after Hattie died. She was as natural at that business as his wife had been. At first he'd worried it was too much to ask of a high school girl, so he'd offered her pay, which she accepted, saying it was only because she wanted to stop his worry.

"I love it," she'd said. "It's just like I know her when I'm out there, and like she knew I wanted to have a garden someday. It's only rock, brick, and cement at my house. I love it here." So, since Hattie's death, not a rose had gone untrimmed, and not a weed had been allowed to exist in the garden, just like when Hattie was there.

But Herb was a wise old goat. He knew there was more to it than dirt and roses. This girl seemed to crave a home. That was his instinct from the first, and he'd found out he was right. Gail and Ron Wallace spent the lion's share of their time running a neighborhood pharmacy, and when they weren't there, they were busy with a calendar-load of commitments. It was a marvel to him that they'd taken time to have a child, and a bigger marvel that it was this child.

Debra was Hattie all over again; she was gentleness and spirit and courage and playfulness. He could no more see her hobnobbing with the powers that be than he could imagine her taking drugs. Once he found her in the front yard socializing with a hermit who made a trek past the house every afternoon. He was a silent, slight, Ghandi-man no one paid attention to; the sort of personage one could easily have ignored by blinking. That is, anyone but Debra. To her, people were like flowers, to be cared for and enjoyed.

She must drive her parents mad, Herb thought.

But just then, she looked like the last thing she could manage was to speak another word, and this led him to conjecture one or two things, piecing together what he knew of the children up until now. They'd been dating since just before Hattie died, he knew that, so at least a year. Michael still talked about her as though he'd found a little queen, wondering how Debra would like this or what she would say if he were to do that. Michael was about as in love as an eighteen-year-old boy knew how to be. Herb, of course, agreed with his grandson. Debra was a catch worth keeping, and actually worth giving up about anything for, but of course he would not tell Michael that.

Michael had a football scholarship going, and if he could keep his pranks and hijinks at a low roar, he'd make a fine living someday. Katherine would slap his hide if he said that even an education was worth putting off if he could hang onto this girl. But that was what he thought. No, that was what he knew, but who listened to an old man nowadays?

Herb took another long look at Debra. Slight as they were, her shoulders were squared. He arrested a grin that threatened his face when he realized her hair was freshly washed, falling down her back in its thick, customary heap of gold and white. She must have had to shower since the ceremony.

Katherine had been in such a dither over the mess on the field, it would probably take her days to recover. He didn't dare tell her Michael had planned the whole thing. Not that he'd been told—he just knew his grandson, and that admirable endeavor had his signature stamped on it, no question. Only a mother could be blind enough to deny it. Looking at Debra, he thought it might be good to keep that a secret from Katherine for a while. From the looks of his girlfriend right now, Michael's parents would have enough on their plate without their son's latest performance to dismiss.

Suddenly Herb was sure. "How far along are you, hon?"

He met her eyes and held them steady with his own. Hers seemed to search for something they were sure they'd find.

She nodded, took a deep breath, and managed to say, "Two months."

As a great-grandfather-to-be will do, although it caused him a little shame, he relished some joy at the thought that the girl was healthy and strong, that she was who she was. She colored a little before she recovered herself and added, "I told my parents today."

"And how did that go?"

"Not well. They think it..." She took awhile to wipe a tear away that had spilled out of her left eye, and a little longer until she sniffed and got her voice enough to whisper, "They want me to...have an abortion."

Herb cringed. It had not entered his thoughts, although he wondered why it hadn't, after all. He knew enough about the Wallaces to have guessed they'd manage things in this way. He also knew enough about these things to know Debra would not be spared heartache, whatever route she decided to take. "You haven't told Michael, you said."

"No. I wanted to talk to you first. I can't abort our baby—"

"And you think Michael might be on your parents' side?"

"No. I think Michael will dump his plans, and...I don't want him to. You know that thing you say all the time, about two wrongs not making a right? I'm thinking about adoption. That's why I wanted to talk to you first. Maybe you can make Michael understand."

Herb took a moment to collect himself, and in that moment he was a little glad he'd let himself feel excited—even a little bit—at the prospect of being a great-grandfather. It gave him a small sense of what she must be going through. Debra's feelings would be a good deal deeper than his own. This was going to hurt.

"We'll talk to him together," Herb said. "But back up a little. What about your parents?"

"I told them, and they gave me an ultimatum. They said if I didn't get an abortion, I was on my own."

What did that mean? Who would do that to their daughter? Herb calmed himself. "And have you really made up your mind?"

What was she going to do? Where would she spend the next seven months? A wandering hope entered his heart, but he dismissed it. Having Debra here would be too good to be true. He didn't dare entertain the notion right now.

Debra turned to face him then. She looked squarely into his eyes. "Two wrongs don't make a right, do they?"

Herb shook his head slowly. "Debra, I know in my heart how I feel because I love God, and I'd rather disappoint the whole world than go against his heart on something like this. Where is your mind on the matter?"

Debra dried her eyes, then searched his. "Herb, I want to know your God. That's really why I came here. I'm going to need him."

There was a sudden garbled rumbling, not quite a ring, at the door. He'd forgotten the doorbell did that sometimes, every other ring, to his shame. Hattie's voice rankled the inside of his memory, saying, *"Love, you've got to fix that thing, you know."* And then he remembered: Jake, his pastor, was due for a visit. Now, wasn't that just like God?

He got up to answer the door. Glancing back over his shoulder, he saw that Debra had sunk back into the couch, and that lonely, homesick expression had returned to her face. "Not to worry, hon. That's my pastor at the door."

Debra

When Jake Highland showed up at Herb's house, Debra was feeling discouraged. What had she expected—that Herb would take her in? She'd told him she wanted to know his God, but what then?

The memory of her mother's words set her on the defensive. *"Debra, you have a mind. I expect you to use it."*

If only she didn't have a heart as well, and a broken one at that. Debra was about to excuse herself and go back home. What was she thinking? That she really had a choice? She couldn't see now how even God could help her.

But she did feel at home here. She loved Herb. However, as much as she wanted him to take over and make things right, she knew: *Love doesn't make decisions for people, it respects their freedom.* That much she'd learned from this child she was carrying. The love she felt for the baby was overwhelming, and he or she had decided to live. Or life had decided to live in the baby, in her. And that made her responsible for the child. The choice had already been made, but who had made it?

Mom, you're right, she thought. *But I have my own mind, not yours. And this child I'm carrying has its very own life and its very own mind, too.* Debra had never been more certain of anything.

She had never gone to Sunday school or church ever, even though her friends had asked her to go with them several times. When she was little, her parents said no, and when she got a little older, she'd bought into their philosophy that religion keeps people ignorant, and that it was responsible for wars.

She'd believed that until they'd told her she could not make her own decision, that their love for her was dependent on her doing what they told her to do...and that was to ignore the reality of this child she was carrying. "Let me get this straight," she'd said. "Religion causes war. You've always said that. But I think indifference causes war."

They'd said, *What about your life? What about your future?* And then she'd remembered something one of her elementary school teachers had said, and she repeated it. "I know this isn't convenient, but my rights stop where another person's rights begin. Someone else has a future here, and I have no right to take it away from them, have I?"

"Debra," her mother had said, "look what you're giving up!"

"Mom, I already love this child. I can't explain it, but no matter how much trouble protecting it will be for me, I have to." She was sure. It was a new concept to her, born into her soul. Love did not demand its own way. It was what it was, and it couldn't change. This love she was carrying inside her was stronger than her parents' will. For that matter, it was stronger than hers, too.

She left the house after they told her what she'd said was nonsense. She felt uncommon strength carrying her away, not just physically, but emotionally. And on the way to Herb's house she tracked her thoughts. She'd made the decision to protect this child, but she had another one to make now.

She knew that Michael would want to get married, settle down, and raise the baby. And maybe he'd be right. But if he was wrong, what would they be doing to their child? She did not know why she was so sure they shouldn't keep it, but she was. And thinking of what it would take to give the child away petrified her. That much strength she did not have, not on her own. She'd gone to Herb to ask him about God. It was not that she was rebelling against her folks. It was because somewhere she'd heard the phrase "God is love." This pregnancy was teaching her what love was. It was supernatural, and that was something she'd been taught did not exist. Now she knew it did. And she wondered how many other things she'd been wrong about.

When the doorbell rang, the courage that had been so hard to muster abandoned her. She knew nothing about God, and maybe she didn't have the right to ask him for help now. At any rate, the whole thing had to be put off, since Herb had company. Maybe it was never meant to be, not for her. So she put her feelings aside and prepared to meet a stranger. She'd have to think about God later.

Jake Highland was blond-haired and stood only an inch or two shorter than Herb at the door. They shook hands and Herb invited him in, then introduced him to Debra. *No,* she thought. This man was not a whole lot older than *she* was. The concept of this lanky kid being some kind of authority figure over the General shocked her into laughing, and she could not stop, rude as she was afraid it might seem. When she tried to explain, she made a mess of it. It was a good thing this guy had a sense of humor, something she assumed pastors did not possess. But then, to her knowledge, she'd never met a pastor before.

When she told him that, by way of apology, he broke into a spasm of laughter himself, then fell into the nearest chair he could find, which happened to be Herb's.

Then she said, "No! Don't sit there," before she could stop herself.

Herb broke up, too. It was a long time before anyone could talk, they were laughing so hard.

After they recovered, Herb told Jake about the baby, and Debra felt relieved. She'd heard of people confessing to a priest, but in the movies it was always anonymous. She could probably have done that, but not this. She trusted Herb, and she sat down, waiting for Jake to come up with an opinion, thinking that if she could wait his visit and his opinion out, she could talk to Herb again.

But Jake's keen eyes fastened themselves to hers, as much as telling her there would be no such postponement. "Do you know that God loves you, Debra?"

"I don't know God," she told him. "We've never been introduced." She dropped her forehead into her hands and blew out slowly. She hadn't meant to be so disrespectful. That tone of voice was the one her parents used when they talked about church people, and their attitudes were what she was trying so hard to sort from her own. They certainly weren't helping her now, but she'd barely decided those attitudes were not hers. She was ashamed. This was a man worthy of her respect. It was amazing to her that anyone could think otherwise.

"I'm so sorry," she told him, embarrassed.

But he only smiled and raised his hands toward her. It seemed an unconscious gesture, but it soothed her. "Debra, let's begin with what you do know. Why did you decide to make sure your baby will live? And why did you decide you want to give her up for adoption?"

"Her?"

Jake explained that sometimes he knew things, or maybe he was just assuming too much, but regardless, he asked her to answer the question.

She told him why, explaining slowly how she was clear on one thing. This baby was its own person, and she had no right to take its life away. And the love she felt would not allow her to be selfish. As much as she might want to keep the child, that wasn't best.

Jake cleared his throat and looked hard at her for a little while. It didn't make her feel uncomfortable, only surprised. She'd expected him to judge her, tell her she'd sinned, and of course she'd have to be punished. He didn't.

Instead, he said, "God has a way of speaking to us before we know him, a way of telling us things so we will listen." Jake took a minute to let Debra digest what he'd said, then added, "You see, he knows his children before they know him. And those feelings you have about the baby, that knowing, didn't come from what your parents have taught you about God, but it might have come from what they've taught you about love."

"They want me to—"

"I know. But I'll bet he's given them a love for you, even if they don't understand what they are asking you to do now. I think it's hard for parents to realize when their authority stops, when their children have to make their own decisions."

Debra shook her head back and forth, slowly. "They mean it, Jake."

"I know. All I want you to realize is that it is usually the child who has to step out and say she's grown up now, and it's time for her to make her own decisions."

"I think I did that, today."

"I know. You did what you had to do, but I think you feel alone, and afraid because you know there is something wrong. You're not meant to be alone."

Debra stared at him. The man seemed to disappear into his words, like they were who he was, and it was impossible to pay attention to what he looked like. Those words were his substance. She listened.

"You know, I believe God gave us parenthood and family in order to show us a picture of how much he loves us. Regardless of how we're brought up, we all long for home. It's those feelings inside us that show us what a real home should be, because there is such a thing, even though most of us have only seen it in one dimension. It's sort of like he sent us out into the world as a baby but tucked a picture of himself inside our heart so we would see it, and remember him. He is what our parents were meant to be, and we recognize that. In fact, we long for it. He designed things that way because he wants us to come home. So he's provided sort of a coupon for a journey, with every debt we owe for the mistakes we've made paid in full, so that he'll be sure we get home safely. And prayer is how we redeem that coupon and get back to him.

"You're going to laugh, Debra, but I don't thank God because my parents were perfect. I thank him that they weren't. Because of that I felt that lack, and I realized there was more, because it was a longing I had, so I searched. And that's when his promise kicked in. He can't lie, and he said, 'Seek and you shall find.'"

She'd heard enough. Debra collected Jake's left hand and Herb's right one in her own, and she bowed her head.

Jake said, "There will be a lot to learn, Debra. This is only a beginning."

"I know. But I've just found a teacher, haven't I? Right now I want to go home."

Jake led her in a prayer that sounded a whole lot like wedding vows, which made her smile and caress the child she carried, confident she'd made the right decision.

Fall 2003

In the morning Debra woke from what sleep she had been able to manage, and was again drawn back into her past. It was still too early to get out of bed, so she reached for the old journal. She'd started writing in it shortly after Annie's birth, hoping someday the girl would read it. Most of the story that had kept her awake was written down there. She skimmed over those early pages, finally settling on a few pages of an entry.

December 1978

I settled into life with Herb soon after I met Jake Highland. As a matter of fact, the day after that Michael and I went to see Herb together, and he invited me to stay with him. I had everything I was going to take from home in Michael's car. That was all I'd ever get, although I didn't realize it at the time. It took me over a month to get up the courage to go back home, but by then my parents had moved, and there was a FOR SALE sign in the yard.

For a long time I was stunned. I've never felt as rejected as the day I went next door to ask the neighbors where my parents had gone, and they didn't know. When I went to the pharmacy to ask where my father was, they told me they weren't sure, but I knew my parents had instructed everyone not to tell me where they'd moved. I was sure my father had simply decided it was time to open another pharmacy. He had often talked about it, saying he would stay right here in Atascadero until his daughter graduated high school and was in college, but he wanted to branch out after that.

I realized then how much of a disappointment I'd been to them. But still, I wondered, hadn't they ever made a mistake? Couldn't they

34

be flexible enough to love me anyway? I went over and over what Jake had told me the day he prayed with me, and it helped. I had to try to reserve judgment for now. But I guess my heart was still broken.

My father was a smart man, and he insisted I make good grades, just like he had. Even though he tolerated my interest in art, he made sure my science was strong. It was in my bones, after all, he said. And he was right. Science came easily to me, and so did math. My mother was supportive of him, but her main concern was that I grow up to be independent, and she didn't see how I would do that if I played around with a paintbrush or clay instead of applying myself to something more substantial. But being independent didn't interest me at all. I decided early on that if I did anything with science, I'd do it because studying medicine would allow me to work with people, not pills.

Anyway, all I really wanted was to have a close family. I thought that would be the most important thing anyone could have. I hope someday my little girl will understand how I feel. I wanted her to have a real family, one she could depend on.

Michael agreed that our daughter should be adopted, but only after Jake told us he'd watch after things and make sure our baby would be all right. I thought it was a lot to ask of anyone, and I told Michael so, but he said he could not give her up otherwise.

The day Jake took the baby, Michael put a ring on my finger and made me promise we'd always consider her ours, that we'd stay together and pray for her every day. I was glad he understood.

I'm still living with Herb. Michael turned down a scholarship to UCLA to go to Cal Poly. He said he really didn't want to play football anymore. He's playing his guitar more, and that makes me happy. He was good at football, but it never made his eyes light up like music does. His mom is even starting to come around. She never liked his playing football, and I'm sure she didn't want to have him so far away. But she will probably never forgive me for giving her granddaughter away. It is something like ice between us, something I just have to accept.

Four

Fall 2003
Chelsea

Chelsea told her editor she was spending the night with the mayor. She was slated, tonight after her first Community Page efforts went to press, to volunteer at the shelter overnight, and so was Al Quincy, Atascadero's distinguished mayor.

The Atascadero Homeless Organization, AHO, had only recently acquired temporary shelter for some of their clientele, twenty-five to thirty people who'd been coming to the community-run soup kitchen for half the year. The organization's director, Paula Frean, had given Chelsea the royal tour the day after Jim Overman let her go and John Milton hired her, so she knew the retired teacher had a way of arranging things bordering on meticulous. Chelsea had the feeling that an interview with this woman would translate into an easily written story, her quotes well arranged and thought out beforehand.

The stage was set when Chelsea arrived at the church. Several of the people who had recently donated blankets and other items were on hand for random comments and photographs. Paula began this interview by gushing over the reporter like a fond mother, telling her how grateful everyone was and how wonderful her stories were, asking why she'd left the television station, if it was any of her business, and never mind, of course it wasn't.

Chelsea wanted to scream, *Paula, I apologized to you, remember?* But she guessed the woman's candid graciousness was as much for the hearing of those around them as to help her get over it. A clean slate was best for all concerned, and best put out there for all to view, in other words.

"We're modeling this after the County Day Center down in San Luis," Paula recited. "They have a social worker on hand to screen people, for safety's sake, you understand." Paula had been hinting hard for Chelsea to stay the night as a volunteer, to ensure another story, no doubt. And she was right: the safety of the proposition had entered Chelsea's mind.

"It's important for the other clients and for the volunteers as well. You know, we have, at last count, thirty churches and service organizations involved on a rotating basis."

Despite Paula's expertise in arranging her stories, Chelsea had questions. "Where do your clients come from, Paula?"

Paula hesitated, having been thrown off course a little. "It isn't what you'd think. There is a new breed of homeless. Sure, there are still those who would rather drink or do drugs than eat, but more and more we are seeing those who simply can't make it in this county. It's become too expensive to live here, and wages have not gone up accordingly."

"Where are you getting this information?"

"The Food Bank carries all the statistics you'll need, Chelsea. They reach out through other organizations, and Hearts & Hands is one of them. I volunteer there."

"I know everyone contributes to Hearts & Hands, even the school children."

"Well, lately funds for utility bills and rent have been stretched to breaking. We send food home with families we know are living in campgrounds, making it on minimum wage jobs, and still keeping their children in school somehow."

"Your overnighters are these people?"

"Some of them are. The soup kitchen was a beginning, and we do serve many of the traditional homeless. When it comes to food, we don't ask questions. In fact, we rely on them to spread the word and bring others in for a hot meal once a day, and we send brown bags home for the times we can't be open."

Chelsea made scribblings of her thoughts, relying on her tape recorder to catch Paula's words. The woman paused, apparently having seen the tape come to a stop, and gave Chelsea time to check it, turn it over, and then beelined back to her original outline for the interview.

"Clients won't stay at the shelter long. If they're here, they're on a list to get into permanent housing of some sort. We have donations and other funding to help, of course, but most of these people have jobs now. With a little time they'll be able to maintain rent for themselves somewhere else.

"And now, Pastor Trukee, with the blessing of his congregation, has graciously lent us this facility." That was a quote Chelsea knew she'd have to use. It was customary not to forget a single service organization in these things. She guessed churches liked their kudos, just like anyone else.

Unfortunately those thoughts had sidetracked her, and Paula's words were becoming unintelligible for that reason. Also, by this time Chelsea had become so familiar with the faint Texas accent she was listening to that it was hard to track. Lucky the tape was rolling, she thought, shaking her head to get her ears readjusted.

"Are you all right, dear?"

"Oh, fine. You were saying?"

"We're mobile, though, for a reason. Someday we hope to have our very own facility. We're looking into grants right now, but in the meantime we don't want to wear out our welcome, and we want all the churches and organizations to be involved to this degree."

Chelsea was familiar with Pastor Trukee's church from the fated interview she'd done most recently. It was a fairly substantial, aging stucco building down the street from the high school, which had at one time been full, but the congregation had aged, and families had thinned. She knew Pastor Truckee had been sorting out ideas to fill the virtually empty space he'd inherited. She guessed this was as good a way as any to do that.

The homeless were now using the two-story classroom building for sleeping quarters, and the huge kitchen and dining area for their meals. Since removable cots were their beds and the clients were on their way before 8 a.m., the buildings were available for church services and activities most of the time. Chelsea had been told that the church membership had dwindled to the point that these rooms were not being used anyway. The facilities here were much too large for the twenty or so Sunday morning regulars.

As Paula approached the second-floor landing, she was beaming—

obviously proud that so much had been accomplished in such a short time. Chelsea was impressed. The new cots Paula had purchased were arranged in two large rooms, separated by a hallway. Neat stacks of blankets, towels, pillows, and even backpacks in a hodge-podge of colors and shapes decorated the head and foot of each cot where residents had left them. A side door led into a privacy room, reserved for families with small children. In there were two cots, a crib, and a playpen. This was meant to provide a little early quiet for the youngsters, Paula told her. Another door a few paces from that one opened into a visiting/television room where schedules and rules were posted, along with a sign-up sheet for volunteers.

Chelsea eyed the coffee pot. Paula smiled graciously and nodded an invitation toward it, so she poured herself a cup, took a gulp, and filled in a blank with her name on the calendar for the upcoming Thursday night. *There*, she thought. *It's in pen. I can't erase it.* Her host had dropped all of seven hints about needing volunteers between the parking lot and the stairs. Why not?

She scanned the puzzled faces of the photo ops who'd come in for the staged orientation, recognizing a few from various stories she'd covered. She would kick herself later, she knew. Had she signed in only to impress these do-gooders? It *was* a good thing, what Paula was doing, what all of them were doing, but was that the only reason she'd signed up, to impress them? Where was her head? It would make a good story; it would be a new experience; it would be different. All good reasons, but she suspected her motive was base, and though she could not identify why, it made her feel ashamed.

And now, here she was, sitting at her desk on Thursday afternoon, trying to edit some gnarly copy from the last Community Page writer's notes on school board policy. She wished she didn't have the added stress of wondering what she was going to do tonight at the shelter. She decided to forget about the night until the hour got closer. But with that thought, the picture of Debra Brown's face came into focus in her mind, and she wilted inside. She was at war with herself over that woman, knowing she owed her an apology. Part of her hoped the woman would be gone, into her own place by now. Part of her wanted another crack at her. She could do that now, off the record. That soft, forthright exterior rankled Chelsea's temper. Seeing that woman was like having someone put a mirror up in her face—a mocking, bouncing, taunting mirror of failure.

That much of what she'd found out was true. The woman had a history of tossing her past away like an old shoe, for someone else to deal with. Who in their right mind would give up a decent wage as a nurse to eke out a living playing with clay? She'd wound up making her bed in a homeless shelter, no less, giving even the responsibility of her living to someone else. *Why didn't she deal with things, just deal with them, like I did?*

But what really hurt, if Chelsea would admit it, was that Debra had married Michael Brown. So why didn't they keep their child? They just went right out and had another one, didn't they?

Chelsea squared her shoulders and lifted her chin. She wouldn't think about that anymore. She refused to. It was all too much right now. With a motion of her hand, like batting an annoying gnat, it was over. She'd say what she had to say to the woman, no more. She wanted nothing more to do with Debra Brown, just like she wanted no more to do with her parents. That was over, best bury it all, and Debra with it. This little adventure had at least carried her away from Louisiana. That, she thought, was enough for now.

She settled into her desk, satisfied. It was comfortable here, and in truth, she'd been uncomfortable on camera, and even more uncomfortable doing live interviews. This was her niche, and a good way to thumb her nose at her parents' ambition for her. She would have her own ambitions, thank you. Yes. It was good to be here. Chelsea loved to write, even though a good percentage of the copy she was required to produce was tedious. And she was left alone to do it. The deadlines kept her mind off anything and everything else.

In many ways a newsroom was the same, whether in print or on camera. Chelsea could not get used to the deference people paid her, or sometimes the frost, when they found out she was press of any kind. It had been more blatant at the station, but it was a problem here as well. There were times it opened doors, but sometimes it was a real impediment. Tonight she truly wished she was just Josie Schmoe, come to lend a hand.

There is the building, now what do I do? It was Chelsea's nature to slow down when she was apprehensive. *Logically, I need to park, shut down my engine, gather my things, and get out of the car.* Looking at the group of men hanging around the front entrance to the shelter, she decided to lock her car doors. *I'll be here all night. Normal thing to do. Still, will they think I'm afraid they'll steal my car?*

She took a deep breath while she retrieved information in her head. *What is it I'm supposed to do now?*

No clue.

She got out of her car and walked toward the barred door to ask. *Now I feel strange. Here I am supposed to be the volunteer in charge— or was that Mayor Quincy?* She scanned the group hanging out near the door. The mayor was on the periphery scratching his head.

Good. Real good.

An erstwhile school bus rolled up about fifty yards from her Taurus and dispatched several people. She noticed they were a diverse group, not what she'd expected. They dismounted in clumps, some of them, and others straggled, singly. One man, late thirties or so, gripped the hand of a little girl, maybe three or four years old. Another one, a black man walked with his head held forcibly up, toward her. She smiled at him, then noticed the driver, and moved toward him quickly, hoping he knew more than she did, at least where the key was and what to do next. She was intercepted, though, before she could reach him.

"Ma'am?"

Chelsea smiled again at the black man, shook his hand, and offered her name in exchange for his.

"Bert," he answered amiably.

Never were last names exchanged.

Almost imperceptibly, she noticed, he dipped his head, and then pushed it back up to show her a determined smile.

"Is the bus driver staying? Do you know?"

"No. He just took us for a shower down the road."

Chelsea caught the eye of the tallish, thin driver, and he too came to greet her. He looked confident. *Not a pastor,* she thought. *Too efficient, too hurried.*

The black man stayed. *This is his home,* she thought, realizing he was trying to be hospitable. The others smiled, too, as they passed her.

The driver approached, grabbed her hand, and pumped it athletically. "Tom," he stated. "I'll open up." While he walked, not to waste a minute—there was one left before seven o'clock—he kept talking. "One of you needs to hold the key and give it to the volunteer who'll close up and check things in the morning."

"Thanks." She had more questions, but trusted the mayor knew more than she did. *Maybe he expects the know-it-all reporter to have the info, though.* Granted, most of it was written somewhere in the mounds of copy on her desk, but not in her head and her briefcase was locked in the car at the moment, because tonight she did not want to be the nosy, pencil-snapping scribe.

She remembered the posted memos Paula had pinned up inside and breathed in a little relief in the cooling air, noticing the dusk pulling down past the hillside houses beyond the parking lot. Chelsea shivered, thinking that instinct causes everyone to seek cover this time of night in the winter. She wondered how these people dealt with it before the shelter opened.

Bert's voice pulled her out of her thoughts. She hoped he hadn't been talking very long because she had not been listening.

"...a volunteer tonight?"

"Yes."

He fell into step with her, and Tom strode ahead of them confidently, nodding to Quincy. The two fell in line ahead of Chelsea and Bert, who continued talking.

"Sure appreciate your comin', Miz Chelsea."

His words caused her to skip a breath and study him again. He was only a few inches taller than she, stout, and he spoke with an accent familiar to her. It came from Louisiana, not far south of Natchitoches, where she grew up. She was sure of it. Not quite Cajun, no French slurs. He must have worked on it, hard. He could be one of her peers at Northwestern, easily. She wasn't used to real hospitality here on the coast, and she'd buried her longing for it, and here it was again, reminding her of a spreading Magnolia on the Cane, drawing her in. He must miss it desperately.

What was that he'd said? Thank you? *You're inviting me to stay in what is your only home, and I'm on my way back to a comfortable apartment tomorrow. This is all you have to give and I know it is not near the comfort you're used to, but you're sharing it—and thanking me?*

She took a few steps forward. "It's good to be here. Have you been staying here since it opened, Bert?"

"Yes, ma'am, I have." He motioned toward the door, which Tom was opening. "Me an' most of 'em up ahead. We have six weeks, an' we're all on a list to find a place. Social worker comes in the mornin' to talk to us. He got me a job; first day's tomorrow."

"Where will you work?"

"Rest'rant—fish place on The El Camino. I've done rest'rant work b'fore."

By then they were at the door. Bert found his way through, and then nodded back at Chelsea before he headed up stairs that rose immediately inside on the left.

She introduced herself to the mayor, and offered her hand.

Quincy shook it, nodded, and offered his name.

He looks more lost than I feel, she thought.

By then Tom was into a spiel that Chelsea did not want to miss. She itched to take notes. The man dangled a set of keys out, wagging it between the two volunteers, who together looked at it like it was a game of hot potato they were playing until Quincy remembered he was the mayor, after all, and reached for it with only a little more confidence than his eyes reflected, which was precious little.

Chelsea took a deep breath, grateful but apprehensive. *I'm not the only one, but unfortunately it's just the two of us, and this guy Tom seems in a hurry to pass the baton here.*

The two volunteers filed into the wide hallway behind the residents and their guide while he explained that if anyone wanted to smoke, they were to go outside, supervised. He nodded over his shoulder, referring to the spot outside the double doors where the group had just been waiting, and said, "One of you is to accompany them for a fifteen-minute break at each cigarette call, every hour, till bedtime…that'd be 10 o'clock. Everyone is up by six, out by seven; at seven, breakfast is served in the kitchen, and before then, everyone has their assigned chores." He pushed a clipboard at Chelsea. On it was a spreadsheet with names corresponding to chores. He told them they were both to keep a roll call, and count often.

She was beginning to get even more nervous, which Tom seemed to discern. He assured her, "They'll tell you when they've finished, and then you just mark it off. Make sure everything is done, but they're good about it. You aren't supposed to do the chores yourselves. They're grateful to be here, and it works out well. After all, it's their home for now, so they're taking care of it."

They'd been paused at the foot of the stairs while several more of the residents moved up ahead of them. Tom ushered the pair of novices past the stairway and down to the ground floor hallway, then opened a door on the left. More clients had arrived and were dismounting bicycles and lining them up against the walls along the hallway. A few of the bikes, Chelsea noticed, had child seats attached above the rear tire guard.

Tom followed her gaze. "The lucky ones have cars," he said. Then, quickly he waved Quincy and Chelsea into a large classroom where two cots were placed along one wall. "This is your sleep room. You'll need to decide which shifts you'll be taking, so one of you can sleep while the other stays upstairs in the day room. One or the other of you needs to be awake all the time. You can keep your things here. The door's kept locked."

Quincy offered to take first shift awake, and Chelsea agreed, but thought she wouldn't be able to sleep early or late, not here in this cold, echoing space with the narrow cots.

With their belongings stashed and the door locked, the two followed Tom back through the hallway and up the wide switchback stairs to the second floor landing.

Immediately Bert was back, looking over her shoulder at the clipboard she held. He pointed, "I'm on laundry tonight. That's me…" He took the pen-on-the-string from her and drew in an X after his name. Apparently in the time it had taken the three of them to view the basement sleeping quarters, Bert had gathered two bags full of dirty sheets. A small closet opened into a washer and dryer area next to the stairs and to the left. One machine was noisily at work.

Chelsea passed two heavy-set women rolling out bedding in the women's quarters, but she was remembering her first foray into this world, and another woman, slim and enterprising, wielding a broom across the room from where the two would sleep, just inside the door. Debra had looked up when Chelsea passed by with the crew that day, and she'd come to the doorway and smiled—a snapshot of serenity—out of place here, the reporter thought, completely odd in these circumstances. And when she'd shoved a microphone into her face, love seemed to dance out of the woman's eyes, and the only thing Chelsea had been able to think was: *How dare she! For the sake of sanity, be sad; that's all I ask. You're in a shelter, for the love of Pete. At least be sad.*

Chelsea looked around for any signs of Debra near the bed she assumed was hers. Inside, the institutional brown tile floor holding up temporary beds had been transformed by a stand of colored bottles neatly arranged on a folding table beside a cot. A small volume, probably a journal, sat on top of a neatly zipped sleeping bag, and a brightly colored comforter was folded perfectly at the foot of it.

But no Debra.

"Hullo!" Chelsea heard a woman's voice call from across the room. "My job...we have to wake up early, so I try to get my chores done at night." But now it was not Debra's soft, cheery voice speaking; it was one of the others.

"Oh." Chelsea looked down at the spreadsheet on her clipboard. "I'll mark it off then. I'm Chelsea, by the way." This time, instead of Debra's bright introduction and handshake, Chelsea received a tired, reluctant nod before the woman put down her broom, turned away, and unrolled her sleeping bag.

Bert caught her attention again. "You'll need to sign in at the TV room. I'll take you there."

At that point Chelsea realized she'd lost sight of Tom, but when Bert led her around the corner, through the men's quarters and into the television room, she found him talking to Quincy. She nodded a thanks to her escort and fell in beside the mayor for more instructions.

The two men were examining the rules posted to the door, and though Paula had reiterated every one of them to her painstakingly at her previous tour, Chelsea glued her attention to them now. She noted Quincy looked more secure. He was gripping the keys in one hand, and Tom was showing him which was which. Apparently they were in charge of a safe in that room, where people could leave small items of value. On the poster it said that all valuables were to be locked up for the evening. She guessed that was meant to alleviate problems, not create them, but what if she or Quincy was accused of taking something? Paula had thought of that, too.

"All items are signed for, both in and out," Tom told them as he opened the safe and motioned to another small clipboard, with spreadsheet and a pen-on-a-string attached.

Quincy was growing visibly calmer by the minute, and by osmosis, she was too, but it was both disconcerting and reassuring that the clients seemed to know more than either volunteer.

She was glad these people had been screened.

Bert presented himself at her side a moment later. "It's time for a cigarette break, Miz Chelsea." He was motioning to his watch.

So much for comfort zones.

Chelsea was up, and it was late. Three people remained in the break room: Bert, reading a Bible diligently, and a woman who sat close to a second man on the couch. John Milton had warned her some of the clients might be parolees, and this one did not try to hide the fact. The man and the woman chatted about old times in lock-up, but as it turned out, the woman had been employed there. The man had not done his time where she worked, but he had done some. They'd both done time in AA. Of the thirty people who'd checked in for the night, these were the only ones who were not asleep. A family, a man and wife with two little ones, were shut for the night into the family suite. Several men

46

snored loudly just outside the break room. She could hear them through the walls. It was no wonder the three lingered where they were.

In the women's quarters there were only about ten individuals, but they included the man she'd seen earlier in the parking lot with his two-year-old daughter in tow. She had noted the teddy-bear studded cots earlier, and Tom had explained the man was on the short list for an apartment, had custody of his daughter, and did have a car and a job. Paula had decided to put them up at a remote end of the women's quarters and curtain them off because the little girl should not be among the men.

Good call, Chelsea thought.

Once again the strong urge came over her to say thank you to these people who were inviting her into their world for the evening. She was glad she was on her own time. This was their world; it was not her story to take.

She slept fitfully, if at all, on the narrow cot in the basement. Ghosts of Sunday schools past seemed to reach out to her in the night from the arc of a lone nightlight plugged into the wall near her pillow. An electric heater crackled off and on, keeping the area just on the cusp of chill and tepid. Her mind caught here and there on random thoughts, most of them closed off with an effort when they came, but one kept surfacing. Where had she seen Bert before? But it was night, and thoughts were vivid anglers in these hours, catching random fish as if they were all prize trout, and not garbage fish. Bert could be one of a hundred men she'd passed in the halls and pathways at school. It was probably a dangling, homesick germ she hadn't washed off yet.

But with that thought cast off, one remained, swimming past her, waiting for an opportunity to fasten itself to her mind. She was almost sure the neatly made cot she'd seen was Debra's. Was it possible the woman was here but had evaded her somehow? There were a lot of residents here, and avoiding contact would not be hard.

Chelsea turned over, tugging at the sides of her sleeping bag with a vengeance, and willed herself to sleep.

The effort was futile, for rest's sake. Thoughts flipped over into dreams, but they were still thoughts. Whether she dreamed it, or whether it was another wakeful memory, she couldn't tell, but there she was in the middle of her parents' home, holding up a statuette—the one that had been on her dressing table since she could remember anything. She'd never thought, until that day, to turn it over and look for a mark, or if she had, it hadn't meant anything to her. She'd never had a reason to care before.

But on that day she'd gone back to stay overnight, having given her husband, Ben, the excuse of being tired, needing a break. Her parents didn't know she was there, and she overheard their conversation. Normally she'd ignore them, but this time she was their subject.

"Thank God she's not like Debra," her father had said.

Her mother answered, "Ron, she is. Exactly. And that boy will kill any notions she has of a career, just as sure as Michael Brown killed Debra's."

Chelsea pushed herself up in bed, training her ears on the door leading into the living room where her parents were talking. Her mother's voice was tired. She said, "I am reconciled to the fact she wants to write, of all things, but this region is a dead end, especially in print. The sooner she gets on the air, the better. She'll want more. I promise you, she'll want more."

Her father's voice was equally tired. "And you want her back on the coast, on television, for all the world to see. What happens when Debra sees her? She's bound to. You know she's still there."

"Chelsea does not know anything about this, not yet. And it's time we made things right with Debra. She has no idea we have Chelsea."

"You want them to find each other..."

Chelsea heard weeping, Gail Wallace weeping. She tried to remember whether she'd ever heard that before. She got up and walked to the door, pressing her ear fast against it.

"I found her work on the internet, Ron. She's back at her sculpting. She's alive! And right now, that's all I care about. We always said we wanted the girls to know each other. All I can hope is she does not hold things against us when she finds out how hard we tried, and what we had to do. In the end, it wasn't good enough, was it?"

There was a long pause, more sobbing. Then Chelsea heard her father say, "Now, Gail, we did what we had to do."

"I know. And we failed, didn't we? But you have to agree. Maybe Debra can help Chelsea now. I'm giving up. It's time they met. It's time, Ron. Besides, if she focuses on something besides Ben, she has a chance of getting over this whole thing and making something of herself."

"So you think finding Debra will occupy her long enough to get her more interested in a career than in Ben? And you think this funk, this depression she's in, will go away if she leaves him? Is that what you're saying?"

"I'm saying that if we ever want to see our daughter again, we're going to have to get this out in the open, and now is a good time to do that. Chelsea's not getting any better with Ben. Maybe she'll get better without him. At least she'll be off that computer and into the real world. He's got her confused, that's why she's depressed."

Chelsea clenched her fists at her side. Her arms were rigid. They were right, she should leave Ben. It would be easier that way, easier for her, easier than telling him what she'd done. She tiptoed quietly back to the bed to get her robe, and the statue caught her attention. She had always loved it and insisted on keeping it there. It was a clay sculpture of a boy with a guitar poised on his knee. His eyes were closed, and his mouth was open in a song she could almost hear. She turned it over. Stamped in the clay was MICHAEL, and under it the initials D.W.

Debra Wallace? What was this all about? Chelsea's head was reeling.

That night Chelsea googled Debra Wallace, artist, and then Debra Wallace-Brown, artist. She also took some pains to research birth records in that area around 1978, but red tape would take some time to cut through if she wanted details. She'd seen her birth certificate and had never questioned it. But then she'd never had reason to examine it very closely. The next day she was on her way to the coast. She decided to take her parents' bait and apply to the television station there, but she didn't bother to tell them. After all, that was the way the Wallace family played things, close and secretive.

It was not until morning, after the residents had packed their things, made their beds, and the doors to the dormitory were locked that Chelsea caught a glimpse of Debra, walking to the cafeteria. She walked lightly, Chelsea noticed, and her shoulders swayed melodically. Her head was raised and poised to the east, probably to catch the sunrise. *No cares,* thought Chelsea. *I spent my night tossing about, wondering what to say to her, and she has no cares.*

Chelsea clutched her abdomen and stared at the woman. The words her mother had spoken that night echoed in her head... *"Exactly like Debra."* But if she was exactly like this woman, why was she so envious of her? Yes. That is exactly what she was, and it was time she admitted it. Debra had not listened to her parents. She could walk down the street with a clear conscience. So, what would she do if she learned Chelsea had done what she refused to do?

Chelsea felt herself shrinking back. Too much had been happening. Still, she felt like a moth drawn to light. It couldn't be helped. Besides, it might be her last chance to talk to Debra. After this, she swore she would not pursue it. She'd move on. So, now she had a line to draw in the sand, and that is exactly what she planned to do.

When Chelsea entered the cafeteria she saw Debra seated at a round table, alone. She squared her shoulders, lifted her chin, and forced herself to make eye contact. When she did, the woman smiled and motioned her to come take the chair beside her. Apparently Bert had seen her, because before she could point to the queue and indicate that she had to get her food first, he was placing a plate full of eggs and toast out for her, next to Debra. Chelsea forced a smile, thanked him, and sat down. An apology was in order, she knew. Fortunately, living with her parents had taught her how to make formal apologies when the last thing her heart told her was that they were owed. Certain things are simply expected, they used to say.

She seated herself, and said, "Ms. Brown, I owe you an apology."

Debra did not answer right away. She waited for Chelsea to look at her, and she did, but it took her a moment to adjust her emotions first. Debra seemed to understand. She said, "Call me Debra, please, and I accept your apology. Paula tells me you've left the station, and you're with the newspaper now. I'm sorry."

Chelsea nodded and then grinned. "My parents will be disappointed, but the truth is, I'd rather be at the paper."

"Pay isn't the issue with you either, then?"

"Not really." She took a bite of eggs and tried to think what to say next, but the food just made her realize how tired she was. A picture of her down-clad, queen-sized bed crossed her mind and kept surfacing, each time more compelling than the last.

But the next words Debra spoke brought her fully around.

Right after Chelsea asked her, "What about you?" Debra answered, "I'd renew my license and go back to nursing, but lately I've had trouble concentrating. I've been having dreams, and they're always about my daughter. I have to find her. Besides, I enjoy having more contact with my patients. I can do that as a CNA."

Chelsea forced herself to continue chewing, making sure she did not bite her tongue or look at the other woman. What would ignorance of the situation say now? She scanned her mind, replaying Debra's words, and finally said, "I'm sorry. I didn't sleep at all last night." She cleared her throat. "Did you say 'find' your daughter? You said she died, didn't you?" There it was again, the resentment in her tone of voice, but she hoped this time it would be forgiven as weariness, which half of it was. She was too tired to control her feelings.

"Not this one. I gave my Annie up for adoption when she was born."

Chelsea breathed in as normally as she could make herself breathe, and then out again. *Annie?*

Chelsea's blood flashed through her veins in a torrent toward her face, and pooled there in a florid heat. No way was this going to happen. This was the end of it if she didn't do something fast. Her heart screamed to ask: *Why do you want to find her now? Do you need her?* She struggled with what to say without jabbing daggers at the woman again, but she didn't dare speak until she could think.

Debra said, "Are you all right, Chelsea?"

Then Chelsea knew what to do, what she had to do. She coughed and moved her face up and down in a panic mime, a way to explain her red face. She moved her tongue back to her tonsils and up, so that it sounded like she was not able to find air when she drew it in. It was her long-practiced childhood ploy; the act had gotten her away from some of the most boring dinners. She'd used it sparingly, but she did it well.

Debra handed her a glass of water, urging her to drink. And when Chelsea had gotten her act under control, she looked up to find the older woman laughing, shaking her head and apologizing. And each time Chelsea looked back at her, she started in again. It was awhile before she was in control of herself enough to talk. She drew in a deep, cleansing breath, and tried, but she had to repeat the procedure several times before she could stop laughing long enough to talk. Finally she said, "You reminded me of something, but it doesn't matter now, I guess."

"What?"

"I used to do that. I mean, I know you were choking, and it wasn't funny, and I'm sorry, but talking about Annie and all...well, I guess it just sent me back in time. You made me think of something I used to do when my parents made me sit in on their dinners or whatever, and I wanted to go home. I used to make myself turn purple. I'd put my tongue up to the back of my throat and pretend I couldn't breathe...I'm sorry, Chelsea. I really am. I haven't thought of that in years."

Chelsea studied Debra's face. Somewhere under that laughter was pain, and she knew that pain. She asked a question. "Where are your parents now, Debra?"

Debra turned her attention back to her food, and answered, "I don't know." A second later a cloud moved over her face and the dimple on her left cheek disappeared. "They left town when I told them I would not have an abortion. I never saw them again. I haven't heard from them in—I guess, over twenty-five years."

Debra eyed Chelsea, as if wondering what to say. "I don't know how, but I knew my baby wanted to live, and I knew it was not my life to take. Just like I knew I wanted her to have a real home, and Michael and I could not provide it for her. And in the end I found out I was dead-on about the whole thing, like someone who knew the future was telling me what I had to do. She would have been in that car with her dad and her sister the morning of the accident. Michael was taking Caroline to school. Annie would have been with them. She would have been fifteen, too young to drive. But now she's alive, and that's only because I somehow knew I couldn't keep her. When they died, it was my only comfort. In the past few weeks it's become an obsession. I look for her everywhere. I even thought you might be her, Chelsea. I'm sorry."

Chelsea nodded, deciding it was time to draw that line, for now at least. "Well, no. I'm not adopted. Mom and I look like clones; you wouldn't believe it, really."

At least she'd told half the truth.

When Debra's face blanched, Chelsea felt ice in her chest. She realized the woman was reacting to her words like one would react to tragic news. And here she was, the confident, cold reporter, sitting with her as a token of her benevolent duty. Before the revelation she'd just made, Debra had evidently thought Chelsea was her daughter. How in the world had she come to that conclusion?

And now what? Did they go back into their separate corners, the homeless woman and the too-busy, uptight career girl?

Suddenly Chelsea realized she did not want that anymore. She reached out and took Debra's hand, holding it in her own, comparing them. The only thing to distinguish them was the manicure and the tell-tale effects of the older woman's work in clay. Chelsea kept her nails short for typing. Debra's were a little longer.

Chelsea said the only thing she could think to say, which was, "I'm glad your daughter's alive, Debra. I really am."

Debra composed herself. "You're from Louisiana? I read your bio online."

"Yes. Natchitoches. Most people know it by *Steel Magnolias*. It was filmed there."

"Really? I saw that. That's the deep South. Your accent is faint, Chelsea. I'd think it would be..."

Chelsea smiled. It was good to be talking small talk again. "I worked on it, believe me. This county isn't too keen on rednecks." She didn't say that her parents had managed to keep their California polish, and insisted she inherit it, something that had cost her dearly. In the south a California accent could be detected on the spot. It wasn't welcome, as a rule.

The inevitable question surfaced then. Debra asked, "What brings you here?"

"Honestly?"

"Honestly."

"I, uh..." Chelsea bit her lip. She needed her mother, or rather the one Gail had never been. "I left my husband, and I wanted a fresh start."

"I'm sorry, Chelsea."

By then Bert had already collected their dishes and was busily sponging down tables.

"I guess that's our cue," said Chelsea, because she couldn't think of anything else to say. She slid her chair out from the table and rose to leave.

Debra's face clouded again, and she looked up, studying Chelsea's face, turning her own slowly, side to side. She looked uncomfortable, as though she'd suddenly remembered where they were and realized there was really no common ground between them, that this might be the last time they talked. "It was good to meet you, Chelsea," she said quietly. "Thank you for coming."

The reporter rose, smiled, and slid her chair back under the table. She looked around her. In one corner she recognized the ex-con, sitting again next to the woman he'd been with the night before. She mentally covered his tattoo littered arms with shirt-sleeves, and realized he could be anyone.

Paula beckoned her over to introduce her to the breakfast crew and to invite her back. Church people scurried around in the steel-festooned kitchen, covering pans and stashing them inside a double refrigerator.

The middle-aged man found Paula and took her hand. His other arm held his daughter, who giggled, and clutched a stuffed bunny, almost her size. Her baby-blond curls were nestled close to her father's breast. Chelsea was shocked back to reality when he said, "Thank you so much, Chelsea. I hope you'll come again."

She nodded and turned to study Paula's face. It was radiant. Suddenly she felt imprisoned in her soul, an intruder on a party, not worthy of enjoying it. But she managed to return the woman's smile, say her good-byes, and thank her for offering to close up. Then she left.

Five

December 24, 2003
Meg

What turned out to be an aborted journey for myself was the same for many who'd flown away from the small terminal in San Luis Obispo the day before. Both my swan and my leprechaun dove were among them. And this time I rode right beside them back to the airport I'd found them in the day before, so that we were able to meet and to chat.

"...so that's it!" I cried when I was introduced formally to the swan. "That's why you had everyone looking your way like you rose from Mt. Olympus when I first saw you. You're a celebrity where you're from." My swan was *the* Chelsea Andressen I'd heard was on vacation and being filled in for at the television station. My hunch or little Omni's insistence had been dead-on.

I learned the two women were headed back to Atascadero for the same reason I was, to check on loved ones or friends. Chelsea, she assured me, had no intention of going back to work or even telling anyone she was home until she was ready to, but I didn't quite believe her. There was a little of the greedy gleam in her eye, the same as probably shines from my own when I can't wait to dig into a story.

"And how is it you two know each other, then?" I asked.

Debra opened her mouth to answer, but Chelsea interrupted to say they'd met because of a story she'd covered awhile ago.

"And here's a misconception on my part," I said. "I took you for sisters. You look alike."

They turned from me to scan each other, Debra with a little half grin turning up the corners of her mouth and crinkling her nose, but I noticed her dimple was only a shadow, maybe my imagination. Chelsea seemed uncomfortable and offered—a little quick-on-the-draw, I

55

thought—"Some blonds tend to, you know."

"Well, I guess you're right there." I had to allow that my mind ventured quickly into things before the facts were known because, of course, I wrote fiction, not fact. The little voice in my ear aside, for all I knew, the chapters I'd written were only that—fiction.

"And you, Meg. What is it you do for a living?" asked Debra. She seemed genuinely interested, so I decided to come clean and told them I was a writer on a quest for a story at the moment.

Upon hearing my confession, my leprechaun broke into a full-on laugh and poked me hard with her elbow, for she was right next to me. "That would explain the nosiness, then," she teased.

Oh, this one I liked.

The swan perked up a bit and said how she wanted so much to drop what she was doing now and burrow into fiction writing someday herself. Oh my, I thought, an animation I had not seen before.

"Oh, it is fun, really," I told her, and then thought, *At least when you're unstuck it is,* which I certainly was now. "I will give you a crash course in bird watching right now if you like," I offered.

"Birds?"

"Yes, character catching. You, for instance, are a swan."

Debra pointed to herself with a question mark all over her face, so I answered it as an audible one. "You are a dove, Debra Brown. And when I see a dove, I know to watch it as if it were Noah's sign from heaven that the waters of confusion are finally receding."

Uh oh. I'd said way too much, and when I do that, which happens often, I keep talking. "...And then there are scrub-jays and owls, wrens, hawks, and quail. I never bother with a quail for a character, but I do watch their antics because they mirror those of a family or a community. Scrub-jays are self-absorbed characters, usually on a mission of some sort, best ignored. They're a smoke-screen."

Chelsea was laughing now. But too quickly she settled back into composure, her comfort zone. It was Debra, I noticed, who possessed a hair-trigger grin and a transparent soul. Rare, very rare.

"But you know I'm right on target with both of you. You are a dove who transposes herself into a leprechaun. You are an illusionist, Debra, with an Irish sense of the comical and the composure of—"

I stopped myself before I finished the sentence because I was about to say "the composure of one who has come through some storms in her life and learned how to weather them." Now, I wasn't sure how much of this knowledge I'd gained from reading her journal. I believe I turned a little red in the face, too, because she raised her eyebrows, but did not prod me to continue. If I'd been caught, I wasn't going to admit it.

"A leprechaun," said Chelsea. "You've pegged her with that one, Meg." I saw a flicker of something in Chelsea's eyes I had not seen before. The slight crack in her exterior had afforded me sight into her well-hidden interior. Was that love? An invitation to friendship? I didn't know. She hadn't a clue it was there herself, after all. This one had little knowledge of who she was, as confident as she appeared on the surface. I believed I'd found the ugly duckling.

It was then I noticed a habit Debra had of caressing a tiny glass encased mustard seed she wore around her neck when she seemed to be thinking. The motion carried her away from us, if only for an instant.

Chelsea wore pearls, I saw, and as I glanced at them she looked up. So I followed her gaze to the aisle and then two seats ahead of us. I gasped but covered it as quickly as I could. I don't believe it was noticed, because Debra was still in her thoughts and Chelsea was distracted at that moment.

Why would the scrub-jay be on his way back so soon? And on Christmas Eve...interesting, I thought, but in truth it unsettled me. And why had my swan cast her aristocratic gaze directly at him the way she had? It wasn't a passing glance, but a familiar one, preoccupied, and a little troubled. My swan had gone back to hiding inside her feathers.

We remained quiet until the plane touched down and we abandoned our seats. Debra let Chelsea take the lead, backing up and motioning her to do so. I wondered why until Debra took my arm and whispered, "I want to talk to you," and then let me pass in front of her as well.

She got straight to the point on the tarmac, saying, "I don't like that man following her."

"The scrub-jay, you mean?"

Her dimple flashed, but that was all. "He seems to be hanging about, didn't you notice?"

"Just a hint."

"He's been watching her since we were at the airport yesterday, and now here he is again."

"I know. I thought he was just a groupie at first. Did she say anything?"

"She did. She thinks he's a nuisance, but I think she's worried he's more than that."

"Then so am I. I have an idea we should stay in touch." I got out my wallet to retrieve a card with my cell phone number on it, and handed it to her after I'd scribbled Charlie's address on the back, and told her, "This is where I'll be."

Then I remembered her journal, and the fact that she was basically homeless at the moment. "Debra, why don't you come with me? You're a nurse. Charlie is eighty-two. I'm worried about her after all that upheaval."

Debra smiled and said she'd be happy to, but obviously she still had the scrub-jay on her mind. She said, 'It's funny, Meg, but frustrating actually. Chelsea said she won her trip at work. So did I. It was a raffle put on by an anonymous donor—a grateful family, I was told. I remember wondering, *Why, Christmas?* But I supposed the rates might be cheaper or something. When Chelsea told me she'd won her trip, too, I got suspicious—and then that man following us like that was too much of a coincidence. I'm just as glad to be going back home."

My heart went numb for a moment. All the while we were talking we followed Chelsea at a distance. The scrub-jay was right there in the way of our view of her, though.

"Where is she going now?"

"Probably to the newspaper. She's a workaholic, I'm afraid."

"Do you know her well?"

"No, not really. It's a long story, but I have something to confess."

I was all ears.

"You know as much as I do. You read all I know about Chelsea in my journal."

I'd have been defensive if I hadn't caught a glimpse of that telling dimple flashing just then. I said, "Busted. How did you know I had your journal? I am terribly ashamed, you know." I reached into my clutch and handed it back to her, relieved I no longer had to hide it or try to figure out a discreet way to get it back to her.

"Shameless, you mean." She was laughing conspiratorially now. "And so am I. I left it on my seat as bait for you, and I hid behind the wall in the plane to make sure you picked it up."

"You didn't!"

"I did. I saw you watching me in the terminal yesterday, and I thought it would be fun. My number is in there, you know. You could have called me right away, but I'm glad you didn't. I was right about you, and now I need your help, and I don't have to ask you to wade through my past with me before I can explain things. Can we talk soon?"

"*Can we talk soon?*" she asked. I believe it is an Irish notion that a leprechaun should not be let out of one's sight, not for a moment. I led her to the roundabout to collect her baggage and then to my car to take her to Charlie's house.

Six

Meg

A s I turned the key in the ignition, Debra fastened her belt and leaned back into her seat. She looked tired.

"You okay?"

"I didn't get much sleep, and what I got wasn't good."

"The dream again?"

"Yes."

Debra's most recent journal entries contained some fretting about a dream she kept having. The train that took the life of her husband and daughter was in it, but a little girl's voice called to her after the wreck was over. It had reawakened her desire to find her firstborn. She was fighting it, she'd written, because she'd looked for so long and had been disappointed so often that she did not want to open old wounds.

"Where did you stay last night?"

"In the airport. We were all the way to San Francisco, waiting for our connection to Hawaii before we heard the report of the earthquake. We'd overheard some strange conversations, but didn't connect the dots until dinner. A television was on at the restaurant."

I already knew some of the particulars because we'd talked about things on the plane earlier. Debra and Chelsea had found out only that day that they were headed in the same direction on the same flight, so they'd decided to pass the time visiting together. Airport chairs do not make a good bed. Debra looked exhausted.

"You can lie down after we get to Charlie's," I told her. "There's a guest house in the back. I keep it stocked with extra clothes and food. It's comfortable and quiet."

"I won't fight you, Meg. You know my situation. I guess that my place at the shelter is taken until I would have gotten back."

I knew. I'd also heard from Charlie again and knew that the shelter was in the middle of a crisis because of the earthquake. The community was shuttling cots and blankets into another building as quickly as they could, but more than one of their host church buildings was closed for repairs.

It was hard to imagine Debra not having a family, and even harder to think of her living on a cot in a homeless shelter. I asked if she was going to look for her daughter, and she said she was not sure. She reminded me that Jake Highland was her only hope, and he had disappeared shortly after the baby was born.

I decided to change the subject. "It's good you're a nurse. Charlie still sounded shaken when I spoke with her this morning."

"I'd be glad to help, Meg."

"In your diary you wrote that you worked for your husband's grandfather as his nurse. Was that how you got started?"

"Yes. I got my nurse's aide training so I'd know what I was doing when his health was failing. He talked me into going after my RN after Michael died. That's part of what made this trip so tempting. I needed a break."

"And now, here you are. I'm so sorry."

"It's really okay. Part of me didn't want to go anyway, and I was able to get a refund, so actually I'm closer to getting settled into a place of my own than I had been before. I wouldn't have known that was an option if this hadn't happened, and I need the money right now more than I need a vacation."

I was surprised, I told her. Airlines are sticklers where refunds are concerned, but she said the prize had included a stay on the island in a hotel, and that was where the refund came in. A good portion of her ticket was refunded, though, because of the circumstances.

"Is there someone in particular you need to check on?"

"My patients, the shelter...I couldn't have just gone off and enjoyed myself, and then there was Chelsea."

"What do you know about her?" What I wanted to ask her was whether she'd given any thought to the off-chance Chelsea had lied, and that she really was the daughter she'd written the diary for, the one she'd given up for adoption at birth. I'd carried on that far with my writing, anyway, and I couldn't get their resemblance out of my head, but I didn't want to bring it up. She must have read my mind, though.

She said, "Meg, trust me, there are a lot of traits that string themselves to the blond gene. Do you know how many wild goose chases I've been on? It's a roller-coaster ride for the emotions, and I refuse to go on another one. I was so sure it was Chelsea, but maybe it was the nightmares making me impatient, a little too quick to draw conclusions. If only these dreams would go away....We did get around to talking at the airport. She convinced me she was telling the truth when she said she was not adopted."

"You're sure? She's very closed up, you know. You've noticed that, haven't you?" I had a hunch about Chelsea, partly because of the back-and-forth I perceived in her persona. But I knew all about up-and-down emotions, so I decided not to share more of my intuitions with Debra. I'd been on my own carnival ride after Patrick's death, and sometimes it was easier to walk around and watch, never get back on anything that looked like a roundabout. My legs felt good under me, moving slowly on terra firma, even if it was in circles. In fact, circles were fine. They were safe.

I asked her about the pastor then. I wondered what became of him, and according to her diary, so did she. After the baby came, Michael and Debra had asked him to watch after her, and make sure she got into a good home.

"We were so young," she said. "We didn't know what we were asking. For a while I didn't understand why he disappeared, why I couldn't find him after that. As an adult, I realize what an impossible thing we'd asked him to do. He was young himself. He was transferred to another church somewhere, as far as I know."

"Herb didn't know where?"

"If he did, he wouldn't tell me. He always said it was best to move on, best for all concerned. I agreed with him, until I lost Michael and Caroline. By then Herb had a hard time remembering things. Losing Michael put him over the top. He had a stroke, so I moved back in to care for him."

"Don't you have other relatives somewhere?"

"I think the diary explained that, didn't it?"

"You don't read it over once in a while?"

"Only a page or two. I found it in my things when I went through the shed in the cabin. I couldn't bring myself to go back through it, but when I started having those dreams, I took to writing in it again. There were some pages left, but I didn't reread the whole thing, no."

"Why in the world did you take a chance on someone you didn't know picking it up and getting it back to you?"

"I'm a good judge of character, Meg. And I was right, wasn't I? Besides, part of me never wanted to see the thing again."

"I think you wanted help."

"I think I wanted to get rid of it, and I didn't care how, but you're right. I did think you might just be interested enough to help. If you weren't, it didn't matter. I was that sick of being alone in it."

I was about to say I didn't believe that, but out of the corner of my eye I saw the first frown I'd seen since I met her. So I asked what had happened to her home.

Debra explained that until her husband and daughter had died ten years ago, they'd lived in a remote cabin together. After that she'd lived with Herb and taken care of him till his death five years ago. After he died, she moved back into the cabin and put every spare nickel she'd earned as a nurse into art supplies and equipment, as well as a four-wheel-drive vehicle so she could get in and out of the place where she wanted to live. Her dream was to go back to the cabin she and Michael had lived in, so she could set up shop and get back to her sculpting and her pottery. The owners were willing. They lived in another state and kept it as an investment. After a year's time, her artwork was selling, but her savings had dwindled to nothing. When the cabin burned down, she found the first job she could get, which was in a nursing home. She was working on a place to live.

I waited for Debra to finish explaining things and to compose herself. Charlie, who is a little hard of hearing, had not heard us pull in, I was sure. I needed to change the subject, and I needed to know something, anyway. I asked her if she knew more about why she thought that man was following Chelsea.

"It's weird, Meg. I noticed him at the airport first, then on the plane, but I thought that was normal. He was eating across the dining room from us in San Francisco, and I didn't think anything of that either until Chelsea said something."

"What did she say?"

"She said she'd seen him before, and he was beginning to make her skin crawl, sort of popping in and out a little too coincidentally in odd places. But she said something else that struck me as a little strange. She said not to worry, she was pretty sure she knew who sent him, and she knew who to call to get him to stop following her."

"That is weird. Let's go in and check on Charlie. I'll call the newspaper, but you should get some rest."

"Meg, Chelsea is a very private person. I don't think she'd want us checking on her."

"Debra, I really don't think she knows what she wants, do you?"

When she opened the door for us, Charlie seemed composed on the surface. I didn't tell her Debra was there to check on her, only that she was a dear friend and she might need a place to stay for a couple of weeks. I shot a look to Debra that said it was better Charlie thought Debra was the one in need, when it was really the other way round.

Debra got to work and made a game out of taking all of our blood pressures, not just Charlie's, with the portable kit Charlie kept at home. She did ask whether it had been calibrated lately, to which Charlie said yes, but I knew it had not been. Debra deftly wound the cuff around my arm and took my pulse, then had me take hers.

"We're all sane, anyway," she pronounced, making an elaborate show of winding the apparatus back into its case and patting it down.

In the spirit of fun we were in, and to which Charlie was responding well, I said, "And I thought you were being honest. You say we're sane? Speak for yourself."

Debra laughed, but then asked Charlie when she'd last seen her doctor.

Charlie told her what I could have told her: She did not like doctors.

"Sometimes I feel the same way," Debra said. "Charlie, how do you feel about my staying here with you, in the house for a couple of weeks? I know it's a surprise, but I'm going to be honest with you. Meg's right. I need a place to stay while I look for an apartment."

This worried me. So honest so quickly, and right after finding out Charlie would rather pass on in peace than to engage the services of a physician. But Charlie was delighted, beside herself with so much enthusiasm that Debra sat down beside her and took her hand to calm her. "Thank you, Charlie! We're going to have a lot of fun."

Debra did not leave her side for the rest of the afternoon, save for a quick whispered admonition to me while Charlie went to the bathroom. "Meg, you cook dinner or call it in. I'm going to call a friend to see if he can stop in for a 'visit' when he's off duty."

"A friend?"

She smiled, found the phone in the kitchen, and made a quick call. I heard her offer some numbers, probably vital signs, before she asked me for Charlie's address and repeated it into the receiver.

After dinner a weary-looking young intern showed up at the door saying he was there to see Debra. Dr. Will James accepted dinner, making a fuss over how nice it was of us to invite him to join us because he was so hungry; he hadn't had a chance to eat since breakfast, he'd been so busy.

I believed he'd missed his calling as an actor.

He turned his attention to Charlie, saying: "Ms. Charlie, Debra tells me you don't like doctors, and frankly I'm hurt."

Charlie looked embarrassed, setting her eyes to her feet to think of something redeeming to say, until Dr. James let out a hoot that could have brought on another aftershock. And then he said, "This earthquake has brought so many people into the emergency room with trauma of some sort that I am amazed you are in as good shape as you obviously are in, ma'am. I do commend you, but I want to leave you with some pills, some just-in-case pills, so that these friends of yours won't have to haul you out to see me in the middle of the night."

Charlie rose to the bait and accepted the bottle offered her. Dr. James smiled, excused himself, hugged Debra, shook my hand, and kissed Charlie right on the nose, which had her looking at her toes again.

Then Debra said, as he was almost out the door, "Will, I'm cooking tomorrow night. I'm thinking roast beef is as good a Christmas dinner as I can think of. Would you join us?"

They must have worked out the script on the telephone earlier, I thought.

He said, "Roast beef, as you know, I cannot refuse. I'm off at seven."

I crossed myself. How could I have forgotten that tomorrow was Christmas? I was glad I'd invited Debra in, at least. And I couldn't believe I hadn't thought of it immediately. When I asked Charlie where her Christmas tree was, because I knew she always decorated, she told me it had been destroyed in the earthquake. I looked around me. The place was tidy, but when I looked closer I noticed for the first time that the panes had cracked above her sideboard in the dining room, and they were almost completely empty. No wonder she was in such a physical state. She must have spent all day yesterday and today cleaning up.

That night, I noticed, Charlie took one of the good doctor's pills.

The next morning, Debra knocked on the door of my backyard retreat. She had spent the night inside at her own insistence, saying to me that she wanted to be near Charlie for a night or two, and to Charlie, "Meg is on a roll with her writing. Maybe she should stay in the guest house, and I'll take the couch tonight."

She handed me her cell phone, saying it was Chelsea who wanted to talk to me.

"Chelsea?" Oh, dear, I'd forgotten to call her. But a second later I remembered what day it was.

Debra explained, "She saw us leave the airport together, and she had my cell number. She wants to see you, Meg."

I invited Debra in, and closed the door. I said hello into the phone and sat down to hear what the girl had to say. She asked to meet me for lunch and I agreed. Chelsea sounded more business-like on the phone than she had on the plane. I imagined her at her desk, hovering over a calendar, but on Christmas? It occurred to me that she must be alone, and that I should invite her to that roast beef dinner Debra was planning to make.

"Are you at work?"

There was a slight hesitation, but she admitted that she was, to which I replied that a little bird had told me she was a bit of a workaholic. I said: "A desk is where *I* need to be, not you." But I assured her I would meet her at Denny's at noon, and after I mimed a question to Debra, which got her head nodding enthusiastically back at me, I told the girl that I would not take no for an answer when I asked her to join us for Christmas dinner. She agreed.

I rang off and handed the phone back to Debra, who looked as curious as I felt. I shrugged and said what she was probably thinking but was too polite to say: "Now what could that young girl possibly want with a nosey old bird like me?"

At a few minutes before noon I drove into the restaurant parking lot, and went inside to find Chelsea. I would not have recognized her had she not hailed me from her seat in the back corner booth. There sat my swan transformed into an elf. Instead of an upswept French roll, she now wore her hair down. It was quite long, and I noticed a generous suggestion of strawberry tint, hinting at red, that must have been hidden in her roll before. As I got nearer, I noticed more changes. She wore less make-up, so that a spray of freckles played across her nose. Her eyebrows were lighter. The polished appearance she'd presented yesterday was completely gone. She looked more honest somehow, and I hoped this would make for good conversation.

"I would not have recognized you!" I told her.

"I know. And I will take that as a compliment."

"It is."

"Well, I'm not at the station anymore. I'm working for the paper."

I didn't know whether to tell her that Debra had already informed me about it; I decided not to. "Isn't that a step down for you, now?" I asked.

"No, because I don't like what I see in my future if I stay at the station. You helped me decide, you know. They want me back, but I'm not going."

"Oh, please don't blame me, dear, but tell me more."

"The writing. I miss the writing. I didn't realize when I applied to television that I would be pushed and pulled like elastic. They told me what to wear, how to talk, what to say. Besides, they pretty much fired me after I interviewed Debra on live television. I blew it. I can't believe she forgave me. I was so rude. I don't know how to make it up to her."

"So, you're already back at the paper, right?"

"Well, let's say that's the other reason I wanted to talk to you. To be perfectly honest, I need your story. 'Meg O'Malley in town doing research for her next novel' sounds good enough to present as my hook, doesn't it?"

"It's Christmas Day, Chelsea."

"I know." The girl seemed to shrink back in her chair, gracefully though—always graceful, my swan. She took a long sip of the water our waitress had set down in front of her, and said, "Did Debra tell you I left my husband?"

"My, no, she didn't. When? Where is he?" I was flustered. I'd said the only safe thing I knew to say. At that moment I couldn't remember how much Debra had written in her diary, how much she'd told me, and how much I had researched online about this girl. "No" was safe, for now.

"He's in Louisiana. My folks are, too. They know where I am, but he doesn't."

"And?"

"And, so I can't figure out who sent this man to follow me. I don't think Ben would. I know he wouldn't. It's gotta be the folks. Did Debra tell you he was shadowing us all the way to San Francisco and back?"

"She said you weren't worried."

"I'm not, really. He doesn't seem to be harmful, just annoying. That's another reason why I asked you to lunch. Make sure Debra knows I'm not afraid. It's nothing. I'm sure of it. She didn't seem to believe me, and I don't want her worrying. She'll listen to you."

I studied the childlike face in front of me, and all I could think of was my novel. Granted, in the thick of things it is hard to stop obsessing on a project. I decided to pretend to change the subject.

Keeping my eyes on the table, I said, "I'll tell her, Chelsea. And about the story...you know my novel is going to be based on Debra's life. She lent me her journal. It was begun in the late seventies, and it's all about giving up her baby for adoption. She's hoping her daughter will find her. She seems to feel very strongly about it. She thinks the girl is looking for her now, and she won't pursue it herself. She says the only link she still has to the mystery is a man named Jake Highland. She hasn't seen him since the baby was born."

I looked carefully at my listener then, trying to discern whether the name would phase her. It didn't seem to. But by that time her face was customarily frozen. She was carefully nodding, visibly coaxing me to say more. I wasn't sure I had much more to tell her, but decided to push the envelope, see for sure whether Jake Highland was someone she did or did not have any recollection of. I told her about his promise to Debra, and then his disappearance.

All she said was, "It does sound like a mystery. Is it?"

"No. I think it's a love story, really."

Chelsea took out a reporter's pad and a pen, and began to take notes. Was she very crafty, or quite sincere? I wondered. She asked, "Meg, why did she ask this man to watch her daughter? Was she in love with him?"

"Oh, no. I don't think so. She married the baby's father, Michael. She says they were madly in love."

"Madly. Why didn't they get married sooner, then? Why didn't they raise their own baby?"

Was the flash in her blue-green eyes only a figment of my imagination, or a reflection from the window on our right? I wasn't sure. I went on. "She said she was afraid if they married so young, things would grow sour, and eventually the baby would have a broken home. And she said something else, too."

"What was that?"

"She just knew it would be the wrong thing to do. She felt very strongly about it."

Chelsea cocked her head, lowered her eyes concertedly to her pad, and cleared her throat. "Jake Highland, you say. Has she tried Googling the name?"

"I'm sure she has." But a second later, I thought better of what I'd said. "Wait a minute. I don't think she would have."

"Why?"

"Well, she said something about Michael's grandfather cautioning her against looking for him or the baby. He was dead set against it, said it was best to move on."

"How does Debra feel about that?"

"I don't know, but my guess is she has mixed feelings. I know if I bumped into the man, I'd get it out of him. But then I don't have Debra's patience, none of it."

Then Chelsea laughed. "That she has, for sure, or she would not have forgiven me so quickly the other day for that horrid interview I put her through."

I decided to cut through any pretending, so I said, "Chelsea, she told me she thought you might be her daughter. She would have forgiven you anything. The truth is, you're right, she's patient to a fault. I would have brained you!"

We were both laughing by then, and she said, "Does that mean I'm not invited over to dinner anymore?"

"No. You'll come to dinner if I have to drag you there, but let me do some more thinking on this interview, this story you want to do about Meg O'Malley. I might want you to show me the piece before it goes to print. You'll be provin' yourself to me. I have my doubts about trusting swans, you know."

Chelsea was hiccoughing by then. She was in the middle of another swig of her water when the word *swan* made her choke. And that's when I saw it. There was a dimple right in the middle of her left cheek, but it was elusive, the kind that never showed unless its owner was in full hilarity. Swans! They could be exasperating—too alluring for their own good, and too aloof for anyone else's.

I groaned, then told her the truth. "I absolutely hate to see articles written about me, not to mention the pictures that always go along with them. But since getting my name out there with publicity about the next novel has to be done, it might as well be by you."

Our waitress refilled our glasses of water, set down menus, and then left us. While we decided what to order, I said, "You know, Debra surprises me. It really is a gift she has with the elderly, I think. She came back to my friend's house to check on her for me, and wound up staying. She didn't want Charlie to be alone last night, and neither did I. She was pretty shaken up."

"A lot of people are. Um…I don't think Debra has a place to stay, Meg."

"I know. She does now, though, and she's talking about looking for a place of her own. In fact, I think she's enlisting Charlie's help tomorrow."

"Rent in this area is steep," Chelsea said. "Even if she gets in somewhere, how is she going to manage on a nurse's aide's salary?"

"She's welcome to stay at Charlie's as long as she likes. Right now Charlie needs her."

"Good. I hope she does. I mean I hope Debra stays, that is."

"Look, when you come over tonight, you can judge for yourself. We're planning on cooking roast beef as an excuse to draw a doctor friend of Debra's back. He was there last night. He can check on Charlie without her realizing it isn't the dinner he's come for, but her. After dinner we can go back to the guest house and do the interview, and you'll have your story."

"Debra got a doctor to come to the house?"

"She did. But I'd be willing to bet it was she who made the diagnosis, and he who took it as sound. Have you seen her in action as a nurse, Chelsea? It's really something to see."

"No. No, I haven't, but I've seen her at the shelter, and I don't want to see her back there, though I'll just bet she goes if only because she wants to be there for the others."

"You know her pretty well."

"We had a good visit at the airport and on the plane. She doesn't seem to be in the least concerned about herself. She came back here without a thought to where she was going to stay, meaning she probably intended to stay in her car again. Did you know she did that for a while? I tried to get her to come home with me yesterday. She wouldn't."

"I know; only if you needed her, right?"

"Right. That would be the only way, and you know...I hadn't thought of it, but I will be trimming the budget with this new job, by half actually. It's a thought. I might need a roommate."

"Well, I'll tell you what, don't look for one just yet. We'll see what happens."

"Deal."

A cell phone chirped in Chelsea's pocket and she retrieved it. "Yes?" She looked at her watch. "Something from home? What do you mean? Who did you say you are?" The girl listened for a long time. I noticed her face tightened a little. After a few seconds she said, "I can be there in about fifteen minutes." She closed the phone and sighed, then looked back up at me apologetically.

"What is it? Do you have to go back to work? It's Christmas, you know, Chelsea!"

"No. Um. It's a surprise. You'll see tonight, I guess."

Our waitress returned, and Chelsea said she'd just have the salad bar and help herself, and then she apologized to me, saying that's all she'd have time for. So I ordered the same.

We said our good-byes. Chelsea grabbed the check and made off with it, waving at me hurriedly on her way out the door. A little enigma she was, morphing back into a swan, off on another one of her flights. And from what or to what was she flying now?

I would have stayed to jot down some notes, had I not seen what I saw the next moment. *Rats! The scrub-jay again.* Out of the corner of my eye I saw his suit, which had become rumpled since last I'd seen him at the airport. He shut his cell phone and rose from a booth within easy earshot of ours, ambled nonchalantly to the counter, paid his bill, and followed Chelsea out the door. I guessed that she hadn't seen him, or she'd grown so used to his shadowing her that she hadn't noticed him this time.

I had a mother hen's instinct to warn him off. Instead, I decided to play the sleuth and one-up him at his own game. It did not feel as good as what I ached to do, which was to grab his collar from behind, shake the livin' daylights out of him, and get him to 'fess up to what he was after, following the girl. But anyway, I was out the door and on his scent easily. The good thing about middle age, I've found, is that the young don't pay much attention to us. This time that fact would work in my favor.

Chelsea was pulling out of her parking space just as the glass door swung closed behind me. The scrub-jay was in the process of starting his auto, and it was luck for me that he was in a hurry. His door was wide open, allowing me to recognize him propped up inside a rental car. He was slow getting it started, not being familiar with the process, probably.

I made a show of ambling and ignoring, making it to my own car in time to start it and be hood-to-bumper with him at the exit onto El Camino. Now, in that traffic, I knew making a left would take time. I was almost certain Chelsea had turned right to get onto the freeway. It was the easier way to get to the newspaper office, where I assumed she was going. She knew the town, while this one probably did not. He'd lost time, lost sight of her car most likely, and if he did turn left, I'd be certain he'd overheard our conversation and be on his way to the newspaper, trusting normal logic for his route to it. Anyone unfamiliar with the area would think the shortest distance between two points was a straight line, and turn left. If he hadn't been following Chelsea and been listening in on our conversation, why would he brave that traffic?

Bingo. The left blinker of his car went on.

Had they talked that loudly? Surely, if Chelsea knew this fellow was following her, it didn't bother her as much as it should be bothering her. Maybe she'd been right when she told me he was simply reporting back to her parents. Any normal twenty-five-year-old girl would be livid if that were the case, but maybe she was used to such control in her life. At any rate, she was not surprised by the concept.

Well, I decided, he'd done no harm so far, save the rattled nerves he'd given us. I decided to leave things as they were for a while and get back to Charlie's. I had decorating to do.

Dinner went well, and afterwards Chelsea led us out to her car, saying she had a surprise for Debra. She lifted the trunk and removed a tarp to reveal what looked like a potter's wheel in pieces. That was exactly what it was, I learned, after Debra shouted as much. In the back seat was another tarp-covered object, quite large. When she uncovered it, she found a set of tools and knives, and what looked like a hundred blocks of potter's clay.

One would think Santa forgot and left his whole world's offering to her, the way Debra carried on. She hugged us all, Chelsea first, and then did it again. "All of this, and I can build my own kiln! How can I thank you? How can I ever, ever thank you?"

Chelsea hugged her, and said not to thank her, that the gift was from someone who had seen the ill-fated interview and wanted to remain anonymous. They had contacted her at the newspaper, and asked her to deliver it as a Christmas gift.

I didn't put two and two together until Chelsea took me aside to say that annoying man had proven to be good for something. This led me to believe he was someone after Debra, not Chelsea. But why? Apparently it was for no harm, at least. Chelsea offered me no more information.

When Debra recovered, she left us for a minute to go into Charlie's extra bedroom, which was really a study. She returned with a small statue, which she handed to Chelsea. And when the girl held it up, I saw that it was a swan in a joyful pose, long neck extended, and beak open and stretched upward, as if in laughter. The wings were slightly spread, but not as if they were about to extend outward. It was amazing to see how Debra had managed to depict the moment in which a bird lights, and then settles itself down in peace, but she had.

It was what Chelsea did next that gave me chills because it was at that moment I realized Omni was more than a figment of my imagination, and that I would not need to go back through my novel and amend it. As lovely and intricate as the object was, it was not until Chelsea turned the statue over to examine the bottom and saw the initials DWD cut into the clay that she cried.

Debra hugged her. "I'd have made it bigger, but there's not a lot I could do without my tools. I hope you have room for something more substantial, now that I have some. Swans are fun."

My word, I thought, *if this is what she can do with a kitchen knife, I have got to see more of her work!*

As Chelsea clung to her, I watched Debra, and I could read her face easily. She was satisfied that it must simply have taken Chelsea time to get in touch with her emotions, and not that the signature might be familiar enough to trigger a memory. After all, how could she possibly know that Chelsea possessed the statue of Michael that she'd left in her own bedroom so many years before?

As the night wore on, I didn't catch another glimpse of that hidden dimple like I'd hoped to, but I did surmise something in watching Chelsea's comportment around the young doctor. His flirting hit stone with her. I thought it was because she was just distracted, as she often is, until I saw her reach into her purse, and then slip a wide gold band onto her left ring finger.

The earthquake had unsettled things in Atascadero as well as in Paso Robles, where I'd seen the city's heart crumbled to the ground on television. But it was a bit less on the Richter scale than had been reported two nights before. In fact, there were several numbers being bandied about regarding its magnitude. I'd stopped listening, figuring in a few days they'd make up their collective mind and settle on something near reality.

Atascadero had suffered a blow to its heart as well, though not visible from the street at first glance. City Hall, the police station, the courthouse, and the museum were located together in a large, four-story, early-days brick building. Various extraneous community meetings were held in the uppermost story, the Rotunda Room. It was a lovely domed round room, so pretty that Charlie's church met there—a small mission, which set up and tore down their paraphernalia every week for Sunday services.

I wanted to see how the quake had affected it, but no one was permitted in unless they had particular business there. This was the case for the church, so I offered to help them collect their things from the building. It was only the day after Christmas, and in truth, I hadn't been that keen on it until Charlie insisted she go herself, and I pretended a great interest in seeing the old building. I told her I would take her place.

Debra understood my concern. She invited Charlie to go with her to the nursing home to check on a few of the patients there. By then the two women had become fast friends. I could tell Charlie was happy for the opportunity to stay in Debra's company, and so it was settled. My leprechaun's penchant for making acquaintances into pals impressed me.

On the way to town I drove slowly. I wasn't alone in my curiosity, I noticed. No one else seemed to be in a hurry either. Signs of the earthquake were everywhere. All around town, chain link fences were up or being erected around older buildings. Some houses and shops held signs of restriction in their windows, which allowed entrance only to residents or shop owners, and only for the purpose of collecting their belongings. Few were open for business.

Here and there entrances to streets were orange-coned and taped, restricted to through traffic. Black-and-whites littered the main drag, some stopped at the curb and some slowly patrolled the long main street, the old El Camino Real, which used to be the highway running north and south. The 101 ran parallel the El Camino, and about a building's breadth to the west of it.

The powers that be struggled to make Atascadero's downtown pedestrian friendly, but the main drag ran so long that this was an all-but-impossible undertaking.

Still, their efforts were admirable. There was a small area of the old downtown, about six square blocks around City Hall, where merchants fought to draw foot traffic from the steady stream of drivers along the El Camino. The Sunken Gardens, a long green park spread out in front of City Hall, served as home to weekly farmer's markets, periodic flea markets, concerts, and other public and political events. I'd been to a few, and remembered children roosting on low branches of spreading oak trees to get a better view of things from the same long, stout, ancient arms that had supported their great-grandparents in another century.

It was a truly beautiful park, boasting a central fountain and statues. On the south side of the Sunken Gardens, beyond the sidewalk and creek, which ran behind the buildings there, was the bowling alley and theater. This had been, only two days before, a gathering place for area youth. Now it too was rendered unusable by the quake.

I pulled into the parking lot across the street from City Hall around 8 a.m. to see a FEMA trailer parked there. Across the street a temporary fence circled the looming brick building I came to see, and a guard with a clipboard waited just outside to admit church members into the building. She was passing out hard hats, I found out, and having us sign a release of liability form before we entered, insisting we not go in unless by twos. I waited there for a spare person to come along, taking my time filling out the short form and signing the release.

Five minutes later a small car pulled up. A man I did not recognize from Charlie's church got out and proceeded to cross the street. I attended services with her when in town, so I knew, I thought, all of the few parishioners at the small mission. This was not one of them, nor did he look like one of them. He was a rather tall gentleman, a farmer type, rugged, tanned, and—I don't know how else to tell it—quietly loud. He whistled as he walked, caught my eye, and nodded politely, continuing his tune, which I did not recognize in any context to do with church. I took him for the gardener. As he crossed to the building I noticed his clothing. Somehow I hadn't before, or I would not have mistaken him for the gardener. They were clean, pressed, and well ordered. He wore leather boots, worn but polished, and as he drew nearer, he removed a tie the exact color of his brown shirt from round his neck, folded it, and tucked it into his pants pocket. He seemed to know what I was waiting for, as though he'd been there earlier that morning and knew what to expect.

He smiled at the guardian of the hard hats, collected one for himself, and pointed to his name, which was already signed on the sheet. The lady insisted, though, that we both sign our names directly beside the time she'd stamped on the sheet, explaining that in this way she'd keep track of who went in, and when.

The man looked to be in his late fifties, and when he shook my hand and introduced himself as Jake Highland, I froze. Was this Pastor Jake? What was he doing here? Did Debra know? No. She'd said she couldn't find him.

I came to my senses in time to accept the hand he offered, which I noticed was work-worn and rough. It was not, I thought, the hand of a man of the cloth.

I gave him my name, explaining I was a friend of Charlie McCullough's, and he must have read the puzzlement on my face because he asked me what was wrong.

"I've heard your name before, but I've come to church here many times and I haven't met you." I hoped that would do for an explanation. It seemed to.

Jake Highland was a transparent character, unlike most people, I thought. His conversation was easy and quickly informative.

"What happened is this," he explained. "The young pastor here lost his home in the earthquake, not just his meeting place. He lives in Paso Robles, only a couple of blocks from downtown. He's lost his equilibrium a little just now, and we'd already been talking about my helping out. I'm manning a little mission down in the South County area temporarily. This event just sped up the process we'd been considering, so we're moving everything to my building so that we can meet together next week."

I was dying to know more, but a little out of breath by then because we were on the stairwell on our way to the Rotunda Room on the fourth floor. By the time we reached the second floor I noticed he was not a bit winded, although I judged him to be a few years my senior. I did manage to ask him what he meant by temporary, though, without telling him that I wanted to know where he'd been all these years, when he had come back, and why. I knew myself better than to imagine I could wait for that information.

"I'm from here originally; in fact, this was my assignment until I accepted a position at a mission and an orphanage not too far from here. When my wife became ill a few months ago, we decided it was time to move near a hospital." He hesitated, and I glanced at him just in time to see the shadow of a cloud cross his face.

I knew that pain.

A half-flight of stairs later, he said, "Anyway, I have always wanted to come back home, and I wanted Marj near our daughter. We'd encouraged Nan to apply to Cal Poly, so she was already here."

I knew most of his life story by the time we'd finished climbing stairs. In fact, I knew quite a bit more than he'd told me because of Debra's diary, and frankly I was struggling because part of me was compelled to be as candid with him as he'd been with me. The timing was wrong, though, because by then we'd come to the door opening into the Rotunda Room. One of the helpers hailed my hard-hat partner as soon as we entered, and he was off.

Looking around, I noticed the beauty of the room was intact, but marred by great gaps in several pillars, corresponding to chunks of jagged wood planks and plaster splatters below. Squares of ceiling tile lay on the carpet too, here and there. Cracks were visible in the walls. It did not look dangerous now, but had been deemed potentially so by whoever judges those things. The ceiling rose in a dome the height of two stories above us. Often, I remembered, birds flew and sang up there during services, but there were none today.

I recognized a few of the men there and went into the storage room to see what I could do to help. I was there for the better part of the morning, packing boxes with prayer books, hymnals, decorations, and the like. As soon as a box was sealed it was loaded onto a dolly and taken to the landing. The elevator was off limits, so four flights of stairs had to be faced with each box. In the end I was enlisted to carry my share. It was a tedious job, and Jake accompanied me each time, reminding me of the two-at-once rule.

By the time the last box was shuttled, we'd had time to talk ourselves a little into the past, and I felt completely at ease telling him who I was, and that I knew Debra. He asked me not to mention to her that he was in town, not yet, but he did promise to give me an interview. I took his card, telling him I would call him soon, probably very soon, if he didn't mind. He agreed.

There was a van outside waiting, with a covered trailer attached, which we filled with the boxes from the stack we'd built at the base of the stairs.

By noon the trailer was packed tight and ready to be driven south.

The guard at the gate counted heads, crossed us off her list, and had us sign out, then locked the gate behind us and shed her official role for a little chatter. She'd take a break, she told us, before the next crew, which consisted of city workers, was due to come later in the afternoon.

We lingered, as much to catch our breath as to visit. In these circumstances, I've noticed, people with no previous common denominator draw comfort in sharing stories and information. She told us that vacant buildings around town were being enlisted for use while a new administration building would be built, she guessed. It was only a couple of days into a situation no one had expected would arise.

The small regret I felt as a transient visitor to the little mission's demise was nothing compared to the regret I saw on the faces of the parishioners who nodded politely at the guard's information and quietly bolted the trailer door on their belongings. Jake Highland stood by, his arms outstretched in a quiet blessing over the others. It seemed to be a purely unconscious act on his part. But for a moment it looked as if conduits of light shot out from his hands. I held my breath. Never had I seen so visible a sign of glory touch a person. Debra's doubts about him, written down in her diary, could not be grounded in anything but her grief, I thought. This was a man of his word.

The vision touched me on more than one level. Here was one of those situations people who question God are always bringing up. Why do unconscionable things happen if God cares about his children? Although for the last year I had put my own doubts in a see-you-later bottle, I had a similar struggle going on inside myself. Why was my husband taken at the peak of his career, and when I was not ready at all to lose him? He was a godly man. I had no answers for it. So, I'd put my faith on hold, being ashamed to approach God with my anger. Still, I feared him. I wasn't sure I liked what he'd allowed to happen to me, but who was I?

I could not get the picture of Jake Highland's blessing out of my head. Here was a man who'd spoken candidly to me an hour before, as though I were his sister, a man I'd mistaken for a gardener. Now he was visibly lit up. I have no other words to explain it here, just lit up. Wasn't Jake Highland suffering even now, with a dying wife? Would he feel the way I had when she passed? Yet there he stood, still in full communion with God, still caring for others. No one could pass such a blessing without feeling it pass through him, could he? And when he turned back to me to wave good-bye, I received it myself, in a lightning-quick rumble and jolt, all but physical. There are some moments in life when no explanation is sufficient. This was one of them. I knew then that I could return to God, and that he'd be waiting. The wall was down.

It occurred to me that Jake's blessing reminded me of something, and so what happened next pleased me right down to my feet. That little buzz in my left ear started up again, and accompanied me all the way back to my car, softly whistling the tune I'd heard from Jake earlier. It had a Native American flavor. "Just what is that song?" I demanded, and I could have sworn I heard a soft little giggle, but that was all. This little Omni person seemed to be there only on a need-to-know basis, and so I was curious about his presence now. I guessed I'd need to get back to my keyboard.

When I returned to Charlie's I called Jake, and to my surprise he was available. After we talked for more than an hour I was ready to write, and I did.

Seven

1978
Jake

Jake Highland had not ever experienced the sense of God's fatherhood in this way. It was intense, and when he looked at the baby through the nursery glass, it overwhelmed him. Small, he'd been ready for—even compelling—but this was someone else's child. He had never had one of his own.

He'd counseled parents through parenting difficulties with young people, drawing only on his education and training, sometimes his experience with friends and family. That was why he was here, for Debra and Michael, certainly not to adopt this child himself. It wouldn't have entered his mind had the young couple not asked him to follow their offspring—make sure she was well cared for. How, he asked himself, would he be able to do that without adopting her?

He had not answered them, but he had not discouraged them either. How could he? They were desperate—and they were, in a sense, his own children. Hadn't he given spiritual birth to them both?

His eyes were drawn magnetically to the two tiny, trusting, blue-as-the-ocean eyes behind the glass, and a little rosebud mouth working questions—silently—into his heart. *Jake*, he told himself, *this is not a puppy at the pound, up for adoption. This is Debra's child, Michael's. And they've asked you to watch over her.* They were just two teenagers in love, asked to do the unthinkable: be adults, and entrust the fruit of their love to another couple they did not even know. Their hearts were breaking in the process. He would have to be a parent if he made this promise, at least for a little while, but he suspected his heart would become as vulnerable as theirs someday, if it wasn't already.

He let those feelings sink in, using them to put himself in their shoes long enough to imagine how he would feel in the same situation.

And then he knew he would ask someone to watch over her. It would be a given. If he were himself in this position, no matter the cost, he would find someone he trusted if he possibly could, and he would only be thinking of the child. If it occurred to him that it was too much to ask, it wouldn't matter. He'd do it anyway.

He understood.

"Penny for your thoughts," Herb whispered from behind. Herb Jentzen was almost forty years Jake's senior, and the baby's great-grandfather.

"Herb, what would you do—I mean, if you were me and they asked you to look after their child?" Jake looked up at the man who stood next to him. His face was a study in dichotomy of love and detachment, riveted to the object on the other side of the nursery glass. A tear made its way slowly down a well-etched path to his chin. He took out a handkerchief that looked like it had already seen enough use to warrant laundering yesterday.

Jake said, "There are papers to sign today, Herb."

"You're signing papers today?"

"I'm going to foster the child—until there's time to pray a little. What do you think?"

"I think it's a lot to ask, and I think you're too nearby."

"I don't know another way to keep my promise."

"Jake, you haven't made that promise yet, I hope."

The pastor's eyes turned back to the object of the conversation, now cooing and turning pinker by the minute on the other side of the glass. "How can I not make this promise, Herb? Look at her. She is their child, and no matter where she goes or what happens from now on, she will always be their child. I understand that much."

"But she's not yours, Jake."

"They're mine, Herb. That makes her mine, too." Jake knew then he'd made his decision. "I'll sign those papers. I have to."

Herb's snow-streaked hair caught light from the overheads so that a twinkle seemed to begin at the top, then fall down to his newly-washed gray eyes.

"Should I tell them, Herb?"

"No, Jake. No. Not if you're thinking of adopting her. If there ever is to be a bonding, it should be a complete one, no strings, especially for a mother."

Jake wondered how the older people in his parish seemed to be so sure of things in life, but in his experience they were often right, and there were few he trusted like he did Herb Jentzen. Even if he had to take this advice by faith, he thought it best to listen and follow it. "Yes, sir. I was only thinking of fostering for now, so I can be sure her home is a good one. That was my promise."

"How will you keep it from them?"

"I have some thoughts. Until they asked for my promise I wasn't considering it, but it changed my perspective on the whole thing when they did. There is a village in Monterey County, a small Salinan tribe. It's not far from here, but it's secluded. I've been asked to take over the mission there. The current vicar has to leave, but he has a handful of children he fosters, and that will be part of the job."

"You're right. You'll need to relocate. But if you're going to take care of this baby, Jake, you'll need more than prayer. And the sooner she is adopted into a family, the better. You know that."

"Yes. A little time is necessary, though, or I'll lose track of her."

"I know, and old fool that I am, that's the last thing I want. Am I selfish?"

"I don't know. I don't think the kids are being selfish. I think they're just being parents."

Herb lifted one eyebrow and turned his attention back to the infant. Whether by reflex or miracle, at that moment the little girl thrust both arms into the air above her head, opened her eyes, and stared straight at Herb. A beatific smile, as only the newborn can affect, displayed itself fleetingly on her lips, and then she closed her eyes and fell back into her slumber.

When Jake returned home, a letter waited for him. It read:

Dear Rev. Highland,

In response to your telephone inquiry to The Christian Adoption Society recently, our efforts to ensure an adoption for the child Debra Wallace is carrying have been interrupted by the biological grandparents, Gail and Ron Wallace.

It seems they have arranged to halt any adoption plans for the present, requesting that the child be held in foster care until they can arrange an adoption on their own terms. I am sorry to inform you that our best efforts to discourage them have failed.

Because of this, the child will have to remain in the foster care system until other arrangements can be made. This is unfortunate. At the moment foster care providers are at a premium.

However, you mentioned your consideration of a position as vicar at the Ta-te mission and foster care facility might qualify you as a temporary custodian of the child. This may be our only recourse in this situation.

Please advise us of your intentions as soon as possible.

We will continue to stand with you in prayer regarding this.

The letter was signed by a social worker from an organization Jake had been referred to as being one that could be trusted. Jake called his bishop to say he would take the position in Ta-te.

A day later Jake saw the baby through her discharge from the hospital. Debra and Michael had already said their good-byes, and today Jake would pack their child into her new car seat and take her home for their last day in Atascadero. By the next morning they would be on their way to Ta-te.

Jake had two concerns on his mind: that this primitive community would be a little difficult to adjust to along with the care of a new baby, and whether to change her name. Debra and Michael had named her Annie. Ideally her adoptive parents would change it, but who knew how long it would be before the Wallaces decided on her future? She would need a name, so he called her Annie. When Jake said it first to the child he thought it was perfect, and he found himself hoping whoever adopted her would keep it. He wondered whether he could insist on the prospect, but he tucked that thought away. It hurt.

He knew that the original document of her birth said only *Baby*

Girl Wallace. But Michael had put his name in as the father. The baby would have his last name written on her birth certificate. Someday, Jake hoped, they would find each other. But the thought crossed his mind that as much as Debra's parents had bent the law to their own will, if they had anything to do with the future, it might take an act of God to reunite the little family.

He wondered whether the kids would stay together. Their love seemed strong, even though they were so young, and then there was the fact of their Christianity. That, he knew, was real. Maybe that would hold them together, but who knew the will of God, or the future?

A thought pricked his conscience. He hadn't remembered to pray for the Wallaces, and maybe that was why he was feeling such resentment toward them. So he prayed all the way up the 101 to Jolon Road.

In the town of Lockwood, which consisted of one store that he could see, and a little over four hundred people, according to a population sign, he turned right. After driving past any sign of life, and then another ten miles, he turned left again and bumped onto a badly graded shale road. He'd driven too many miles past Lockwood to be counted. The map was little help to him, save a penciled arrow with the words *Nine more miles* scribbled above it. It corresponded to a hand-painted wooden sign in the shape of an arrow pointing north, which read *Ta-te.* He set his odometer, and rolled on.

Sheets and layers of time peeled away until he felt he was not traveling in miles but in time, backward. There was no sense of past, present, or future, to be sure. In this place there was only an eternity of rock and dust, sagebrush, and the hint of green here and there between inhospitable insults of brush and stubble. The road dove deeper down endlessly, not bothering to turn or wind. No need, no obstruction of hill or rise anywhere that he could see. Just cut rock road separating gray stalks of weedy ground and more rock.

This resembles a desert, he thought. His spirit tumbled, dejected. Until now he'd been excited for the adventure, but this road was demoralizing. After some time he saw that his down-turned ride led to water, and there was no bridge to buffer it from his car. Luckily the stones were well worn by water that must at times have covered them, but not now. There was only a trickle meandering lazily across the road. The car went through and laboriously climbed a matching incline on the other side before it leveled out. By the odometer Jake had gone only three miles past the crude arrow drawn on his map; six to go.

Oh well! He decided to make himself hope that the end of the road was nothing like this. Six miles was an eternity in this varied country. It might take him an eternity to drive it, too. The road was horrendous. He wished he'd asked more questions about the village. Was there a store, for instance? Driving back to a town on this road was not something he would want to do often.

The clock moved faster than the odometer, and with one mile to go he found he was going to be all of an hour later than he'd planned, maybe more. The road had gotten even worse, if that were possible, but the scenery had redeemed itself with periodic oaks and pines, a jungle of Manzanita stands, and boulders the size of trees, whose shadows protected wide carpets of plush green natural lawns. Although he had not seen a sign of human life since passing Lockwood, a variety of creatures began to show themselves now that the terrain had changed.

A red-tailed hawk sat alert on one oak branch that stretched out over the road, and a moment past that Jake slowed to allow a darting roadrunner passage. To his left, out of the corner of his eye, he saw antlers nodding curiously at him from behind a wall of granite.

Jake's apprehensions lifted layer by layer as his car crawled along. Finally he crossed another creek, which looked more like a shrunken river. This one had a wood bridge built across it, wide enough for one car to pass. It cleared the water by several feet, leading Jake to decide the river would run deeper in the spring. A glance at the odometer told him Ta-te must be just up the rise.

Just then Jake froze. He took his foot off the accelerator and the car stopped. A bald eagle stared down at him from a rock only four yards from his windshield. He met the knowing eyes of the creature because he couldn't do otherwise, and then it settled itself into rest, spreading its wings over the rock. At the joints, the wings formed shoulders. The sharp eyes closed. Jake watched for a long time until the bird reawakened, rose up, and launched into an updraft it had apparently been waiting for. It flew. He watched it as long as he could see it, until its wings held steady and soared, and until it was a small black dot in the air, and then he restarted the engine and drove ahead.

They were almost there. This, at least, would be a good place to wait upon the Lord. And for the time being, this little one would be safe on his shoulders.

Annie cooed and hiccoughed occasionally, but she'd slept the better part of the trip away. Just past the river he found the village, then the church, and pulled his car into the driveway of the adjoining vicarage. Within seconds, three children bounded out the front door of the earth and wood structure all at once, crying a joyful welcome. Vicar Townsend followed only a little more sedately than his charges. One of the children, a small adolescent girl Jake thought must be Pia, took immediate control of the situation, opened the rear car door, and extracted Annie from her car seat, singing as she did.

Jake had not heard such a voice, ever. Annie seemed to respond to it as though she had found a mother at last. She nestled herself happily into Pia's bosom, and the young girl looked to be in her element. Jake grinned at her, wondering whether he would get a chance to hold the baby himself from time to time.

Then he saw little Benito, Pia's five-year-old blood brother. His serious eyes fastened themselves to the baby, and he tickled her tiny feet all the way back to the door. He, too, would become a little watchman over Annie, Jake thought.

The other child, a boy, stood straight like a man and held his hand out to shake the new pastor's with. "Welcome to Ta-te," he announced proudly. His smile was slow but genuine. *This must be Martin,* Jake decided. The eight-year-old stood straight as an arrow, though he had the diminutive build of his people. He was not much taller than Benito, though three years his senior.

Jake thought he had never felt as much a man or ever as pleased as this. In one day this thirty-one-year-old vicar had become the father of a household, and the spiritual father of a community. His bishop had given him full charge here, and the title of vicar was now official, even though a small ceremony would still have to be held in Ta-te when the bishop was able to arrange it. Judging from the drive in, it might not be soon.

The air around him spoke of another culture and another time. Again, a certain quiet peace overtook him as it had when he'd gotten out of the car at Herb's retreat. It was another kind of beauty, that of a granite-concealed oasis. The little village evoked thoughts of another century, close and real. Jake was at once relieved of his fears and his care that tending for this baby would be a monumental task. It seemed the most natural thing in the world to be here, and to trust these people.

Vicar Mark Townsend smiled and extended his hand in greeting after Martin's, then proceeded to explain Jake's new duties and what to expect.

"You will be pleased at the openness of this people, and their sense of family, as you saw by the way the children greeted you. It will be all we can do to keep from meeting the entire village tonight, but we will try. I've arranged a community get-together tomorrow, and I'm hoping their preparations will keep them occupied until then. They will be preparing food through the evening, that's sure."

When Jake entered the house a delicious aroma assailed his senses. He hadn't realized he was hungry until then, but he was famished, and very grateful for whatever was bubbling on the stove and baking in the oven. As though Pia could read his mind, she scooped up a large colorful ceramic bowl filled with tortilla chips and set it on the table, then motioned for the two men to sit down. A bowl of salsa was already there. She then filled two large glasses with lemonade and set those out. When Benito and Martin pulled out chairs of their own, she gently reprimanded them.

"Boys, you will need to help me in the kitchen. The men will talk while we serve the meal." The girl still held Annie on her hip, but the baby was fast asleep, her tiny head resting on Pia's chest. Jake wondered whether he should suggest she be put down, but he remembered her bassinette was still in his car.

Pia had anticipated this, too. She said, "Reverend Highland, I have a small basket for the baby. Don't worry, she will sleep, but I want her to be close by. It is good for her to hear noises and learn to sleep through them. It is not good for her to be alone while she is this young, either." With that, Pia strapped a basket around her middle and placed Annie in it, receiving blanket intact around the infant, who continued to sleep.

Mark smiled, then turned to the new vicar. "You will find our Pia is quite the little mother. She is all that Benito and Martin know, at least. They have accepted her as such. I have tried to encourage her to be a child, but I am powerless. She is who she is."

"You don't know how grateful I am for that," Jake assured him. "It was only yesterday I brought Annie home from the hospital. You can imagine how concerned I was about taking on these responsibilities all at once."

"I know, but with Pia here it will be much easier. I knew that when I heard of your situation, and it is the only reason I felt it would work out."

"I'll need to know all about the children, Mark. You've told me that Pia and Benito are brother and sister, is that right?"

"Yes. Let me explain now, while they are busy. Their mother, Espiranza, left Ta-te when she was very young and went to the city. When Pia was eleven, Espiranza, or Espi, as she was often called, returned with her. She was expecting Benito. Apparently the father had finally abandoned her and she had nowhere else to go. No one ever found out exactly what happened to him. Espie died giving birth to the boy, and Pia took over as surrogate mother. They became part of my little orphanage because Espie's father had died when she was quite little. Her mother hadn't lasted much longer. The girl had no one when she left the village, other than Old Mother, who belongs to everyone. She is Espie's biological great-grandmother, but she was much too old to take care of the children."

"You wrote that they were up for adoption?"

"Yes. The tribe is open to it, and so we have looked around a little. Many times in the beginning I had offers to adopt Benito. I turned them down. Pia is as much a mother to him as he could ever need, and the offers did not include her. I thought it best they stay together. If we ever receive an offer for the two of them, I'll recommend you take it—carefully—but it will be good for them to leave the village one day."

"Why is that?"

"Pia is like a visiting princess here. The people love and admire her, but they have told me they believe she will leave one day, that she is a gift to be shared. These children are part Anglo—obviously so, and she was not born here. Benito simply belongs to Pia in their eyes. They treat him as though he is her son. Although the laws are changing to suggest now that the tribe has first rights to adopt them, the tribal council has considered the matter and they agree that Pia should be shared with the world. You've heard her sing."

"Yes. Her voice is lovely, to say the least. But how could they simply let her go?"

"It is not that they want to. There is a good deal of wisdom in these councils they hold. You'll see. They listen to the children as respectfully as they do the adults. They love Pia. They want the best for her, and they are realistic."

"And Martin?"

"Martin is another story. His mother died in childbirth as well, but his father is unknown—at least officially."

"But he is full blooded…"

"Yes, I think so. The community seems to take it for granted, which means they probably know who his father is, though it is never spoken of. Martin is a true son of Ta-te, and though he may never be offered adoptive parents here, it really doesn't matter. As long as he stays here, he's family. He knows that. Besides, it's in his heart to stay."

As though she understood the men had finished the private part of their conversation, Pia sang out, "Supper's on!" She nudged Martin, who carried a steaming pot of beans, and Benito, with a basket of tortillas, ahead of her back into the dining room. Pia carried what must be the main dish herself, with Annie still asleep against her midriff. Jake noticed the basket held Annie comfortably, so that her head was slightly elevated; the baby slept easily, as if she were in a crib, though swaddled close. Pia shifted the basket to her side and sat down to eat. Mark took her hand and Benito's; Jake took Martin's and Benito's, and then bowed his head gratefully.

After a huge going-away celebration for Mark the next day, which doubled as a welcoming for Jake, the new rectory was established. Vicar Highland was accepted as *Da*, Mark's former unofficial title among the villagers. The children made the adjustment easily, it seemed. Pia continued to care for Annie as though she were her own, and Benito stayed only inches away from her himself. Jake was grateful that part of his job was to homeschool the children. He didn't want to be without Pia's help.

Martin proved to be a good student, but Jake noticed it was much easier to teach him his lessons when he could tie them to Ta-te's history, geography, and culture. So Jake developed a curriculum to use, which he decided he might as well extend for Benito later on. He rounded out this effort, beginning with the third grade, so that Martin would have what he needed, and then he completed a curriculum for the fourth grade as well. With this done, he decided to fill in the gaps, so he began work on lessons for preschool through high school.

When he taught Pia her lessons from the state textbooks that Mark had left, it was as if she were the teacher. He learned to simply plan her daily work page by page, and then oversee her progress. He was never disappointed, but he prayed he could include music in her studies someday. She had already taught herself to play the guitar, and often invited friends over to play with her. If they did not know the chords, she taught them, and if they knew more than she, she learned. In this way she seemed to make steady progress. But there was no one in the village who taught voice, something Jake felt was imperative, given her natural talent. It was easy to understand why her people knew she would leave them. Her hunger to learn was voracious.

All these things occupied his prayers at night, and the presence of Annie reminded him to pray for her natural parents and grandparents, too. In the back of his mind he knew he should pray for her future, but it was hard to do, hard to imagine her leaving.

He had taken to caring for Annie during the time Pia was studying. He joked that this was the only time she would let him. At first he simply tied the basket around his own waist. As Annie grew and became too active for this, he fashioned a large, gated play area for her next to the dining room table where her sister and brothers worked.

While the older children were occupied, he played blocks with Annie, stacking them, one for each prayer he thought of—reminding himself to tie each prayer to Scripture and to say them out loud to her, hoping the supernatural quality of the God's words and his promise to perform them would extend to these baby ears and hold her in God's protection.

This became such a habit that he was surprised to hear little Benito reciting his oft-spoken Scripture verses back to him. *Well,* he thought, *there is good in this no matter what.* Though the boy had his own curriculum, he preferred playing with Annie and sometimes took over with the blocks, praying exactly the same prayers he had heard his Da pray every day. This sobered Jake, who realized that truly God wasted nothing of his work. *If these prayers are being multiplied before my eyes,* he thought, *what is happening with them in heaven?* He could only imagine.

Pia, too, was mindful of Jake's ministrations, and her faith seemed to grow daily. The process was not lost on Martin, either, not to mention the housekeeper.

At Mark's insistence, from the beginning, the church had employed a live-in housekeeper at the vicarage, and this became more appropriate as Pia matured. Angelina scoured the floors regularly, kept the bathroom spotless, and saw to the laundry, with Pia's help. She was a widowed grandmother, whom Mark had said needed the income as well as the room where she stayed. Though Pia insisted on caring for the children and cooking, Angelina was mindful of Pia's need to study, and during the day she took broom or dishtowel away from the girl, insisting she get back to her music or her books.

Often Jake noticed Angelina scouring slowly and thoughtfully near Annie's enclosure while he prayed. He caught her more than once looking over his shoulder when he taught the boys their letters and helped them read, so he made sure he included her as their "tutor" at every opportunity. Later, in a letter, Mark told him Angelina had not ever had the opportunity to go to school, had been married at age fourteen, and before that had been enlisted as foster mother to her many brothers and sisters.

This fate, he knew, would have been Pia's, had she not been in the orphanage and had grown up in one of the larger families. It was a way of life that no state law had managed to override.

It was a blessing and an anomaly that English was the language spoken in Ta-te, despite the prevailing Salinan influence. For this he had the Catholic missionaries to thank. Though they had long since left off their travels to Ta-te from the mission, bequeathing it to the Reformed ministers, their influence was still felt in the community.

We Christians certainly are a patchwork people, Jake thought, remembering long afternoons at his grandmother's knee, watching her stitch one of her many quilts, using pieces of various garments. She had once told him that the adjoining thread in a quilt represented the blood of Christ, the batting, his Spirit that touched all, and the backing was the fatherhood of God, which bound it all together to make it what it was. He looked around and realized that for now, his contribution to the design was to guide the needle that held that miraculous thread through the tiny snatches of colorful fabric in the lives of these children, as well as those of the citizens of the village.

After studies Jake allowed Pia, Benito, and Martin to do what they wanted with their time. He knew this meant playing with Annie, so that the time was usually his to visit the sick or prepare his sermons for Sunday. On Wednesday nights he offered a Scripture study for adults at the church, and on those nights Angelina relinquished her duties to Pia and attended.

By now everyone called him Da, and he often chuckled about it. He was younger than many people in the community, had never been married, and had no blood children of his own. Still, somehow, since Annie's birth, he had considered himself a father, and he could not imagine being any more attached to his own blood children than he was to these four. Perhaps this was God's way of preparing his priest. A priest, after all, had to be a father of sorts—and actually, if truth were told, a better father than most. He had to represent Christ. Jake could not think of a better proving ground than the situation he was in now, even if it was temporary.

He tried not to think about that, remembering not to concern himself with tomorrow—that it would take care of itself when it came.

But sometimes that was hard.

Shortly after his arrival, Jake began receiving mail addressed to

Mark Townsend, but forwarded to him from an adoption agency connected to the church. They were signed by a Marjorie James, and they were inclusive of whatever correspondence had preceded them, so that Jake was updated more fully on the progress of finding homes for Pia and Benito, something he hoped would not be necessary immediately. Even so, he needed to look out for their welfare, and if a family was found that would accept both children, he would have to consider it. He decided to write to Ms. James and be honest.

Dear Ms. James,

I am in receipt of your letter dated July 29. Vicar Mark Townsend has accepted another post, and I am his replacement in Ta-te, and therefore the guardian of Pia and Benito now. I understand you have been involved in their case for some time, and I would like to continue the communication with you on their behalf.

I know you have the best interest of the children at heart, but I am unaware of how much Mark has told you regarding them. He did inform me of his insistence they stay together if at all possible. I agree with him, having seen the relationship these two share. Pia is a mother to Benito, having filled this role since his birth. He responds well to her, and she is quite firm and loving in her training. In fact, it is uncanny what a magnificent job she is doing with her little brother. I believe—for both their sakes—Mark was right in deciding to make sure they stay together.

I understand from your last correspondence that as long as your organization feels the children are well cared for, there is no reason to hasten the adoption process unless an ideal situation arises. For my part, I am extremely happy to fill Mark's shoes here. I am also foster father to a baby girl and, of course, to Martin as well. I believe the church will keep you abreast of my qualifications.

The children remain in a homeschooling situation, as they had been under Mark's tenure here. I am quite comfortable with this, and I do possess teaching credentials, so there should be no legal problem with the situation. In fact, there is talk of creating a Christian school here in the village, in which case the church will be involved, of course.

This is only a matter of prayer at the moment, and I will mention any progress in subsequent letters in case it needs to be part of your report regarding the children.

I look forward to hearing from you in the future.

Sincerely,
The Rev. Jakob Highland
Ta-te Mission

It was late August and Annie's second birthday had come and gone. The children had made good progress in their studies, and Jake had completed work on a curriculum designed specifically for Ta-te children. Both Martin and Ben had completed two years of their studies in this. They were both well ahead of their peers, not only in Ta-te, but in other parts of California as well.

Angelina had taken over the reading of bedtime stories to the children, and though Pia made a show of complaining about it, she was often right there beside her brothers and little sister, listening. Angelina combined her growing knowledge of Scripture with her reading skill and an uncanny storytelling ability to create riveting tales akin to Christ's parables. She had her audience almost as enthralled as Jesus' little ones must have been long ago. She would always begin by reading a story from the children's Bible, but then she would tell another as she drew colorful pictures to illustrate the truth she'd just read. Jake was pleased. Recognizing her gift, he put his housekeeper in charge of the children at church on Sundays, and he was not disappointed.

He started working Pia out of her regular curriculum and into the eleventh-grade program he had at last completed for her. The girl was working so quickly through her lessons that he planned to forge ahead and finish the twelfth-grade curriculum immediately. But what of her music? Lord, what was he to do about her music?

He wasn't to wait long for an answer.

A week later he received another letter from Marjorie James. He had kept up a steady correspondence with the woman since Mark had left the mission, so she was aware of Annie's situation and was now working as his liaison to the Wallaces.

Dear Rev. Highland,

Thank you for your recent letter regarding Gail and Ron Wallace. I have contacted them, and they answered my letter, asking me to inform you of their intent to begin adoption proceedings for Annie themselves. They have begun the proceedings through another organization but have agreed to work with us simultaneously.

I have informed them of the situation, that Annie has formed close bonds to her foster sister and brother. I emphasized the fact that Pia had been her surrogate mother for over two years, and I believe they will respect that relationship and try to do what they can to accommodate the children.

I have other news, however, which will complicate the matter. We have found a suitable, and I think exceptionally good family for Pia and Benito. I know your wish for Pia to study music and continue developing her talent is important to you, and because of this, I think it would be best for you to consider this family seriously. Mark and Susan Mitchell are music teachers in Natchitoches, Louisiana. Susan is an exceptionally accomplished soloist, and Mark plays several instruments. Both play the piano and guitar.

I have spoken with the Mitchells, and I believe their faith is genuine. They have raised one child and are unable to have another. When they heard of Pia and Benito through their church, they were quick to contact me and offer to begin the paperwork in order to adopt both children.

I know this will complicate your desire for Annie to remain close to her foster siblings, but I don't know where to begin looking for a solution. The Wallaces have priority where Annie is concerned, and, as you may know, they now live in Southern California.

Please contact me when you receive this. I will be calling you soon, but perhaps this will give you time to consider the situation before that.

Sincerely,
Marjorie James

Jake received a call from Ms. James the day he received the letter by overnight mail. He had only read it through one time and was about to reread it when the telephone rang.

"May I speak with Reverend Highland, please? This is Marjorie James from TCAS."

"Yes, Ms. James. This is Jake Highland. I just read your letter, but I haven't had time to digest it yet."

"How does it set so far? I am sorry to rush you like this, but I'm afraid we need to discuss this right away."

"It's that urgent, is it?"

"The Wallaces have made up their minds. I believe the Mitchells can be stalled if necessary. They have their heart set on Pia and Benito, though. They really are good people, Reverend Highland. We've checked all their references, spoken to their pastor, and all seems to be positive."

"Is there no chance they will move to California?"

"None."

"Then the Wallaces will have to move to Louisiana."

"Reverend Highland…"

"They are pharmacists, aren't they? They'll find work wherever they go."

There was a long silence on the other end of the line.

"You think I'm being unreasonable. I'm sorry. I moved to a Native American village in the middle of nowhere, changed jobs, and began raising four children because the Wallaces abandoned their daughter two years ago. Forgive me if I seem presumptuous."

"Reverend Highland, perhaps you need a little time…"

"I do. You're right. I had no idea that this was still so close to the surface. I've been praying for these people. I thought this would be easier, but I certainly didn't expect them to up and decide they would adopt Annie themselves. Where did that come from?"

"You've been blindsided. I'm sorry."

"It's been over two years. They could have adopted her earlier. Did they tell you why they didn't do that?"

"No, but Jake—I mean, Reverend Highland—perhaps it is the Lord's will. Annie has had a great deal of love and prayers for two of her most formative years."

Jake was reminded of his determination not to take thought for tomorrow; it would take care of itself. "How much time do we have, Ms. James?"

He heard a long sigh, and then her quiet reply. "We have enough time for me to visit the children, take pictures, and gather some information for our records. The Mitchells have applied for a temporary foster care license so the children may be enrolled in school for the fall term. Ideally, they could begin with the rest of their class, but I told them nothing could be done that quickly, and they understand. They are considering continuing to homeschool the children if you will extend the curriculum they are used to. Susan has decided to retire in order to devote all of her time to them."

"That's good. I'm glad. Now we'll see whether the Wallaces will move even as soon as that."

"You are—um—as unflinching as your letters. I can't hold out any hope to you for this to work out the way you want it to, but no matter the outcome for Pia and Benito, Annie is sure to be adopted by the Wallaces. It's a done deal."

"I'll pray. When are you coming out?"

"I'll be there next month, on the first Saturday in August. I wish it could be a weekday, but I can't miss work here. We're swamped. I have to take an extra day and get this done."

"Okay, Saturday, then? We'll look forward to meeting you, Ms. James."

"I wish it were under better circumstances. I really do."
"So do I."

Jake dropped the page he was reading and the sheet behind it. He wanted to cry, but the children were nearby. It was a sweltering summer day, and though the fans were going, the close air made him more irritated than he would otherwise be. He decided this was the perfect time for a siesta.

"Angelina," he called out to his housekeeper in the next room, "the children are outside playing, and I am going to take a nap. Can you watch them, please?"

"Yes, Da. I'll be here. You rest."

Eight

January 2003
Chelsea

It was a week past Christmas. John Milton's crew had met deadline the day before, and the paper was out. Fridays were quiet for them, usually. This was when the local biweekly rested, allowing the county daily to feed on hard news that happened in the lull between meetings and schedules on weekdays.

Chelsea faltered at her keyboard, considering ideas for her column. This she could do only when there were no pressing hours. She'd gotten to her desk shortly after noon, still groggy from covering a service club meeting the night before. It was already four o'clock.

Only James Avery remained at his desk, hammering out mass quantities of text per minute, editing press releases the high school coaches had faxed him about their hopefuls, their stars, no doubt. Chelsea smiled, glancing across the room at the sports editor's computer-shielded head.

That is a writer, she thought. He'd stay at his desk until he had to leave for Friday night's football game. *When does he sleep?* she wondered, but she knew exactly how he felt. There was ink in her blood, too.

John and the two other writers on staff were gone for the day. The office girls were busy enough with paperwork to keep them at their desks till five, when they were supposed to lock everything down. The low buzz of the police scanner was the only noise to harmonize with the peck-tap-peck duet of plastic keyboards.

A beep and crackle woke up the scanner, though, and a careful, tinny voice—a woman's—took the air. "All units, be advised, RP advises, robbery in progress, suspect is armed, 1049 ECR."

James continued typing, but said, "Chelsea, that'd be something you want to listen to." Her beat by default, in other words.

Chelsea trained her ear on the reply: "10-4, 92 en-route, Code 3." The low buzz resumed until the dispatcher responded, and outside a siren's wail began and grew in intensity outside.

"What's your 10-20, 92?"

"Uhh...SB and ECR, ETA one minute."

"10-4, 92...All units respond. Robbery in progress, confirmed— 1049 ECR."

"James, that's nearby."

"Check the book."

Chelsea fumbled for her phone book. How would that help? "We're 1040. It's right across the street," she yelled.

The wail was now a roar. Chelsea split the shades beside her desk and looked out the window onto the El Camino. "It's Hastings!"

Jessica from Classifieds and Lou from Circulation had heard the siren and gotten to the newsroom from their desks. Lou turned up the volume on the scanner.

"What's going on?"

Chelsea froze.

"Crimanee," James yelled, "it's an armed robbery!"

All Chelsea could think to do was to grab her notepad and pencil; then she pushed in for a place near the scanner. Now it was James, Jessica, Lou, and Ruth out of graphics huddled there, not sure what to do next.

"Anyone call John?"

"I did," said Lou. "He's not picking up."

Everyone looked at Chelsea. She groaned. "He takes his scanner everywhere; he'll be on it."

James eyed her hard, nodded, moved back to his desk, and locked his zoom lens onto his camera, then waved them all aside, heading for the door. "I'm going."

Chelsea's face colored as she watched James chase outside. This was her responsibility, but she'd frozen.

Painters had been at work that week, and left scaffolding on the south side of the building. James climbed the apparatus up to the roof with the grace of a large cat. The four women watched his movements till they couldn't see him anymore, then turned their attention to the plate glass window above Chelsea's desk, which faced east. From there they had a wide view of Hastings Fish House.

A noise like a firecracker sounded then, and a second later a faint concussion hit the newsroom, seeming to ripple the glass on the windows. Jessica and Chelsea gasped, but Lou said *SHHH*, she wanted to hear. Chelsea couldn't breathe, much less make a noise at that point, anyway.

Gunfire.

Four seconds passed, and then another, louder crack—closer?—could be heard. Ruth and Jessica backed in slow motion away from the window. The pair dove instinctively, one under Chelsea's desk, the other under Karl's metal corner unit. Chelsea and Lou were on the ground but climbed back up to the window to watch the scene unfolding outside.

Clad in black over bulky, hot armor, Atascadero's finest had been first at the scene. Chelsea recognized Rodney Black, a rookie, just as the second shot was fired. She'd been his ride-along the week before. *Oh, dear GOD! Please,* she begged...*Not Rodney.*

NO! The gunner, who had been standing in Hastings' doorway, fled before Chelsea could tear her eyes away from the policeman long enough to focus. All she saw was a blur of black leather gloves, a revolver, and a masked head crouched in flight.

Back-up should be the TAC team, but they weren't there yet. A lone siren grew louder as they watched dark blood pool under the young guardian's head. On the street, which no one had taken time to block, brakes screeched, then a pickup careened out of control, trying to avoid the black-clad body. It slid sideways onto the walk in front of the news room, burning serious rubber trying to stop. At last it bounced off the brick planter under the window just above James's desk.

Chelsea swallowed air and choked. Lou yelled at the top of her lungs for her to "Get down! Get down, Chelsea! NOW!" A loud metal-on-mortar crunch could be heard inside the newsroom, and then an ear-splitting crash exploded inside the room; this time it was the plate glass window above the targeted planter, blown in all directions, inside and out.

Instead of diving under a desk, Chelsea ran to the back. Clearing the newsroom before glass flew, she bolted down the hall to the water cooler. She couldn't breathe. In the distance she heard a siren wail, or were there two? *An ambulance. Someone has to call for an ambulance!* But her voice was impotent. She gulped down a paper cupful of water, fought for her breath and finally recovered it, then ran back to the front. Only half-able to whisper, she grabbed Lou, who was still crouching down, half under the desk. Her head—eyes only—slanted above the window sill, peering east.

"Lou—call an ambulance!" Chelsea croaked.

"I did."

Just then Chelsea realized the road was still open. Another vehicle —a bus —was headed in, this time from the north. Giving no thought to anything but the danger of a bus headed toward the policeman's defenseless body, she ran out the newsroom door into the middle of the street. She began waving her arms over her head and down, again and again. "There—there's a body in the street!" she tried to yell, but her voice was still hoarse.

The next thing she knew, she was head down, spread-eagle on the pavement—underneath a suffocating load. Her knee had snapped as she went down, and now screamed out to her almost audibly in a burst of excruciating pain. Sirens overpowered the sounds of shouting, brakes locking. Closer in she could hear a hiss in the ear that was not pressed against asphalt. "Stay down!"

Chetty

Chetty Armstrong leaned back as far as he could stretch himself into the corner booth where he sat across from his pal, Sam. A plate of fries, in a paper bowl in the middle of the table, was dwindling. Sam picked up the slice of lemon on top of his water and ice and squeezed it. "This stinks."

"What—bein' on the outside or the water?"

"Both. Smells like fish."

Chetty snickered. "It is fish."

"My daddy used to say guests stink like fish after four days."

"Ya. Well, we been out more'n four days, and it *is* startin' to smell."

The waiter, a muscular man with a big grin, came round to refill the water glasses. "Y'all need anything else?"

Chetty's eyes widened. He opened his stubble-lined mouth and sneered, revealing a row of ragged yellow teeth. "Well, now. Let me just think on that 'un here a minute."

The waiter lifted his head but lowered his eyes, averting them to the floor, then back up, as if forcing himself to make eye contact. "More water, sir?"

Chetty spat his mouthful of half-chewed fries on the floor. "Haw!!! Yessuh! Mo' watteh theaya. Mo' uh dat freeee watteh. Tha's what we need he-ah, yessuh!"

The waiter poured Chetty's glass full, then Sam's, nodded and turned to go.

"Wait a minute!"

The waiter stopped, his shoulders drooped a little.

"Y'all wouldn't have any more o' these here 'free' French fries in the back, now wouldya?"

Bert

The waiter looked back over his shoulder and caught a glimpse of something shiny, laying half on the table, half in the man's right hand.

He understood. "In a minute, be here in a minute. Yes, sir."

"I like a boy whut know 'is place," snickered Chetty. "Yes, I do."

"What!" hissed Sam. "You crazy?"

"Nah! May as well have us some fun 'fore we go back. Besides, that ninny's not gonna do nothin'. You watch."

"Oh, I'm watchin' all right."

Bert walked calmly back to the counter, moved behind and called out so the customers could hear, "Sarah, two orders of fries!" And then he picked up the receiver, and surreptitiously hit #1, speed-dial for 911. The place was noisy. No one would notice it hadn't rung.

After hearing the faint voice of a dispatcher answer from the receiver, barely audible, "911 emergency," he said, "Hastings Fish House," then waited a moment, pretending to listen while he wrote in a fake order on his pad. He recited the address into the receiver, as if he were giving directions to a takeout customer for pick-up, and said, "Okay, then. We'll be expecting you." Just before hanging up, he shouted the fake order over his shoulder to the kitchen: "We got a number 64-G for takeout, Sarah. ASAP."

The man named Chetty interrupted him at the counter, and in a low voice growled, "Listen, boy, forget the fries. I'll take what you got that's green!" He was holding the revolver in plain sight now, but with a glove, and he was pulling a mask over his face with his free hand. His buddy had already retreated out the back door.

"You want money? You got a gun. It's yours, man!" Bert said calmly but loudly enough for the other customers and Sarah to hear. The few who had come in for an early supper scrambled then. Glasses tumbled, and food flew as some of them hit the floor under the tables. Others ran for the front door or the back. Sarah dove under the sink in the kitchen.

Bert pushed the *No Sale* button on the register and lifted his arms in the air.

"You gettin' uppity on me, boy? Put it in a bag. Do it quick!"

Bert reached for a to-go bag and opened it, collected what cash was on top, and loaded it in.

"Lift the bottom. I want it all!"

A faint whine grew audible, and then louder outside.

"You called the cops! You'll pay for this, boy!"

Chetty grabbed the brown bag with one hand, the waiter's arm with the other. "Come with me!"

There was dead silence in the restaurant, save the scuffling of the two men as Chetty pulled Bert around the counter and shoved the revolver into his back. The only other sound was the whine of a siren, close and loud.

"Move!"

Chetty's plan worked. A big black man pointing a gun at him from the doorway was apparently all the officer saw.

"He thinks it's you, boy. I'll just humor him here." With that, Chetty lifted the waiter's right hand from behind, slipping the gun under it and training it on the cop. A loud crack reverberated on the street, and the black man slumped to the ground. Chetty ducked quickly, took aim at the cop's head, and pulled the trigger.

Bert bent double and groaned, but then managed to push himself back inside the door, shut it and lock it. The man called Chetty had vanished, but he wasn't sure the other man had, so he got to his feet with a mighty effort. Blood, he could see, was seeping out his shirt, low. It felt like a block of cement was pulling him down, but he made his way behind the counter to check on Sarah. She was hysterical, on the floor under the sink in a fetal position, sobbing.

There was a door at the back of the kitchen, with a window in it. He could see to the street. Traffic was going crazy. One pickup had just bashed into the building across the street and more cars were coming from the north. It was then he saw the woman fly out the door where the truck had come to a sliding stop and hit the bricks. "Oh, no. She's gonna get herself hit…it's her!"

He ran.

Somewhere between the restaurant and the street Bert heard another shot, then another. He heard it or he felt it, he wasn't sure. The traffic wasn't Miz Chelsea's only danger now. He couldn't stop. He wouldn't let himself, but the cement center of his abdomen pulled him down as hard as adrenalin was pushing his body forward.

With all his effort he lunged at his target, trying with all his might to push her as far from the city bus he'd seen coming as possible. Then there were the bullets, the squeal of frozen brakes, and the smell of rubber burning way too close.

And then it was night.

Chetty

Chetty Armstrong ran for his nearest cover, a white stucco building just north of the front door of Hastings. He'd seen the black and white out of the corner of his eye from the front door of the restaurant. It was parked on the opposite end of the building, south. He stopped and turned only after he'd cleared the few feet of wall leading to a dumpster behind it. A parking lot and the fishery blocked his view, but he could just see a figure—a woman—yelling and jumping up and down like a crazy thing, at oncoming traffic. Then the black boy—still alive, but running heavy—was limping, fast.

That wouldn't do. No witnesses. He knew no one had paid much attention to him in the restaurant before he'd had a chance to pull his mask on. No one, that is, except the waiter. No, sir, it wouldn't do to have that boy live. He had five shots left, may as well go for broke. He leveled the revolver at his target. No problem. If it had been his bullet that hit the boy, well—he'd be down without a prayer now. That cop was a lousy shot, or he wasn't aiming to kill.

Chetty thought his own marksmanship keen, talented really. He was long on that. It was honed by hours, days of practice. Lately Sam and he hadn't had much else to do. Since the day they left the slammer they'd been holed up in the river bottom, where there were lots of places to hide and to sleep, and to practice. It was easy finding the revolver. Drunks sleep hard, and they play cards indiscriminately. The riverbed was full of drunks.

This would be an easy mark. He trained his right hand over his left for balance, but the dumpster he was leaning against chose that moment to roll. He missed. Then it dawned on him that his cover was lost if the downed cop's partner figured out where the shot came from. Sure enough, he heard another report ring out from somewhere near the street. He quickly wiped the handle and trigger of the revolver with the front of his T-shirt, dropped it into the dumpster, and ran up an embankment. The dirt hill was hidden by the wall of another long building: a boarded up, deserted laundromat.

Safe enough.

He pulled off his gloves, and then the mask, stuffing them into his jacket pocket before he reached the summit. Then he was off the main road, invisible again. He knew where to find Sam; that's where he'd go. The water in the river ran deep. There'd been no rain to feed it that showed, not this time of year. A man could hide himself just like that river, deep and long till the seasons changed. Then he could be gone.

Nine

This time *The Examiner* had seemingly lost its rightful weekend scoop. Only James Avery's sports-seasoned eye had caught every aspect of Atascadero's weekend highlight from his perch on the roof directly over his own desk. All that was left by the time the North County crew arrived was a pile of bricks and glass.

KSLO sent a camera crew on its way as soon as the code was heard on their scanner, but all the footage shown that evening on the news was of Massey's Towing Service loading a pick-up onto a tow dolly and pulling it away from the shattered window and planter outside the newsroom.

They did, however, manage to get a live interview with Chelsea Andressen from her stretcher; she was covered with blood but not badly hurt, so left for the last ambulance on the scene to pick up.

"What were you doing on the street, Ms. Andressen? What did you see?"

The answer was inaudible, but viewers could see the woman was shaken. She was crying.

Chelsea

That's my payback, Chelsea supposed when she watched the six o'clock news later, *for all the times I've shoved a microphone in front of people with one hand and stolen a picture with the other.*

Officer Black had been taken away in an ambulance first, then the waiter in another unit. Both had lost copious amounts of blood, and the pools of it were fodder for both KSLO and *The Examiner.*

Friday night, after Chelsea's knee had been x-rayed and the blood had been cleaned off and found not to be hers, she was advised to stay overnight at the hospital for observation. She had a good-sized goose egg on the left side of her head—the side that had landed on the street. The doctor informed her that she had a dislodged kneecap and torn ligaments—they didn't know the extent of the damage yet—a concussion, and a nervous condition to do with shock. Any of the above, they told her, was cause for concern.

"Ya have to, Chelsea. Sorry," John Milton told her. "This is Worker's Comp."

"Okay, but are you sure? When they see the headline 'Stupid Woman Flies Into Street to Stop Bus,' are they gonna pay for this?"

"It's *our* headline. Let's see: *'Courageous Reporter Runs into Street to Save Police Officer Down from Gunshot Wound.'*"

Chelsea couldn't make herself smile. The picture in her mind of Officer Rodney Black's prone body on the road banned the humor her editor was trying to evoke in her. "How is he, John?"

"He'll be okay. He's young. There was a lot of blood, but the bullet hit the ear and only grazed the brain. If he hadn't fallen straight back like he did—he hit his head pretty hard—he'd be the only one going home tonight."

"Where is he?"

"Recovery, down the hall."

"There was another man. They had to pull him off me..."

"That was the waiter from the restaurant."

"Is he okay?"

"No. Lost a lot of blood. They don't know why he ran out and pushed you out of traffic like he did, or if he meant to. They're saying he was on the run, and you were in his way. He took another shot going down, from Rodney's partner."

"How bad? And why do you say 'if he meant to'? Why else would he have done that?"

"The police have one witness, and that's his story. James's pictures tell another one, though. The first bullet hit him way below the heart, under the rib cage, and exited. They haven't found it. The second hit his side, lucky again, but he's lost plenty of blood—and that bullet lodged. He's in surgery right now. Word is they found the bullet, but they're having the devil of a time getting at it."

"James got pictures."

"Some good ones, yeah, he did."

"The crazy lady?"

"That too, but like I said—it stays in house."

"Plastered on your wall, no doubt."

"Art." John pulled a stack of papers out of his shirt pocket. "Here are the prints. Thought you'd want to see what the paper would look like Wednesday."

"You know, you could sell these for big bucks to *The Examiner.*"

"Not on your life."

Chelsea took a few of the prints and began examining them. It was like looking at frozen action figures in black and white. One was of Rodney Black in shooting stance—his gun trained on the front door of Hastings, at a man—a black man. The photography was superb. Every feature was detailed in well defined, graduated tones.

"Oh!"

"What's wrong?"

"I know this man. He was at the shelter when I spent the night. He said he had a new job—at a restaurant. He robbed Hastings?"

"They're not sure, but I don't think so. See the right hand there?"

"Ya, I do. There's a gun in it."

"Look closer, and take a look at the blow-up. Here…" The editor handed her another print.

The details James had managed to get with his zoom were very close, and he'd taken several. One of the prints was of the right hand by itself, blown up to the size of a melon. "There are two hands there, one looks like it's gloved—under—right there." Chelsea pointed to a thumb clinched around the revolver. The black hand above it seemed to be flat, not touching the gun at all, a detail only a sharp zoom could have caught. Obviously Rodney Black's 20/20 vision hadn't caught it. Bert had been shot because the officer assumed he was holding a gun.

"Clever robber, eh?"

"That's what it looks like. I'm going down to the station right now, that is, if the chief isn't here poking around. He'll need to see this."

"You kept a copy."

"Of course, and the negative. James used film, not digital. There shouldn't be a problem, but that's what we're here for—keep 'em in line."

Chelsea thought of James's logic at climbing the scaffolding and of his ability with the camera. *If it hadn't been for that....*

Then she thought of a phone call she had better make.

"Paula?"

"Yes? Oh, hello, Chelsea! Are you all right, honey? I saw the news! I can't believe you're on the phone! Did you lose a lot of blood?"

"I'm fine. The blood wasn't mine. That's what I'm calling about, actually."

"Blood?"

"Yeah. Well, the man who tried to save me—he was from the shelter. Paula, it was Bert. He's been shot."

"Bert Jackson? Our Bert?"

"Yes. He's in surgery."

"Is he going to be okay? How bad is he hurt?"

"John says he's lost a lot of blood. Listen, there is something I want to show you before any of this gets much further. Can you come to the hospital?"

"Oh, of course, dear. I'm on my way."

Ten

Chelsea

In a rare moment for the newspaper, James Avery had insisted on writing something other than sports. After almost a full morning of clearing glass from his desk, he was hard at work at his computer, oblivious to the chattering and pounding of two workmen installing a new window above him. Chelsea knew he would finish his story, and then stay late getting the sports pages ready as well.

She was working on her column, or trying to, with her right knee swollen, bandaged to the size of a cantaloupe, and her leg extended out and up, away from her desk. Yes, she would write a story on the shelter now, but at least in this forum she could inject her own perspective. This story would tell about the man who greeted her at the shelter—homeless, yes—but also the man who risked his own life to save hers.

In the hospital overnight, she could think about little else. Who was this man, and why would he do so much for a woman he hardly knew? More than that, she was obsessed with making sure the whole story was told.

After talking to Rodney Black, Chelsea knew he was adamant about Bert having been the robber. In his mind, and in his pride, he could not let go of the idea that he'd done the right thing. Chief Curry had no reason to doubt him at this point, save the blow-up of two hands John had managed to make him look at. Unfortunately, that was after Curry had been accosted by KSLO and *The Examiner.* "All I see is what looks like a glove," he told John.

It would take more than James's genius photography to override the statements made by APD, since they'd already been unleashed. She hoped John's insistence that the newspaper held public officials accountable was true, but she'd seen the power of a little choice ink spilled on newsprint, and it could be scary.

While John Milton saw to it all Atascadero's public meetings were covered consistently, the larger, more widely distributed *Examiner* sent their reporter to these meetings selectively. Their North County coverage was spread thin between one full-time and one part-time reporter, making it impossible to paint a consistent picture.

What was worse, *The Examiner* had recently hired a new, young editor, who often sought out articles with a negative slant. Rumor had it that if a story was turned in without it, it was sent back for a "sexier" version. Chelsea still hadn't decided what "sexy" meant in news circles, but she did not like the implication. It was one of her reasons for leaving the air. Still, she had a healthy fear of the new wave of marketing stories. Was it "sexy" to imply a homeless man had gotten a job in a restaurant and then decided to rob it?

If only there had been more witnesses, she thought. But the diners had fled before much could be seen. All they could do was identify Bert as their waiter that day. No one, apparently, had paid much attention to things until they heard him shout (one said unnaturally loudly, as though in a play—not real) something about having a gun and wanting money. No one had stuck around for the second half, and the manager had hit the floor in the kitchen when she heard the word *gun*. Sarah did tell James, and later the reporter for the *Examiner*, that Bert had programmed 911 into speed-dial his first day at work, one of the first things he did. She had thought it was strange, a little too coincidental, and, of course, a sexy "coincidental" version of that hit the presses and wound up in Saturday's paper. James's version wouldn't see light until the following Wednesday.

Common sense would ask why Bert would want the police to show up if he was in on the heist. Unfortunately, that might be up to a judge to decide at this point, because common sense was not what prevailed when the press printed before facts were sorted. And between Friday when the robbery occurred and KSLO arrived, and Wednesday, when James's version of the robbery would be in print and less widely circulated—a whole lot of rhetoric would have already fallen out, true or not, in no less than four issues of the *Examiner*.

As for Bert, he was swinging perilously close to the other side at this point, and whether or not he'd pass over was anyone's guess. The truth needed to be considered, for Bert's sake, but for the sake of the shelter as well. This lie that was being suggested could cost AHO its fledgling reputation, and its future. All Chelsea could see in her mind's eye were the faces of those she'd met at the shelter, faces relieved to be out of the cold for the night, faces she had not wanted to paint with printer's ink.

Her resolve to write about it in her column came only after the statement was aired—on the nightly news, no less—that allegedly "Officer Black was shot by an African-American male, who had just begun working at the restaurant that day and was living at the local homeless shelter."

The wall the department seemed to be keeping in place to protect itself would rob Bert of his just due, at the very least, if he lived. She hoped it wouldn't rob him of his freedom as well.

The Examiner's Saturday exclusive was plastered on John's window for all to see. Lou stood by it, scowling at what she read.

"Hey, was anyone contacted by *The Examiner* here?" she asked.

It was Monday morning, and all John's minions were at their desks working.

"You kidding?" from Karl.

Chelsea was still reading. "Their 'source' was Curry. He wasn't there, was he?"

"Nope. They regurgitated his 'exclusive' next to the picture of the blood in the street—no doubt stilled from KSLO's 'late breaking' on Friday."

"Did anyone see Mitzy there?" asked Chelsea.

Mitzy was one of the North County reporters.

"No, not a trace," offered James, without skipping a beat on his keyboard. "And I had the expensive seat, remember?"

Chelsea smiled, but this reminded her of something. "James, did you see Rodney's partner shoot Bert—when he was running at me, I mean?"

"What?"

"John said Bert had two wounds. There must have been two shots, and there was an officer on the scene. Lou, do you remember hearing three shots?"

"I don't remember much after the window went out; then you ran out there. Let's see...I saw you go down, and Bert was flying. No. I wouldn't have heard anything. That bus sounded like a train wreck trying to stop like it did. That's all I heard. But, you know, I think he did jerk a little—Bert—when he was in the air coming at you, I mean. It was slow motion for a minute there—like it gets in an accident sometimes, and I remember thinking, *That's really odd, the way he jerked again.*"

"Where was the partner—Rodney's partner? Do you remember?"

"Maybe by the black and white? I don't know."

"That was on the south side, across the street, if he was still in it. James?"

"I had the camera on you, Scoop. I don't know. Things were happening pretty fast. I never saw the partner."

John rounded the corner then. "It'll all come out in the wash, you watch. I don't have the money or the time for investigative reporting...let's get back to work."

On cue the clatter of James's keys grew intense, and soon the other keyboards joined in. Karl was working on the police log, which would include Friday's incident. John went back to his desk, where he was teasing out an editorial with the same emphasis. All desks were concerned with the same subject, and all hoped it would somehow make a difference.

Only Lou couldn't be intimidated by the boss. "Johnny! You write the best little ole'editorial we've ever written, ya hear?" She headed down the hall toward her own office, but on her way, dramatically she threw back: "This one's for truth and justice. You go, team!"

At three-thirty the front door of the newsroom swung open, and from the high counter above Chelsea's desk she could see Debra looking down at her. She noticed the serenity that usually characterized her was shaken today. She wore hospital scrubs, so she must have just come from work.

"Something the matter, Debra?"

"It's Bert, Chelsea. I've been at the hospital. I got off early to go check on him. He's awake and he's talking. He's asking for you. Paula sent me down here to let you know."

It was Monday. She could afford the time today. Chelsea looked over her right shoulder, into John's glassed-in office. He was looking at her, nodding and shrugging, which she knew meant "It's your decision, just finish your pages on time." Nothing escaped that man. She grabbed her bag and her jacket. "Let's go."

Debra hopped and Chelsea hobbled into the Taurus, because Chelsea said Debra's car would be safe where it was till they got back. She'd have to return anyway. After they were settled in and belted, Chelsea pulled out, made it to the intersection, turned right and right again onto the Highway onramp, headed north toward the hospital. She waited until she'd merged into traffic, then asked, "How is he?"

"He's in pain. They've given him a morphine pump to use, but he refuses until it gets pretty bad, I can tell. He wants to see you. He keeps saying that."

"What do you know about him, Debra? Where did he come from? He looked so familiar the first time I met him. I guessed it was because he must be from Louisiana. Am I right?"

Debra seemed to be pulling at files in her brain and examining them. "All I know is he's trying hard to make a start in a new place. That's what he told me."

"That's all?"

"That's all I know. He does have a Southern accent. Do you really think it's Louisiana? Can you pin it that close?"

"You'd be surprised. I'd be willing to bet he's an old neighbor of mine. He talks on the solid side of must-be-able-to-speak-clearly and Cajun, which means he's probably well educated. I'd bet my swan statue on it, and you know how much I love that thing."

Debra laughed, but had a puzzled look. "What do you mean by 'must-be-able-to-speak-clearly'?"

"They seriously run help-wanted ads like that down there. They have to. Cajun is a mixture of French and deep Southern drawl. No one can understand it unless they speak it, trust me."

"I do remember one thing," Debra offered. "He told me he had some things to do for a friend."

"He was in his Bible a lot, wasn't he?" Chelsea added, thoughtfully.

"Yes, he was. He still is. He had Paula bring it to him as soon as he woke up from surgery. She's been reading to him."

"Paula's there?"

"She hasn't left him that I know of. They've started taking the bus around to the hospital before showers now. Bert has a lot of friends at the shelter."

"Smokin' buddies." Chelsea smiled, remembering the group that huddled and chatted on the front porch together, twice on her watch.

The air grew quiet inside the Taurus.

"What have you heard, Debra, about the robbery and all? What are the others saying?"

"Paula says Bert wasn't the one who shot the officer."

"She's right. He didn't."

"That's not what the paper is saying, you know."

"I know, but it's the truth."

Quiet again. They were approaching the hospital off-ramp, which would put them a quarter mile from the building.

"I'm only trusting my instinct on this, Chelsea. It's strong. I know he didn't do it. You seem to think he didn't. There's something you need to know, though, if you haven't seen him since he woke up, I mean."

"What?"

"They have a guard on him, and there's talk he's being investigated. When I left, Paula was really upset. That's why she asked me to come get you."

Chelsea pictured Paula in a tizzy, frustrated with the authorities, and with herself for not being able to commandeer the situation and make it better. But she realized that having this woman on her side— on Bert's side—had a calming effect. It was reinforcement to her that Bert could not have had anything to do with this robbery. Paula was sharp.

The memory of a voice in her ear, her left ear, told her the same thing. Bert had not been running away, and he could not possibly have been the robber. She could replay it perfectly in her head, and she wondered if it wasn't something she needed to listen to even now: *"Stay down!"*

A uniformed police woman stood at semi-attention beside the door to Bert's room. She nodded to Chelsea and Debra as they passed her. It wasn't as if the suspect was going anywhere. Chelsea recognized her, vaguely, as one of the drug team officers she'd met recently on the high school campus.

Paula Frean sat in an institutional chair next to Bert Jackson's hospital bed. His head was held back hard against the pillow, as if in concentration, his eyes closed. He looked old. The yellow glow of light that fell in an innocuous circle on the bed was unnatural. Subdued rays emanated from a fluorescent light under a shelf, which was screwed into the wall directly above the head of Bert's bed. The yellow bounced lazily up to muted walls and pale striped curtains, half pulled to simulate a mock privacy.

The click of Chelsea's heels on hospital tile alerted Paula; she looked up and breathed in deeply, closing her eyes in relief. Her lips formed a silent *thank you* upward, and then another audibly to Chelsea and to Debra while she nodded to them in turn, as if to say, "Let's be quiet. He's not so good."

Paula got up, and Bert opened his eyes. He looked weak, Chelsea noticed. She hardly recognized him, and since she hadn't known him well, it was difficult to be comfortable. After all, she was at the hospital bed of a man who'd saved her life four days ago, a man who might not live because of it. But he seemed to know exactly how she felt, because he lifted his head slightly from the pillow and smiled. That was what she remembered, his smile. "Bert. I'm so glad you're awake. You saved my life. Do you remember?"

"Miz Chelsea!" His voice was a whisper, and it came slow, but he hadn't stopped smiling. "I have…somethin'…to…tell ya."

Chelsea had pulled out her hand-held tape recorder and set it to run; she was close to him, coaxing. "What did you want to say, Bert?"

"Man's name was Chetty...heard the...other one say it."

"The gunman?"

"Yes...Chetty had a...gun." His smile had turned serious now, but when he exhaled, it was labored and long. He seemed to be gathering strength from somewhere. "Ex-cons—way they...talk."

"There were two of them? What did they look like?"

"Thin...short...shaved head." He took another long, shallow breath. Bert was exhausting himself, she knew.

Then, as though by some magic, the room appeared lighter. Bert took a more natural breath, and a peace came over his face which made it look younger. "Miz Chelsea, call...Ben."

"What?" She saw his exhaustion again overtake him, but she couldn't believe what she'd just heard. She asked, "Ben? You know Ben? How?"

"Paula knows. She'll...tell ya." Bert closed his eyes and turned his head toward Debra then, and she crossed over to his bed, took his hand and pushed a button close to his wrist. "Good night, brother," she whispered.

"Wait," Chelsea cried. "Wait! Bert, what do you mean?"

"Chelsea, you'll have to ask Paula," said Debra.

Chelsea looked frantically at Debra, and then Paula. She couldn't read them, or maybe she didn't want to. She said, "He's not coming back, is he?"

Paula reached for her hand, and said, "He needs rest."

A few minutes passed while the women watched the slow, unsteady rise and fall of Bert's chest. After a long lull in the rhythm, Debra checked the pulse at his neck, and shot a look back to Paula, then at her watch. She pushed the call button for a nurse and reached for a pen to write down the time that Bert Jackson passed on.

Chelsea finally broke down. With the overnight work at the shelter, the stress on Friday, her hospital stay, and now Bert's passing, she was completely spent, and she let herself cry. Nothing seemed to matter anymore. She fell on the floor next to Bert's bed and lay there in a heap.

It was Paula who called John at the paper and arranged for Chelsea to have the rest of the week off. The staff, he told her, would take over and get her pages on for her. "Just get her home, but don't leave her alone there," he'd told Paula.

Chelsea made her way through the hospital corridors, supported by Paula and Debra. The three paused at the Intensive Care waiting room to tell the others, the thin bus driver Tom included, that Bert was dead. There were no dry eyes. Paula decided it would be best to sit for a while among the others, even though Chelsea was beside herself. Debra agreed, and the group made room for them on the padded seats in the quiet room. Paula went out to get water for Chelsea.

It was good to talk. Each one, in turn, had a story to tell about their experiences with Bert. None of them had known him long, but when they put their stories together, they added up to quite a lot.

The woman from the state hospital offered, "He used to say, 'You study hist'ry, an' you'll see—only thing that ever done good is love.' I thought he was crazy. I think I just didn't want to listen—he always had that Bible out, and I was afraid he'd quote it to me."

An elderly man Chelsea hadn't met said, "That's why I think—well, there's a reason he died 'n' all. Someone like Bert don't die for nothin'."

"He saved my life, you know," Chelsea managed.

"He did that," said Paula. "He was so glad he did that."

"Anyone know more about him? His past?" asked Chelsea.

Paula nodded and looked around at the others. "We're not supposed to talk about what we know about clients, but he did give me a word or two for you, Chelsea. We'll talk a little later."

"If it was us, Paula," said the middle-aged man, who held his little girl in his lap, "We'd want you to share—just now." The others nodded their agreement. "And we know Bert would feel the same way."

Paula stood up and hugged them, one at a time, and whispered something in Tom's ear in the process. He stood up and looked at his watch. "We need to get to dinner soon. Paula will join us later, and we'll talk," he said.

Slowly the visiting room emptied, save the three women. Debra tried to excuse herself, but Chelsea asked her to stay, please. And then Paula reached in her bag and pulled out a thin black leather wallet, opened it, and passed it to Chelsea. A laminated card on top read *Bert Jackson, Private Detective*. She scanned the rest of the card for more information and learned that her hunch had been right on the money. He was from Natchitoches, Louisiana. *Ben...what did he say about Ben? What was going on?*

"Paula?"

"Chelsea, Bert was at the shelter because I asked him to stay. He came to me early on and offered his services, and I asked him to go undercover. I just didn't want anyone nervous. He was in town temporarily anyway, and he needed a place to stay."

"What was he doing here?"

"Working for a friend."

"What friend?"

"Your husband, Chelsea. Ben sent Bert to see whether you were all right. He was worried about you but didn't want to crowd you." Paula looked at Debra then, asking her to check on things in Bert's room, saying she'd join her there later to take care of arrangements.

When they were alone, Paula continued. "Chelsea, he was working for Ben Mitchell. His card was in Bert's wallet. It was the only contact I could find, so I called him when Bert was in surgery. He said Bert was a friend of his, but you didn't know him."

Chelsea reddened, trying to decide what to say. How could she tell Paula what she was thinking? This was one of Ben's new friends from church, obviously, one of the people she'd worked so hard to avoid.

"Then he took that restaurant job so he'd be close to my office?"

"Probably."

Chelsea buried her head in her hands and sobbed.

On Wednesday *The Acorn* published its exoneration of Bert Jackson, complete with the photo of his hand extended forcibly over the gloved hand that grasped a revolver at the door of Hastings Fish House. Chelsea had made sure James included the information about a man named Chetty, and he had even cross-questioned some of the diners, and found out there had been an exchange between the waiter and this man, a rude one. There had been two men at the table, both thin, and sporting tattoos on their upper and lower arms. One of them had a shaved head.

Paula had made sure Bert's history was included, and that he was actually someone she'd hired to guard the shelter, not a resident. James had dutifully put her quote in verbatim in a prominent position in the story, then for good measure, into a pull-out—just down from the headline, and to the right.

To the sports editor's credit, *The Examiner* had called up to congratulate him, and to ask for the use of his picture of the two hands on the gun. He'd given his consent, and so had John Milton.

Unfortunately, *The Examiner* managed to slant backwards again, stating that "a good percentage of the homeless are parolees from local prison facilities, so of course Ms. Frean's decision to hire an undercover agent was warranted." In the same paragraph, they made reference to the up-and-coming Atascadero Homeless Organization shelter, where Bert Jackson had been housed the day before the shooting. They called him "one of those involved in the shooting" rather than a victim of the hold-up. Any reader might contribute guilt by association, which is exactly what was implied.

"Unbelievable! Do they know just how to muck up the water or what—they're like vipers!" Chelsea cried when she saw the headlines in Thursday morning's county paper—front page, no less.

"Say what?" Debra asked. She was at the kitchen counter, cleaning up after breakfast. She'd stayed with Chelsea, rather than going back to Charlie's after Bert died.

The arrangement had been Paula's idea, and a logical one since Chelsea lived alone, and John had insisted she not be for a while.

"Here. See what you think when you read this," she said, handing Debra the A section of *The Examiner.*

Debra took it but motioned Chelsea down, commanding her to rest. She had the day off because she'd be working Saturday and Sunday at the rest home. For now she was helping out where she could, at least making sure Chelsea kept her knee elevated. The x-rays had shown no permanent damage, but the knee was traumatized. Debra was finding Chelsea to be a hard patient to work with, though. It was a challenge to keep her off her feet.

Her heart sank when she saw *The Examiner*'s assessment of things for herself. She fully understood Chelsea's anger. It upset her, too.

"Why would they do this?" she asked.

"It sells papers. The more circulation—newspapers you can prove are sold—the more you can charge for advertising, the engine that runs the machine...m-o-n-e-y."

"Why was your paper able to print the simple facts, then?"

"Our publishers have a little more conscience, and they have to live here...hold their heads up in town. I think *The Examiner*'s higher-ups live in New York, so it doesn't matter to them, not from where they sit."

"Couldn't you write a letter to the editor or something?"

"Oh, they'd love it. Those sell papers too—and the nastier the fight gets, the more papers they sell. I wouldn't give them the satisfaction."

"How's Paula gonna take this?"

"Not sitting down, if I know her, but what can she do?" Debra smiled at the thought. "It'll be interesting to find out."

Paula

Paula didn't take it sitting down. She wrote. She made phone calls. What she did, though, that brought real results, was to open the shelter to television again. With the consent of all the clients, Paula baked *The Examiner* with the only local oven that cooked faster and hotter than they did, KSLO. She invited television crews to do an exclusive, handing them a statement—signed by no less than every client—that KSLO could come in and film their evening, with live interviews with whomever they chose.

The Examiner, Paula knew, would not like the television station airing something they hadn't even been aware of, so Paula made it her business to see to it they did not know until it aired. When they sent their reporter around to demand interviews, Paula told her, "Well, yes, of course, dear, but only if I may approve every word before it goes to print. You understand. There has been some bad publicity. We can't afford that. And, to be sure it doesn't happen again, I'll need your signature and the signature of your editor and your publisher on this agreement before the interview is granted. You understand."

The county paper buckled, and printed the first straight-up story they'd run on their pages about the robbery since it occurred. That wasn't enough to satisfy Paula's sense of justice, though. She followed it all up with another letter campaign, involving every pastor, choir member, and service club president who'd ever pulled a ladle out of a soup tureen for AHO. In short, she created an echo of sorts, a resounding one that didn't stop reverberating for weeks.

Even though his body was to be sent back to Louisiana for burial, Paula held a memorial service for Bert. She called him a local hero who deserved the best that could be done for him. She insisted on selecting the best polished wooden casket, and then proceeded to pay for it by looting the pockets of hundreds of contributors at a massive silent auction held at the Park Pavilion. The fundraiser netted a hefty profit, with money left over to start a trust fund for the shelter in Bert's name.

All of the above was well publicized, Paula Frean-style.

Chelsea said she wondered whether Paula planned these things out from start to finish in little "what if" scenarios. She'd managed to get KSLO to cover the fundraiser, the funeral, and then the shelter—all in less than a week. And she had *The Examiner* tamed to reporting the straight truth by then, at least where AHO was concerned.

Debra reminded her that Bert's funeral and his exoneration were not all Paula had taken care of, and that it wasn't all planned out—not by Paula, actually—that it was just the best plan, and maybe God had something to do with it. Chelsea didn't say anything to that, but she knew what her new roommate meant. It did seem impossible that a human being could have woven things together so masterfully, on purpose. But then, there was no one quite like Paula Frean, was there?

Eleven

Debra

It was Saturday, and Debra was back at work after securing a promise from Chelsea that she would stay put for the day. There was a new admit to the nursing home, and a room to prepare. Marj Highland was a fifty-seven-year-old woman who'd had an early stroke and was deteriorating. The family couldn't take care of her anymore. When the daughter had brought her into the lobby earlier Debra noticed she was a strikingly pretty woman with strong features. Her smile was rare and barely perceptible because the muscles on half her face did not respond. It seemed Marj was able to communicate, one way or another. Either someone had been working with her, or the stroke hadn't stolen any more than her mobility and some of her speech. *She's probably depressed*, Debra thought, *but who can tell at this point?*

It would take time and special care to read her emotions because the stroke had rendered her face almost blank. But the staff was in the habit of treating patients as though they were responsive even when they were not. It was rare, but sometimes they were surprised, and patients would pipe up a week after they'd been told something, say they didn't like what someone said to them, or ask why someone did something, or they'd just act like they knew it all along, out of the blue.

Debra and one of the orderlies fussed over Marj's room before the aide was left alone to accommodate the move. When the daughter arrived she introduced herself as Nan. She was in her early twenties, Debra guessed, freckled and blond, where her mother had the coloring of a raven.

"I've had to go back to work," Nan explained, presumably apologizing for the fact that she had to admit her mother at all.

"It *is* hard, I know," Debra told her, but the girl still looked regretful. She helped Debra settle Marj into bed, then ran back and forth bringing in boxes and suitcases, and spent the rest of the time hanging clothes in the closet and placing pictures artistically on the small bulletin board above her mother's bed. Debra lent a hand where she could and chased down some scissors and tape to give her from the nurse's station.

"Do you have to be at work today?" she asked the girl.

"No. I took the morning off, and I have until after the lunch hour. I'm fine."

"I'm sure your mother appreciates what you do for her."

Debra looked at her watch. If it was true the girl had until after noon, she had another hour to kill here in her mother's new room. Marj was asleep, she noticed.

"Tell me about your job," she said to the girl.

"I just started, actually. I'm a social worker. I teach job skills for the county and I help people find work. I only finished school recently. A few years ago I went home to stay with Mom because she needed round-the-clock care. But then she started deteriorating physically, we don't know why. We moved here to be near the hospital, and I was able to finish my courses and graduate."

"Has she lost any ground with her speech?"

"No. Not really, but I'm not sure because it seems like she doesn't want to talk now, even though she can—a little." Nan bit her lip and wiped at her eyes.

Debra decided to change the course of the conversation. "Do you teach younger people or older at work, Nan?"

The girl took a deep breath and answered, "It depends. Most clients we get are either laid off from their jobs or returning to the market after having children, or even completing college."

"What do you teach them?"

"Well, we assess them first, and then we have a library and staff to help get them started on resumes, contacts, and everything. I basically find out what they need to do to get started and help them do it."

"A job is a blessing." *Truly*, she thought. It would be her job to help with activities soon, her favorite chore. She had an idea. "Nan, why don't you come to the dining room with me? Marj is going to sleep, it looks like, for a while. I'll show you what we do with our residents. Some are struggling just like your mother, and you can see how we work with them—how they respond. Would you like that?"

Nan brightened, and Debra could tell she was relieved at the prospect of getting up and doing something else, anywhere else.

"Let's go."

At the nurse's station the head nurse foraged among papers at the counter, her ear to the telephone. Debra nodded and waited for her to finish her conversation before she said, "Kathy, I'm taking Marj Highland's daughter to crafts for a little while. Marj is asleep, and I showed her the buzzer, but I'm not sure she'll remember where it is— just a heads-up."

"Okay, Deb." Kathy looked up and smiled in recognition as she extended a hand over the broad blue counter for a shake. "Good to see you again, hon. Oh, could you please tell your father we need to see him about a few things when he gets a chance?" The charge nurse had a friendly manner, but she was all business with her time. No one ever witnessed her wasting a minute if there was something she could slip into it. She added, "I've left word at his office a few times, but the pastor leads a busy life, doesn't he?"

Marj Highland's husband was a pastor? Debra's ears perked up. Was this a coincidence, or was Jake Highland back in town?

Her mind wandered. She looked at Nan more closely. If her father was Jake Highland, couldn't it be that Jake had simply adopted her himself? She looked a little young, but it was possible. Oh, she refused to go through this again! She would not ask Nan's age or whether she'd been adopted. She wasn't even going to ask whether her father's name was Jake. She said a silent prayer, half closing her eyes, and trusted Kathy's attention was focused on the girl she was talking to.

Lord, take this idea away for now. I really can't do this again.

Nan's voice was unusual, Debra noticed as she returned her thoughts forcibly to the conversation. It had an unusual cadence, a sing-song, earthy lilt. She strained to draw back memory of Jake's voice, but could not. It had been too long. Jake had been blond, and that would explain why Nan's coloring was not like her mother's. Besides, Marj looked Irish, which meant she probably had blond genes hidden close under the surface. *I'm doing it again*, she told herself. *And I am going to stop. Now.*

"Yes," Nan was saying. "He's always busy, and the earthquake has added to his workload now. I'll let him know to call when I see him. Is there anything I can do, though, while I'm here?"

"I don't think so, but you said you'd be here awhile?"

"Till noon at least, yes."

Debra steered Nan to the dining room, and in conversation managed to find out that she had an older foster brother, and that they'd been raised in a village too far from town to commute. Her father and mother had taught them. Marj had once been a social worker, and Nan decided she wanted to be one, too. Debra did not ask for her father's first name, but when the girl was gone and all the work to do with mealtime was finished, she found Marj's chart, and her curiosity was answered.

Twelve

Chelsea

It was good having a roommate, Chelsea decided. Having Debra around during her forced vacation had made it a lot easier. Today, finally, she was headed back to work in a couple of hours, and relieved at the prospect.

Debra got up early and had already left for work. So Chelsea was alone with an hour to kill before she had to shower and get ready. The coffee pot was half full, smelled terrific, and was still hot. She poured herself a cup, stirred in some chocolate cappuccino, and went into the hallway to retrieve her jacket. She'd sit outside and let the cool air wake her, she decided. She slipped on her boots and went out to light the clay stove on the patio.

What's this?

Next to the stove, on the cement, lay a notebook. It wasn't the journal Chelsea was used to seeing Debra write in. It was thicker and very worn. She noticed the pattern on the outside cover was an outdated blitz of black, pink, and more pink. She picked it up, thinking she'd better put it away. It wasn't like Debra to leave things around, and rain was in the forecast. It shouldn't be left outside. Well…she'd just read a little.…

At her desk again, Chelsea satisfied herself that she'd written up every spring-off story from the last school board meeting. Not all of them had run, but they were written and the ones left over could be run for filler material. None of it was urgent information. She filed them and made a memo to John about what she had so he could plug them in when he needed to. There. She was ready to face another meeting.

The community pages were another matter. She quickly perused what she had in her inbox. It wasn't enough. She decided Paula's treatment of Bert's funeral could use a follow-up. She reached for the phone.

"Paula?" How was this woman so accessible to her? Most of her other contacts were hard to track down. Paula was phenomenal.

"Yes? Oh, Chelsea! How good you called just now. I was thinking of you."

"Paula, how do you do it?"

"What, dear?"

"You should be the busiest woman in town, but you're always there when I need you."

"You just have good timing, that's all."

Yeah, right. "I could use a follow-up story. Can I see you today?"

"Let's see…when?"

"From now till four I'm open, today if possible."

"I'll meet you for lunch—Hastings okay?"

Chelsea shuddered, but at the same time, she thought it was appropriate. This could be her first demon faced. "Good. Is noon okay?"

"Yes. I'll meet you there, then."

The rest of the morning was taken up in going over the school board agenda, and then editing material for the calendar, and setting the few obituaries and wedding announcements that came in. She had to chuckle. She enjoyed this work, but it was entry level stuff. She'd done it as an intern in Natchitoches. If her parents knew she was back at the keyboard—and they probably did—they'd be mortified. Well, they'd better get used to discomfort. She was about to "topple their little boat on the Cane" again. That was a paraphrase of what Ben had said to her after getting off the phone with her folks, telling them they'd eloped. He'd said, "Chelsea, I'm afraid I've just toppled their boat on the Cane again."

It conjured up a brightly colored picture in her mind of two small children sitting in her father's boat. It was tied to their dock, just down the hill from their house on the Cane River downtown. Ben and she made a game of stretching themselves out lengthwise, dangling their legs over the sides, and rocking back and forth until it almost, but not quite capsized. The day it finally did was the day Ron Wallace's wrath fell down hard on Ben. They were teenagers by then, which meant they were old enough to know better, and big enough to cause some problems.

What Ben meant by tippling their boat on the Cane was that they were both about to catch time away from each other, if her parents could possibly arrange it. They'd arranged it then, and they were still doing it.

Wow. Chelsea stared into her monitor, seeing nothing. A solid, sinking thickness fell inside her from her head down to her legs, and she could feel her blood coursing through her body like an alarm. By not standing up for herself she'd allowed her parents to separate them again. She thought she was being independent by running to California, but it wasn't true at all. She was just being a child, letting her parents make her decisions.

What was that she'd read in the diary this morning? Something that pastor said about it being the child's responsibility to let the parents know when it was time to stand on her own. Well, that was long past due now. It was time she stopped blaming them for what she had done, and face it.

Chelsea got back to work, realizing she was so comfortable doing it that she didn't have to stretch herself much, if at all. Today everything seemed to be pointing to the fact that she needed to take responsibility for her own life, stop running, turn around, and face things. She might be running, but as far as her life was concerned, she was running on a treadmill.

By the time the noon hour neared, she was pretty sure the pages would be full by deadline the next day. She made two calls because there were a few more minutes to fill, and set appointments for interviews for features John had asked her to do and photos she needed to take, routine. And then it was time to go.

Chelsea found Paula waiting for her in a booth by the back door of Hastings. The woman smiled and waved at her as she entered. "Over here, dear! I've already ordered for you."

"Thank you!" She was relieved. This would save a good deal of time.

"I remembered what you said last time."

"Last time?"

"Yes. We ate here the day of the first story, remember?"

"Good heavens, you have a memory!"

"I do, but only for important things. You ordered and then you said: 'Fish is fish. I always order fish 'n' chips, but replace the chips with salad, and sweet tea, please.' I remembered that only because when you said 'sweet tea' the waitress didn't know what you meant, and you said you guessed you'd just have to 'sweeten your lil' ol' tea glass yourself, then. You know, I did not know you were from the South until you said that? The waitress thought you were being rude, but you weren't."

Chelsea was incredulous. That had to be over a couple of months ago, or more. She had assumed Paula was a manipulator, not really genuine. But then, after the work she'd done for Bert's memory....

Again Chelsea felt a tug at her heart. What did this say about her? How could she be so ungenerous? How could she be so judgmental? She was embarrassed, and all of a sudden she felt a flush run to her cheeks. She said, "You are a genuine person, Paula Frean. You really are."

Paula laughed, obviously surprised. Chelsea realized she was getting to know a lot about this woman that was in direct opposition to what she had once assumed about her.

"I mean—I—well, all you do. I guess I can't find fault with anything I've ever seen you do."

"Listen, you aren't *The Examiner*, Chelsea. It isn't your job to find fault. And you never have, to my knowledge. You've been a good friend to AHO, and to me."

"You're kind."

"I'm just a gopher. If I'm kind, it's the boss's fault." Paula pointed one finger up toward the ceiling, and Chelsea understood.

She dug out her pencil and a reporter's notebook. "Is there any news on the robbery?"

"You haven't heard?"

"What?"

"They did discover that the bullet lodged in Bert's side was not from a police firearm. We've cleared Bert's name but only in the popular opinion around here. Law enforcement won't pursue this because there was only one fatality, and he was 'homeless.' What they tell me is that they've hit a dead end, and unless more evidence crops up, the case might as well be closed. To them, homeless is homeless, and until I can get the community convinced that these are real human beings, just like themselves, I'll hit resistance in everything I try to do. People know the riverbed is full of transients and vagrants, and they know some of them show up for meals. We are not going to stop feeding them. But the public has got to be shown the shelter is safe, and it works. It is helping people get back on their feet. Otherwise we'll hit snags until the laws choke us out."

"How much of this is on the record, Paula?"

The woman raised her eyebrows. "All of it, dear, especially my determination to find this robber. It's time to use whatever leverages the daily media's granting us. I'm not naïve enough to think they're permanent. But I don't like being the heavy."

"You don't? But you're so good at it!"

Paula frowned. "I think it's my old nature—I tend to push—but I don't like it, at least afterwards. I feel bad about doing it, and I wish I didn't have to."

Chelsea studied Paula's face carefully and said, "Mind if I quote you?"

"Are you kidding? Why would you use that?"

"A new angle. Maybe no one perceives you as reticent to, uh, push, like you say."

"Is that the way *you* feel, Chelsea?"

Chelsea raised her eyes from her tablet and looked apologetically at Paula. "Not at all, but I did at first, and I'm probably representative of some of our more skeptical readers. And those are the ones I assume you are trying to reach. Am I right?"

Paula smiled, but she was visibly shaken.

"I didn't mean to hurt your feelings, Paula. I've been a little surprised at my true nature today. It isn't so good, what I see when I look at myself. I may have been wrong about a lot of things I was cocksure about yesterday."

The food had arrived. Chelsea noticed Paula had ordered two

identical plates. Only Paula had water, not tea, in front of her. Her lunch mate's thoughtfulness in ordering ahead reinforced Chelsea's discomfort.

"I should explain."

Paula looked puzzled.

"I used to think people like you—people who say they're doing things for God, I mean—I used to think they did those things to get attention, so everyone would think they were better than the rest of us. I'm sorry. I don't mean to come off so abrasive. It's awful. It makes me sick to think how mean-spirited I've been. Today I read about someone who did something I would never dream of doing, just because he really believed God. He didn't take himself into consideration at all. I just can't understand why anyone would do that. It's almost like it isn't human. I know I couldn't be that unselfish."

Paula smiled. She put the forkful of salad she'd speared back into her bowl, folded her hands under her chin, and propped her elbows on the table. "How isn't it human?"

Chelsea sighed. "I couldn't imagine doing something like that without an ulterior motive."

"Chelsea Andressen, what was your ulterior motive in running out into the street to stop a bus from hitting a helpless man?"

"That was knee-jerk. I knew Rodney Black, and I felt guilty for not going out there to do my job in the first place."

"I don't understand."

"James went out there for me that day. I was supposed to be the one taking pictures."

"Would you have thought to climb up on the roof?"

"No."

"Then the picture of those hands configured like they were under that gun—they would never have seen ink, would they?"

"No. But, still."

"Want my opinion?"

Chelsea's eyes dropped.

Sarah came by then, water pitcher poised to refill the glasses on the table. "You ladies doing all right? Need anything?"

Paula met Sarah's eyes and motioned to Chelsea, hoping the

woman would understand they shouldn't be disturbed. The message was missed entirely.

"Oh, Chelsea Andressen!" the girl blurted. "I've been meaning to come tell you how nice your articles about Bert have been! I wanted to thank you!"

The praise proved too much. Chelsea's eyes brimmed, and she couldn't speak except to say, "This is the one you should thank." And she motioned to Paula.

Sarah appeared perplexed for a minute, wondering how her compliment could draw tears. She eyed Paula, who was just sitting there, biting her lip.

"This is Paula Frean," Chelsea managed to say. "She was responsible for the articles, and all that was done for Bert."

"Oh, Ms. Frean," said the waitress. "It's good to meet you. Bert talked about you —before he...."

Paula seemed pleased. "How nice! He was here for such a short time."

"He was so grateful for the shelter and all, you know."

"Yes. I know. Thank you, Miss..."

"Sarah," the waitress offered, extending a hand. Then to Chelsea, "I really do enjoy your writing, Ms. Andressen." Then she excused herself and hurried back to the kitchen.

Chelsea was composed by then but had lost her train of thought.

Paula hadn't. "Chelsea, my opinion is that we all have opportunities. It's *why* we use them that causes them to prosper, not *how* we use them."

"For ourselves or for others, you mean?"

"In a sense, that's true, but only in the sense that we are helping others because we see God in them; we see their true value. We make a choice because we recognize another person is just as important as we are, no matter what other people call them or think of them. And we act. We defend them, we protect them, or we help them because of the love God plants in all of us. We're closest to him when we pay attention to that love. And speaking of love, dear, I want to talk to you about something."

Chelsea, poised over her salad, decided it was time to dig in, but before she did, she said, "What's that?"

"It's Ben. Have you talked to him?"

"No. Not yet."

"He sends his love. He's called me a few times, asking how you are. He says he's worried about you, that when you left, there was something wrong. He'd like to come see you."

Chelsea worked at her salad, and then her fish. And Paula did the same until the silence between them grew awkward and Chelsea broke it to say, "I couldn't face him. I made a decision without asking him. It was a very selfish decision, a childish decision. I guess it was easier to do what I thought my parents expected of me than to stand up and be an adult. I've hurt him, Paula. I've hurt him badly. I've hurt us."

Paula finished her meal before she said, "Can you trust me?"

Chelsea eyed the older woman sitting across from her, someone she'd grown to trust and admire. Well, she asked herself, was she going to keep on running, or was she going to face things?

Just then Paula reached out and took her hand. "Why don't you practice on me? It will never go any further."

Chelsea took a minute to gather her courage, and said, "I had an abortion, and Ben doesn't know I did. When I went to my parents, upset because I'd just finished school and didn't think I was ready to have a baby, I guess I knew what they'd tell me. And when I think about it, that's why I told them first, and not Ben. If they made the decision, I'd have the excuse of saying it was their fault—to myself anyway. Ben will know why I went to them first. It's going to kill him."

"When did you realize you couldn't blame your parents any longer, Chelsea?"

"Today. I finally faced myself, I think, and my responsibility. Two wrongs don't make a right. I read that somewhere this morning. You're right. I owe it to Ben to talk to him, to face him."

"Well, I'm glad to hear that because he's here. He drove out a couple of weeks ago. But you have to know something else. He's talked to your parents, and he already knows what happened."

Chelsea went cold. The blood drained out of her face, and she couldn't speak.

Paula squeezed her hand and smiled. "He loves you. He told me you grew up together on the Cane River. He said he cried when he heard about the baby. When I told him I was going to have lunch with you he said, 'Tell her from now on we'll have our own boat to play in.' I don't know what that means, but he said you would.

"You know, Chelsea, there's a little book I carry around with me just in case I need to explain things like this. My gift is not writing, but I'm not above relying on those who do it well, as you of all people know."

Chelsea couldn't squelch a giggle, and with it one of the tears brimming in her eyes fell down to her chin. It occurred to her that Paula was one of the few people she knew that said what she meant and meant what she said, so she must not know that the articles she'd written for her had been predominantly Paula's own words—steered and juggled, but only a bit, usually.

After allowing herself a good cry, a feeling of relief began to grow in Chelsea's heart. She felt light, even though she was apprehensive about meeting Ben again. But now an excitement was taking hold of her. She grinned at Paula, who still looked innocent. Apparently she really had meant what she said about not being good with words.

Chelsea shook her head incredulously. "Oh, you could write, Paula, you just don't know it—or you're busy doing much more important things. What I can't figure out is why you are always there for me. Most of the people I try to interview aren't nearly as available, and they're not nearly as busy as you are, either. Why is that?"

"There are things that can't be explained—um—in the usual way, I guess," said Paula. "But I've noticed that too, and it surprises me just like it surprises you." And then she pulled out a very thin paperback book with a profile of a small nun in an Indian habit on the front cover. She handed it to Chelsea, saying, "Mother Teresa wrote this, and it explains just what I'm getting at about whom we do things for and why, I mean. I want you to have it."

Chelsea accepted the book, *Words to Love By,* which was no thicker than a quarter of an inch. When she looked inside, she noticed the writing was sparse. It would not take long to read.

"Thank you, Paula."

"Now, what was the story you wanted to interview me about,

dear?" she asked.

Chelsea's jaw dropped, and then she looked down at her notepad for clues. "I'm so sorry, Paula. I really don't remember."

The first thought that hit her was that she'd wasted such valuable time, but the woman sitting across from her burst out in laughter.

"Oh, Chelsea!" she cried. "You've made my day! But I remember, and I'll get some material together for you on the investigation follow-up. It will help me push more, if I have to. Aren't you going to ask me where Ben is?"

Chelsea's eyes widened into a question, and Paula said, "He accepted a job in San Luis and has moved there. He said it would be best to be away from your parents for a while. I think he's right. He's waiting for you to call him. You have time, though, Chelsea. Take your time if you need to."

Chelsea rose and hugged Paula. All she could say was thank you. All she could think of was Ben.

Thirteen

Ben

Ben Mitchell looked up from his desk to see a red-and-gray-haired, sprightly woman staring at him. As soon as he noticed her, she threw out a friendly hand and smiled, saying her name was Meg O'Malley, and that she'd like to talk to him if he had a minute or two for it.

He did, he told her, and asked her to please sit down, which she did.

"I'm a friend of Chelsea's," she announced. "And I'm also a friend of Jake Highland's. I'm going on the hunch that you remember him. Do you?"

"Yes, I do. His daughter works here, you know: Nan. But what do you mean by a hunch?"

"Jake told me about Ta-te, and that you were his foster son there until you moved to Natchitoches. You were adopted?"

"Yes."

"Then you are Benito?"

Ben laughed. No one had called him that in years. But why was this woman here? He said, "Tell me a little about yourself." In other words, why is this any of your concern?

The woman seemed to read his mind. She grinned and settled more comfortably into her chair. "I know I seem nosy. I am, actually, if you will forgive me. But I'm just here to get some memories from you."

"Memories?"

"Of Ta-te. You see, I'm writing a book. Have you read any of my husband's novels? Patrick O'Malley?"

"Of course. What Christian hasn't? I was so sorry to hear he'd died. My condolences, Mrs. O'Malley."

"Thank you. And please call me Meg." She sighed and squared her shoulders. "Patrick left me a project to finish. Listen, this is awkward. What I'm going to do, since I told you I'd only take a minute or two, is to leave you with this." She pushed a folder across the desk.

Ben opened it to find a short manuscript. He didn't understand.

"I'd like you to read it. I think you will want to help me after you do. My card is in the folder. I'll wait for you to call me when you have the time." With that she rose, and nodded.

Ben furrowed his brow. What a curious woman. Patrick O'Malley's wife was writing a book, and here was part of it on his desk. For his part, lately, he was game for any distraction he could find. He looked at his watch. In a little over an hour he'd be home. This would be a nice way to spend the evening. He stood up, lifted his right hand to his forehead in a friendly salute, as though tipping an imaginary hat, and said, "Thank you, ma'am!"

Meg

Meg could not suppress a smile of the sort that stretched taught across her face. Here was a Southern gentleman with a Native American composure and strength. He was easy to like, and easy to trust. She hoped that after finishing the few chapters she'd left with him, he'd feel the same about her. She was depending on it.

Three hours later Meg received a phone call from Ben. His earlier reserved manner was gone, and he asked her whether she might be a night owl herself, as he was, and if she was, would she like to meet him tonight. She said that yes, she was a night owl, and that she'd love it.

"What is it you want to know, though?"

"Oh, a little more about what your childhood...and...may I be nosy?"

Meg heard a chuckle on the line. "Okay, I know. I've already been that. Your childhood in Ta-te will be enough. If you want to share more, I'd love to hear it."

"Meg, I have nothing to hide, and I think what you're doing might be a good thing. But how did you know all that you've already written? I can't imagine Chelsea being this transparent with you."

"She hasn't been, but this is fiction, after all. And I'm not going to say otherwise. If it happens to touch square on reality, I'll ask for permission from all concerned before it goes into print that way. The names will be changed, of course, and whatever else would be a problem. Regardless, I trust that nothing I write will be a secret to anyone concerned by the time they read it, and they will have read it before it's in print."

"Well, what you have so far intrigues me. I knew nothing about Debra. But I think I can shed some light on Annie, and from what you left with me, it looks like it is time that gets done. Didn't Jake tell you about Annie?"

"He did, but he said he needed to speak with Debra before he said any more than he did."

"Well, maybe I do have a piece or two of the puzzle for you, and after reading this I have questions myself."

Ben

Ben hung up after giving Meg the address of a late-night coffee house near his apartment where they could meet.

He leaned back in his chair, tugging at the knot on his tie to loosen it. He had heard from Bert Jackson that Chelsea had made friends with a woman at the shelter. He guessed, then, if Meg's story was running along the side of reality, that woman was Debra. If she was who Meg seemed to think she was, putting their stories together might clarify things for both of them.

Chelsea had not called, although he'd hoped she would after Paula called him to say she'd told her he was in town. And until Meg showed up at his office, he'd considered going back to the river. It had been his only solace since arriving in California.

Paula had invited him to the shelter the day after he arrived, to show him the place and ask him whether he'd volunteer his time to interview clients, since he was a social worker. What he saw there drew him in. And then she'd said, "Ben, I have one or two contacts that live on the riverbed. They are the only ones who can convince the others down there to come here for help. The ones on the river find it hard to trust, and it is the only way I know how to reach them. It's rough down there, and now that it's winter...well...every year we lose people. I wonder how many we could help if we could just draw them out and get them here."

He decided to spend time at the river, and after that made a decision that might further distance him from his wife. Although he was anxious for Chelsea to call him, his feelings were mixed about it. She had leaned back into her parents for support a year ago, after he made a commitment to Christ. How would she react to a deeper commitment?

Her annoyed resistance to his faith had turned venomous in the end, and that was telling. He'd wondered why she'd opposed it so bitterly; now it was obvious. His faith said taking a life by abortion was wrong. So, in adopting her parents' obstinate, progressive attitude, she formed a veneer against what she felt would be his scorn.

He wished, of course, that she hadn't left, but if it put distance between her and her parents, it was probably best. It would, at least, allow her space and time to think for herself. It was their only hope. Otherwise, she might not forgive him for what he knew he had to do with his life now. It had come to him only last weekend, on the riverbed. He leaned back in his chair to recall the experience.

The sun only hinted an approach from the east, barely outlining oak and willow forms on the opposite bank of the river. Deep underground, the Salinas rushed northward. This was the end of its hidden season. Eventually, when clouds broke loose, water would surface in torrents, and those who lived there would seek higher ground along its banks. The lucky ones would find shelter in a car, a cheap motel, or an empty house. On that day they'd shored up to dry earth and sand at its crusty shores, and huddled in tents of tarps and blankets held up by boxes, branches, or whatever could be found discarded. Real estate under the bridge, always at a premium, was developed pylon to pylon.

Ben's camp was several yards north of the bridge. He was first to stir and emerge from his cover, which was a dug-out in the cliff on the west side of the river. Making his way to a round pot of embers, he stirred it with a stick, dropped chips, a branch, a log, and last night's trash in, and sat down on a rock nearby.

The noise of early traffic hammered his ears. A short distance from him tires raced, slowed, stopped, and accelerated. The high whining and grinding of tired brakes and gears complained of exhausted semi-truck drivers, nerves thin with caffeine or worse. Quartet after quartet of these drivers paused their rigs, boasting shots of ear-splitting exhaust into the morning air. When the signals turned, they pushed up to life again, one after another at the four on-and-off-ramps above him.

Insults of diesel stench drifted relentlessly down in foggy sheets. Ben bowed his head and pulled the hood of his army-green coat over it in protest, more in response to the the diesel fumes than to the cold. His hands were shielded from the chill by thick brown gloves, his feet by heavy boots the color of sand. By now, because he'd hiked for some time before settling down, their too-new condition was hidden.

After the sun rose, the traffic thinned, and he leaned toward the lazy cloud of his campfire. He imagined himself back in his village, camping along Big River, where he remembered Old Father saying of the earth, "Listen to her, grandson. She is talking to you." So he did listen, and she was weeping for the discarded souls of the homeless.

The night before, when he arrived with a pack on his back, his offering of fresh pork chops to cook had been accepted. Later, by the fire, there was talk of the earthquake. One said he knew things were different that morning, because the air was almost pregnant. By instinct several moved out of their tent-homes under the bridge and into the open to hike up river until the highway was more distant, and the banks were steep and far from structures.

Now they slept soundly, back under the bridge, settled in sleep under sedatives of one sort or another, and all they owned. They slept to pass the time, and to forget the cold. So he was the only one awake. It was Saturday, and he had been there only overnight. By Sunday night he would be back in another world where he would bathe, dress in clean clothes, and sleep in a soft bed; there would be a thermostat on the wall. And on Monday he would go to work and fill out forms for people who would not be helped, because it was their souls that starved, not their bellies.

He gathered his thoughts and stilled himself again. *"Listen to the earth. She is speaking to you."*

He pulled his blanket around him. It was patterned and woven by Old Mother from his village, and it was warm, even though he'd used it every day of the twenty-three years since he'd seen her last. She'd been past a hundred years old, waving her fan over her fruit and vegetable stand the day she simply fell asleep, and her fan stopped moving. But he hadn't been there to see it. To him she was still alive. When he closed his eyes he could hear her low, chanting voice, and see her wrinkled face lifted to heaven, her eyes closed in concentration. Old Mother's songs were a mixture of native chants and Da's hymns.

He lifted his head and saw a leaf floating gently down from the almost empty branch of an oak across the river. It rolled, as though kin to the air, and hitchhiked on a lonely breeze, probably only a gust from a semi above his camp, and made its way to him, then caught by its spurry edges on his blanket covering. He touched its brittle, browning body and traced the now useless veins with his finger and smiled, remembering the watchful village woman at her work: Old Mother, who called her discipline out to the children over several generations.
He pulled the leaf off his blanket, and gently placed it on the sand. Old Mother was dead, and Annie had been wrenched away from him, but the river and his people were courting his heart; the earth had spoken.

Ben arrived at the coffee house at eight, just in time to see Meg drive up. As she climbed out of her Rava, he smiled, noticing she'd let her hair down, and it fell almost to her waist in a tangle of red and white curls. She looked younger. Apparently she'd dressed up to meet him at the center. Now she was wearing blue jeans and a green parka. She met his smile with one of her own, and any awkwardness vanished.

Music met them as they entered the coffee house, low guitar strains, mellow lyrics. They bought a pot of herbal tea and two scones, collected cups at the counter, and then chose a booth at the back of the place, and sat down. When they were settled, Meg asked whether Ben could tell her a little more about his present circumstances.

"Meg, I don't know where to begin. I came here to be near Chelsea, or at least that's why I thought I came. Now, I think Ta-te drew me, too. I was thinking about it just before I left my apartment. You know Ms. Paula, I think—"

Meg smiled. "Paula Frean? I know of her. She's a mover and a shaker."

"Yes, ma'am, she sure is. She invited me to the shelter to work, and I became fascinated by the efforts they're making to be available to more of the needy. So I stayed at the river a night or two just to see for myself what it's like for the homeless down there. You mentioned you wanted to know more about Ta-te. Well, I want to go back soon. Would you like to see it?"

Meg

Meg studied the chiseled lines of Ben's face. The intense black-brown eyes and aquiline nose were the only features belying his Native American heritage. His complexion was olive, his hair medium brown and wavy. Jake had said his father was Scandinavian, and this was the reason Ben stood several inches taller than most of his people. But from what she heard beneath the surface of his words, his heart was planted in that village.

"I'd love to, Ben. And I think you might be the perfect guide. But first, tell me a little about Chelsea. She's a puzzle to me."

His face softened in intensity for a moment before he said, "Sure."

He took another moment to draw his thoughts away from his village, and then another until his eyes softened. "We grew up next to each other along the Cane River in Natchitoches. Her parents owned a pharmacy, so both of them worked until they dropped most days. My parents took care of Chelsea when she was little. But she worked at the pharmacy as soon as she hit junior high, after school and on Saturdays. They never cared much for me, probably because my parents went to church. I think Chelsea's job was their way of weaning us away from each other, but it didn't work. We eloped while she was still in college.

"Meg, how did you know about the abortion? Did Chelsea tell you?"

"No. It's an awfully long story, Ben. I'll tell you sometime. But, no, I don't think Chelsea's told Debra, either."

Ben nodded. "Well, her parents talked her into it. And after that everything spun out of control for us. She became distant—depressed I think—and then she left. I had no idea where she'd gone until Bert Jackson confronted the Wallaces. He'd offered to help me find Chelsea, and they were his first contact."

"Did they know where she was?"

"They had a fair idea because they'd suggested California to her. I think they even contacted KSLO and convinced them to call her. They know the station manager, I guess. Bert couldn't get any more out of them, so I went over there. They were so angry at me that they said some things they shouldn't have. I put the pieces together, and they fit. Chelsea had gone to them when she became pregnant. I guess she wanted to keep her options open, so she didn't tell me. I'd just gotten serious about my faith, so she probably knew what I'd say. My church going made her uncomfortable, so things were bad for us before she got the abortion, and worse afterwards. She was hurting, and I thought it was just her frustration with my new life."

Meg could see the weariness etched in his face, and she decided it was time to change the subject. He looked relieved when she said, "Now, tell me about Ta-te."

He leaned back in his chair and took a long swig of his tea before he said, "Let's see...first I'll tell you about a day I remember most. It was the day I realized things were changing, our first autumn celebration.

That would have been 1980 or '81...."

After an hour had passed, Meg made another date to see him, saying she wanted to hear more, but it was getting late.

The following morning Meg told Charlie she'd be staying in her room to write....

1980
Ben

A woman I'd never seen before came to our village. She had jet black hair that curled, and her skin was very light. It made me self-conscious for the first time in my life. I'd seen different skin and hair because my foster father and one of my foster sisters were fair, but they were part of the village. This was different. I had the oddest feeling that she was coming to take everyone away who was like her. And I was like her. My skin was lighter than my foster brother's, and my hair curled.

I wondered where she came from, but I knew it must have been a good distance. The road leading into Ta-te is long, and it's crude, or at least it was then. Miles of desert, like empty land, had to be driven before getting to the bridge over Big River. After that things are green, and it's a different world.

Days in the village were tedious until autumn, with hard work in cruel heat for everyone. Big River was our only relief. For those families without wells, it was a source of water for their household. For the children it was our playground, downriver of course.

It was still warm the day the lady came, but the day before cooling breezes had begun to blow in, and the women were excited. They got out their garlands from rafters in their huts, and declared the next day to be the first Saturday celebration. In the fall, after the harvest, every Saturday was a parade and a picnic with lighted nights full of music, stories and games.

By Saturday the village was decorated. Woven garlands hung from the rooftops, across the street like a canopy. My sister Pia hung bits of shell and rock and tin on them to make chimes. And she sang.

In front of the grocery Old Mother pushed her palm leaf fan above her fruits and vegetables, daring insects to light. The leaf fan swung on ropes—Old Father's invention—so that Old Mother's gnarled hands would not hurt so much. Old Father pushed melons into openings among beans and corn. The children dipped cool, lemon-flavored water from a wooden barrel into gourds cut into cups and painted especially for that day. Martin, my foster brother, helped with the lemon water booth, but it would be his last autumn, he told me. The next year he would be ten, old enough to build floats on wagons for the donkeys and goats to pull.

Da, which is what we called Jake, because he was our foster father, stood sentry on the village. I am sure he was unaware of it, but he was blessing us.

Amy and Quay danced by, holding hands. They were like wind, overturning our water gourds in their play. Martin righted the water spill and cleaned the gourds because they'd dropped into the sand. But he didn't complain, and I knew it was because Quay was his favorite. I had seen him looking at her, and I knew my guess was true because the year before he would have chased her down the road and yanked her braid for causing him trouble. But on that day he was shy.

That was my first thought of change. It stuck in my gut like a lump of mud, the thought that things change and they can't be put back the same again.

I was sad and I guess that translates into angry for a kid. I kicked at the water barrel and it made a deep, satisfying thud, but hurt my foot, so I pinched Annie, who was two. She yelled and her round cheeks got red and wet. I felt bad and hugged her.

Martin shouted at me to bring him a clean towel. I took Annie's hand and we walked to Old Father's booth for towels.

"Benito, wash your hands and hers too!" Old Mother commanded from her seat at the fruit stand.

"Yes, Mother."

Annie copied me, saying "Nes, Muds."

A breeze kicked up and Pia's mobiles danced, throwing sunlight in patterns down to the boardwalk and filling the air with music. Annie got excited. She laughed, and we hopped together, trying to capture the light shapes with our feet. Then I forgot that my foot hurt, and the lump of disappointment in my stomach dissolved.

Down the road guitars strummed in rhythm and castanets clattered intermittently. These sounds overshadowed the music of Pia's random shells. It was a signal the evening was near, so there would be relief from the heat, enough cause to celebrate. My sister's voice blended into the new melody. It was strong and clear and she became the focus of the festivities. She was not comfortable singing by herself, though, and she gathered others her age, insisting they sing too, so that the music became as wide and as long as the street because everyone joined in. I knew some of the words and Annie copied me in her baby language. With the next song, though, the instrument players gathered in a circle around Pia, insisting that she sing with them. They made a band. There was dancing.

I remembered to wash our hands and that we had a job to do. Annie danced but would not leave my side, so we danced together around the water barrel after Martin had his towel.

And that's when the lady came to our village. She took pictures, especially of Pia and of Annie, and I didn't understand. Martin was not impressed with my worry. He said it was just because I was too young to remember other autumns, and that strangers were bound to come. I looked down at Annie and wondered if she would remember this one.

Da gathered us together and Pia followed. Then the musicians and the others did, too. I took Annie's hand and pulled her to the green in front of the church. Martin had joined the other boys his age, and had already found a spot to sit just within eyesight of Quay, I noticed.

Da began to tell stories and I forgot my worry about the lady, but it remained in my memory, because while Da spoke she continued to move around the outside of our communal circle with her busy camera. Da did not seem to notice, which was his way. His stories were strong, because he was in them. He didn't seem to think of anything else while he told them.

We were quiet. I could almost hear the river's low moan as it sucked through below the undergrowth along the riverbank. I could hear soft music from Pia's ornaments whenever a breeze sent relief.

That was all, besides the stories of Da's Bible. Annie was quiet, but this was because she was asleep, with her head on my lap. I noticed her hair, sunlit almost to white, and I wondered for the first time why it was so. I reached for my own. It was grown out a little, and it curled. I wondered about this, too. I wondered about my mother who was dead, they told me, though to me that only meant she was not there. I never knew her. Da had one picture of her alone. No one ever mentioned my father. My mother had gone to the city and she came back. That is all I had been told. Da said he didn't know more than that, but he was my father for now and he would look after me.

Later that evening I noticed Da talking with the lady from the city. They exchanged papers of some kind, and they shook hands. They were close, and it worried me. I wondered later whether that was why things changed so suddenly after that Saturday.

"Pia needs to go to the city. She needs a good education," Da told me. He was on his knees more than I'd noticed before, and he was quiet, even when I asked him questions, as if he did not hear them. I had to ask why twice before he told me, "We are going to look for a family there, for you and for Pia." I asked about Martin and Annie, but he said Martin would stay in the village. He didn't say anything about Annie.

I knew the lady with her camera was a bad thing. I told Martin. He ran his hand through the curls in my hair, which was not as dark as his own. Neither was my skin as dark—as he showed me by lining up his forearm to mine. "You can learn to be an Anglo," he told me, "but I have to stay. Besides, little brother, Da will take care of you.'"

What was an Anglo? I thought of Da with his long legs and light hair, and my world began to define itself by color and shape, as it had not before. *Only the others can stay*, I thought. *Pia's hair curls too. Perhaps this is why she must leave the village.*

On Monday a council was called. I knew only because the church bell sounded in the early evening, just after supper. The sun was going down, and Old Father stood at the center of town, dressed in his ceremonial shirt. I could see him from the window of our living room. I also knew that he would have a fire built, which would be burning warm enough to heat us all by the time we dressed and made our way to his side.

I pulled on my beaded shirt. It was new, and this would be the first time I wore it to a council. Pia had sewn the beads on it for me, and she was standing by with a proud smile, anticipating her little brother looking so grand at the council fire.

She had sewn Annie a little dress and beaded it to match my shirt. Of course, while I dressed myself, Annie insisted her new garment be put on as well. Pia could hardly hold her still in order to get the dress over her bobbing head, but she finally accomplished the task, and then threw up her hands, insisting I finish the chore for her. "Annie will stand still for you," she said, and motioned me to my job, which was to button her dress. I didn't mind. Annie did stand still for me.

The lady had stayed at our house in our housekeeper Angelina's room. She would attend the council, Da said, as a guest. I asked him what she would wear, and I was told that Pia and Angelina would take care of it.

I hoped they could not find a dress for her.

Tribal councils were special times. Sometimes they lasted well into the night, and that meant the village would sleep until the sun was well up into the sky the next morning. Autumn was a good time for councils. The nights were still warm, and the sky was often clear, and so it was studded with a million stars. The skies were magical in autumn.

Annie was excited, and the few other children in the village that were her age were, too. Still, I knew that before the music was over and the talking began, she would be asleep, with her head on my lap. It was good that she was asleep, I thought, when her busyness stilled after only one song, because at the council every child was given as much respect when they spoke as any elder. This time I might be called on to talk. It would not do for Annie to imitate me when I did.

Old Father waited patiently for the last strains of a soft flute to move gently through the gathering, and he gestured to his son to throw the largest log onto the fire. When it caught, there was silence. All that could be heard was an occasional note coming from the garland trinkets when a rare breeze moved through the village, and the crackling wood and night creatures that seemed to be part of the ritual, too.

"My people," he began in his slow, soft tone. "We are here to talk about our children, and we will all be heard."

Again there was a slow silence within the circle. Somewhere an owl called out, and a blanket of dread came over me. Still, it was exciting to be at council. The fire popped, and the large log was engulfed in flames. I hoped it would not be consumed too quickly.

Soon Old Father continued. 'We have been told that Pia and Benito are offered a home among their father's people.'

There was a rush of hushed voices, and none were happy sounds. My limbs stilled like the log in the fire, helpless at my own involvement. I looked at Da, who sat rigid and silent next to me. His face was like flint. I looked at Pia. Her eyes flamed wide, and a tear flooded her eye, rushed over the lid, and spilled down her cheek. But it was not until I looked down at Annie, peacefully asleep, curled into my lap that my eyes began to burn and my chest began to heave for air. I pulled Annie closer, as close as I could.

Then Da rose to speak. He quietly looked down at me, and at Pia and Annie. "Two years ago I made a promise to myself, to God, and to Annie's mother, that I would watch over her. I came to this village to care for Pia and Benito and Martin. Pia became a mother to Annie, and Benito and Martin became Annie's brothers. I will honor those relationships forever, I promise. But now Pia has been offered an opportunity to learn more about music in a family who would like to adopt her and her little brother. They are music teachers, and good Christians. They will make sure she has every opportunity to learn. She will be able to go to college, and so will Benito.

"Still, it is entirely up to the village to decide this matter. Legally, because the children are half Indian, the decision is up to you all. I do need to say for Pia and Benito's benefit that I am doing everything I can to make sure Annie is placed near their new family. The village has no say over Annie's fate, and unfortunately neither do I, now. Annie will be living near them. I am doing my best to make sure that when her parents are ready to take Annie, they will move close to Benito and Pia, and I believe they will."

Da sat down, reached for my hand, and then passed his other hand over me to Pia. "A promise is a promise." Da's eyes were set like gleaming stones in their sockets. I took courage. Da always kept his promises. Always.

Martin stood up next, his body ramrod straight. It took several seconds for him to speak, and when he did, his words were cloudy, like they were forcing themselves through water to be heard. "I do not want my brother and sisters to leave!"

A muffled roar of agreement sounded out around the campfire, until Old Father raised his hands in a motion for silence. "Martin, you may say all your words now. All of you will have a turn. But remember, we love them, and we show love when we think of what is best for others, not only ourselves. So we must consider this. What is decided here tonight will affect many lives."

Martin tried to speak again, but he couldn't. He simply looked at each of us individually for a long time, then sat down.

Old Father spoke again. "It is right what Fr. Jake has told us. We do have the right to keep these children as our own. They are our blood. This is the law. But we must remember that we love them, and love never seeks its own, just as it never ends."

Again, there was silence. Then Pia rose and shook her head as if to throw the tears away that clung to her face and still welled in her eyes. She pointed her chin high, and spoke. "I love my village," she said. "But Annie is like my own daughter, and Da says she must go. I know that I speak for Benito when I say we will follow her if we can. But I am torn in two pieces." Then Pia sat down and wept.

Peter John, Pia's friend, stood up. He looked over at Pia and then at Da, and said, "'Love is patient, love is kind.'" His chin trembled and it took him a long moment to continue. "'It does not envy. It does not boast, it is not proud. It is not rude, it is not self-seeking, it is not easily angered, it keeps no record of wrongs. Love does not delight in evil but rejoices with the truth. It always protects, always trusts, always hopes, always perseveres. Love never fails.' Da, you have taught us this. We know Pia and Benito love Annie. We do too."

Then Pia's best friend, Maria, stood. "There was a time when the blood of our village was one blood, but that has changed. Now it is Christ's blood we share, and our village includes all those who share this blood. We are not Anglo or Indian any more. We are all one in

Christ. This law is greater than any other."

Again there was a long silence. Old Father raised his hands to heaven and began to chant. His eyes too were brimming with tears. All began to follow in song, blending perfectly with the now vibrant sounds of the night. I knew Old Father's song was a blessing for us, and it would follow us, wherever we went.

The council log cracked and split into embers and coals, but we would stay long into the night, close to each other in silence until the warmth of our last council fire was gone. More was discussed, but I still remember Peter John's words. Da had patiently taught them to us, all of us. I had recited them many times. This time they stirred my soul.

I looked down at Annie and pulled the brightly colored blanket Old Mother had made for us tightly around her shoulders. I would go wherever Annie went. I would always love Annie.

Fourteen

2004

Chelsea

Debra was working late at the rest home. The apartment was quiet, and Chelsea thought about calling Ben. Paula said he knew all about the abortion, and that he'd forgiven her. It was a relief to know she would not have to tell him, but it didn't make it better.

She drew her thoughts back to what had been running through her mind just before she met Paula for lunch. She would have to grow up and take responsibility for her own actions. Regardless of her parents' role in her decision, she'd been the one to carry it out. It was the role of a child to eventually face her parents and stand on her own two feet. In a sense, she'd done that by leaving. But now, it was up to her to decide whether what they'd convinced her to do was wrong. If it was, then she had been wrong, as wrong as they were. And that meant there was pain coming. At some point she would have to allow herself to be eclipsed by it. Not even Ben could help her, because running to him now would be avoiding the issue. No. She wanted to face it before she faced him, or she would not be able to accept his forgiveness. And she certainly would not be able to forgive herself.

Only a day ago it would have been easy to laugh the whole thing off, saying, "Y'all have faith, and good for you. It's not my thing." And then get back on that treadmill, call it her life, and move her legs up and down until she tired herself out and could sleep into another day, and then another, without Ben, without Debra, without Paula, and without God.

A tiny tug at her heart brought her thoughts to a new concept. To deny God was to deny everything these three people stood for, and they were probably the strongest examples of selflessness she could name. To deny God was to deny what seemed to be their lives. She had already denied him in the life of her child, and it had shipwrecked her emotionally. Was she denying God because her parents did? Was she following them and all the rest of the progressives like a lemming? It certainly felt like that. She had fallen over a cliff and was drowning because of what they preached. Yes, they believed it and their arguments were convincing, but they'd never had to live it out, had they?

But Debra had. And because of that, a woman was alive now that would not be otherwise. As much resentment as she still felt toward Debra sometimes, she could not help admitting that truth. A person was alive because Debra managed to be strong and make a choice. Debra was still in some angst over it, but then so was she. Was there a right and a wrong to this choice, like some said? Would she rather be feeling Debra's angst or her own emptiness right now?

Chelsea folded, bent double in a pain that could not be described. Who had she let down? Her baby? Ben? That was enough to kill her. But what if there was a God? If there was, he was the only one who could save her now. Chelsea remembered reading one of Paula's letters to the editor. It said there was nothing too difficult for God, and that he loved even the worst people, homeless or otherwise, and his blood was strong enough to pay for anything they'd ever done. Paula had been sure, and the woman was a rock. She'd also written, "God is as close as your next breath, only a prayer away."

Chelsea was still aching with the self-inflicted wound she felt inside her gut, but she bowed her head and prayed.

Fifteen

Monday was a very long day for Chelsea, a school board meeting being the frosting on a rigid afternoon schedule. Trustees were not in any hurry to complete their business, and the teachers union had chosen that night to show up and debate their contract. That extended the open forum time before the formal agenda got underway. Then, the budget issues were introduced—at length. Both topics would have to be written up by the next day in order to be included in Wednesday's edition. This meant an even longer night for Chelsea, because her notes and ideas would have to be in rough draft by the time she went to bed. If they weren't, the chore would be agonizing tomorrow. The tape recorder never picked up in a meeting like that. She had to depend on her memory and her notes, and her mind tended to dump details if she slept on them.

She got home at 10:45, bone weary, ready for anything but typing. But that's what she did. It took only about thirty minutes to blurt out her thoughts onto the computer screen and tag her notes for confirmation. Then she poured herself a cup of hot apple tea.

Surprisingly, when Chelsea was ready for her tea, Debra came out of her bedroom, eager to join her.

"Aren't you tired?"

"I took a nap. You were late!"

"School board."

"Put your leg up. It isn't swollen again, is it?"

"Nurse Debra. All right. All right. It's up. See?"

"You're a case, you know it?"

"Maybe so, but I'm done, and it feels real good right now."

"You like to finish things, don't you?"

"I do."

"So, what's new with the investigation?"

"I have a feeling the police are dragging their heels—or it's just beyond their scope. I don't know. John thinks they'll just let it go if they can—and that's where I come in."

"How's that?"

"I should say that's where Paula comes in. She pushes, and I put it in print, basically."

"I'm glad. I've been praying for justice, and there's more at stake than just Bert's memory here. There's the shelter. Did you read *The Examiner?*"

"No time. What'd it say?"

"They're still running letters to the editor about the robbery, and they always seem to bring up the shelter, implying it's a liability for the area."

"Liability. How can they do that after all Paula's done? I know. I know. I'm the one who said it. That's what they do."

"Apparently."

"Ouch!"

"You've got to stay off that leg, Chelsea. When did you go in today?"

"Nine."

"It's 11:30. I've been around hospitals enough to know you're pushing here. Keep that leg up—and I mean it. I'm going to get some liniment. *And*—no more shop talk. I'm sorry I brought that up. Let's talk about something else." Debra went to her room and came back with a small white tube. She knew better than to think her roommate would be in bed before midnight. It never happened. She sat down and began to unwrap the bandage on Chelsea's knee. "Look at that! You are working from here tomorrow, girl."

"It's deadline, I can't work from here."

"There's e-mail, you know."

"I'm not set up for Quark here; I have to set the pages."

"So, you can work part of the day here."

"Sorry. Most of what I've got is already set. Just have to fill in some holes."

"Now she tells the truth. So, fill in the holes, and then come home and work from here."

"We'll see."

"Make me a deal. I'm going to measure this knee of yours. If it is any larger in the morning, you're home by noon, understand?"

"Yes, *Mother,*" Chelsea said—then realized she shouldn't have.

Debra's face tightened. She got up and returned with a piece of string and wrapped it around Chelsea's knee. After a while, she looked up into the younger woman's eyes. "I...I wish you *were* my daughter." She could hardly talk. Tears clouded her throat. "I was so disappointed when you told me you weren't adopted."

Chelsea's heart caught in her throat. How could she be so cold? How could she do this to Debra? She said, "That's what my birth certificate said. I checked it before I came out here. I'm sorry, Debra. I'm so sorry. There *is* something I haven't told you about that. Please forgive me for being so cold. I was so selfish."

"What do you mean? Why did you check your birth certificate, Chelsea? And why *did* you come out here?"

Chelsea studied her face for a minute, then took Debra's hands in her own. "Our hands are the same. We look alike, we walk alike, and we almost talk alike. Have you noticed?"

Debra choked. All she could do was nod in agreement. She lifted Chelsea's hands and kissed them.

"If it weren't for that document, I would think you were my mother. I'd have every reason to believe it, too. Debra, sit down. I haven't been honest with you at all. I've been arrogant and mean, and I hate that I've hurt you. But here are the facts. My birth certificate says I am Chelsea Wallace, born to Gail and Ron Wallace, in Los Angeles, California."

Debra's jaw dropped to the floor. She couldn't speak for a long while, but then she managed to say, "My sister? Chelsea, are you my *sister?*" She tried hard to arrange her thoughts before she spoke again. After a minute she said, "How did you find out about me?"

"I overheard a conversation the day before I left. I didn't talk to them after that. I came here to find you. They wanted us to meet each other. They seem to miss you terribly. It's breaking Mom's heart. From what they said, I think they're hoping we can help each other. I can help you forgive them, and you can help me in ways they couldn't after the abortion."

"Abortion?"

"I haven't told anyone except Paula. It's why I left Ben, and it's why I was so angry at you. The folks said something about their leaving you because you wouldn't get an abortion. It is why I was so angry when I first met you. I resented you standing up to them like I hadn't been able to, and when I thought you might be my mother, I was angry you hadn't kept me. Oh, I think I was just angry, period."

"Wait a minute. You thought I might be your mother?"

"It's crazy, but I made myself believe for a while that they'd forged the document and adopted me, and that you were my real mother. I think I wanted it to be that way."

Debra brightened. "Wow. Chelsea, we're family...we're really family! Oh, my sweet Lord, Jesus, I have a sister." She jumped up, gathered the girl into her arms, and held her close, squealing. After a minute the room was quiet. Still holding on to Chelsea, Debra asked, "Honey, you must hurt. I am so sorry about the baby. Are you all right?"

There was only one small thing Chelsea could not understand. It was not that the birth certificate seemed to mean Gail Wallace had been pregnant with her when she left their teenaged daughter in her own pregnancy all those years ago. It was Ben's pet name for her—the one he told her no one else was ever to hear—Annie.

She shook herself slightly, as though to dismiss the train of thought that seemed to carry her into more questions than she had answers to right now. Chelsea held onto the shoulder Debra offered her and said, "I'm all right now. The folks were right about wanting us to find each other. Will you pray with me?"

"Of course I will."

Chelsea woke refreshed, and without the alarm. In fact, she was up an hour earlier than she'd planned. *All right, then*, she thought. *Maybe I'll actually see Debra before she leaves today*. This thought cheered her even more than waking up chipper. She lifted the covers and examined her knee. It didn't hurt. Everything, in fact, felt new. She tested it by hopping out of bed, not favoring her leg as she'd been doing. It really was better. She couldn't wait to show Debra.

"Hey! Nurse!" she hollered across the hallway, "Guess what?"

Her answer was a groggy "What?"

"Oh—my—gosh! You're still asleep? Why are you still asleep?" Chelsea got up and went into Debra's room. "Don't you have to go to work?"

"Not this morning. I thought I'd make sure you were all right before I went in. I called the hospital last night."

"Ta-da! See? I'm good as new. Now you can go to work."

"No pain? That's great! But I'm not the workaholic here. I've got till just before noon."

"I see, so you're taking advantage of my infirmity to stay home?"

Debra groaned. "Yes. Are you making coffee?"

"I like yours better."

"Bring me coffee, and I'll make breakfast."

"Deal."

Within five minutes Chelsea was placing a hot cup of coffee on Debra's night stand. She said, "You know, I have two hours before I have to go in. You have more...can we talk?"

"We talked last night." Debra was no morning person. Even though she woke up early to go to work—a long quiet time was usually necessary before she felt up to anything. "I can't think in the morning, Chelsea. Let me have a few minutes with my coffee. I'll be out in a little bit, okay?"

"You know, you're no fun. I'll make breakfast while you meditate —or whatever it is you do to wake yourself up—but you owe me."

"I owe you. Now go away."

A half hour later the aroma emanating from the kitchen was straight out of a Pillsbury box, but warm and delicious anyway. Debra got up off her knees, made it to the shower, and was out within five minutes. "Smells good," she said. She pulled on her scrubs and shook out her hair to dry. "Can I have some?"

"Sure. Sit."

"You wanted to talk?"

"You wanted to measure my knee, remember?"

Debra glanced over. "I don't believe this."

Chelsea's knee was down to its original size—it matched the other one, and it wasn't red anymore. It was almost flesh color, too. "How'd you do that?"

"I'd like to take credit for it, but I think it belongs elsewhere."

"Don't look at me." Chelsea pointed a finger to heaven and grinned.

Sixteen

Chelsea stared for a long time at the vase of roses placed on her desk—seven of them, each a different color. And, just under the vase, was an envelope.

Lou breezed in from the back and announced: "Lover-Boy struck yesterday while you were out, Chelsea. You gonna tell us who this guy is?"

Chelsea only smiled.

"Come on, girl, 'fess up! You send these to yourself to make me jealous."

"Yup. Is it workin' yet? You green with envy?"

John came in to add, "Who's the stalker, Chelsea?"

How could she get them to quit? One more comment would send her back into tears, for sure.

Lou and John exchanged glances. John tossed a stack of papers into Chelsea's inbox and returned to his office.

Lou stayed. "Hey, kid, you wanna talk?"

It was tempting, but to risk office gossip about this was unthinkable. "Shoo! Maybe later."

Lou pointed to her extension typed on Chelsea's desk list, and mouthed *Call me*.

When Chelsea settled into her desk, her morning projects advanced quickly. She finished the school board stories first, and then set her pages. It looked like she would be able to take an extended lunch break, even though it was a deadline day.

She thought of the conversation with Debra that morning, and then how she would explain those same things to Ben.

It had been muggy and hot, typical of Natchitoches in June. She'd gone down to the local Planned Parenthood office, just for counseling, she told herself. But they'd made it sound so easy and scheduled her right away for an exam. The doctor had come in at one point and told her that it would be a simple procedure, since it was so early in the first stages. "Painless," he'd said.

It hadn't been. But his well-chosen words matched her parents' earlier explanation. As for her own mind, what she wanted was not to think about it anymore, so all she had to do was take their word for it and make an appointment. Then it would be over, and she could forget about it. The "problem" would go away.

It didn't. There were complications. Worse than the scar tissue forming because of a "slight slip-up" in the procedure, was the uneasy feeling in her conscience that seemed to grow in her womb in place of the baby. Each day she would wake up wondering what it would be like to be three, six, nine months along. In the end, on the date she likely would have delivered, her feelings became unbearable.

The whole thing had driven a wedge between her and Ben from the beginning. There was something awful about not being able to share the most painful experience of your life with your own husband. Worse, his continuing excitement about church was like a knife going into her womb. How could she share faith with him? She was certain that if she told him what she'd done to their child, he would hate her.

Glancing up at the standing roses—one for each year of their marriage—she was drawn into their beauty. It was what their marriage could have been. She and Ben were more than friends; they were companions who knew each other with a child's instinct. They'd grown together like side-by-side saplings, finally merging at the stem. How had they grown apart? One side of the plant had found a source of life by reaching out, while the other resisted, clinging to old ground until it died. What kind of tree was dead and alive at the same time?

But today, she felt alive. By some miracle, death had turned into life. She hoped Ben's faith would receive her, just like God had done last night, with absolute assurance that the past was completely paid for, over and done. She felt a joy rushing through her, a knowing. No matter what happened next, that life would not leave her. She was no longer determined to free herself from Ben, an impossible task. Instead she was determined to cling to another source of life, with him.

Debra had prayed with her last night, and relief had come over her to a degree, but the thought stuck that her soul's salvation was not all she needed, not all she wanted, at least. She wanted—badly—the salvation of her marriage to Ben. Thinking about that, she'd cried herself to sleep, and when she woke up, her knee was completely healed. Looking at the roses gave her the courage she needed to pray again. She plucked out the center rose, a white one, and prayed, *Lord, please bring life back to our marriage.*

She decided to give it a day, and see what God might do. She wouldn't force the issue or try to do it her own way. She'd wait a little while. *But, Lord, don't let me wait too long, for Ben's sake. It's been too long already.*

Finally, she gathered enough courage to open the note attached to the roses. It said, *I love you, my Annie. Please take good care of yourself. When you're ready, I'll be waiting.*

Debra

"Hey, Marj!" Debra swung round the door, as she was used to doing, hoping the surprise would at least cheer the patient. But Kathy was there tapping Marj's hand, saying her name—almost shouting.

"Debra, call the family, and get Dr. Ochley down here stat if you can! I think she's had another stroke. Tell him she's unresponsive."

Debra made the necessary calls and went back to the room to see how things were going. It would take Jake and Nan at least 20 minutes to arrive.

She had met and talked with Jake by now, of course, but there had not yet been a time she felt comfortable pinning him down as to where Annie was. He seemed reluctant to go into the subject whenever they got near mentioning it, and so she decided to let things ride until Marj's condition leveled out. Right now it did not look like it would.

Marj was in a coma when Jake and Nan arrived, and she passed an hour later. They said she'd gone peacefully enough. It had been another stroke. Debra was glad she'd come in late, and that she'd gotten some extra rest. This was going to be a long afternoon. She asked Kathy whether she could tag a second shift onto her half-day, and there was no problem, given the circumstances. She was, after all, the aide assigned to Marj.

It was always hard when a resident died, but Marj was comparatively young. The routine was the same, though, and Debra busied herself at the task of steering the family through the arrangements, something that in this case was delegated to her. Jake was clouded with grief, so she simply took over. Nan brought a friend with her from work, who seemed to know the family well. It was good to have Ben on hand for the hour he was able to spare. He made what decisions he could on his own and somehow managed to coax information out of Jake about relatives to call and choices that had to be made.

She picked up the phone, called Chelsea's extension at the paper, and found her in. "Hi Chelsea. Is it possible to come down here and walk a family through an obituary? I know you usually don't do that...but this would mean a lot to them...and to me."

She looked over at Ben, who had followed her to the nurse's station. His features had frozen. He looked on the verge of tears.

After she hung up, he said, "I need to get back to work, Debra. Tell Nan I'll cover for her, all right?" Then he quickly left the building.

Ben

Ben hadn't been completely honest, he knew, but he could not stay and risk running into Chelsea this way. The woman inside must be Meg's Debra. She looked so much like Chelsea that he had little doubt she was. When she called the paper, he decided to leave. He hadn't seen his wife in over five months. This wasn't the time or the place for a reunion. He hadn't realized until now how afraid he was of finding out that maybe there was no chance left for them. Maybe she was happier without him.

Now he sat alone in his car, resigning himself to rerunning

memories. After a while he forced himself to put the too-often rehashed thoughts away, start his engine and go back to work, but he broke down. Tears flew to the surface, and the harder he worked to wipe them away, the fiercer they became. From somewhere deep inside, a groan made its way up, and he could not suppress the expression of it.

Chelsea

Chelsea heard a loud wail as she parked the Taurus and got out. A shock ran through her. *What's that?* She looked in the direction of the sound and saw a man inside his car. She walked toward him and heard him sob again.

Oh, dear Lord, she thought. *This is not going to be an easy grieving for anyone; Debra was right to call.* She decided to see whether the man was all right. The helplessness of the sounds coming from the car broke her heart. She had spent time reading Paula's book. Mother Teresa's thoughts had filtered into her heart on several levels. She wanted to learn how to love like that, to see Christ in everyone, and to minister to him by loving his children.

Chelsea made her way to the man whose cries were beginning to wound her. When she could not get his attention by tapping on the window, she opened the passenger-side door and sat down next to him. It was his hands she noticed first. They were gripping the steering wheel, and his head was on them. And there was something about his dark, slightly curly hair....

"Ben?"

He wiped his eyes and turned his head to look at the woman sitting next to him. Pain....relief....fear....frustration were all there on top. No anger. Acceptance. He would accept what was to come. He would trust God. He smiled, then leaned slowly over to his wife and kissed her.

Chelsea leapt into his arms. She was crying now, but she was still in her husband's arms. She willed him to hold her a little longer, and he did that.

When he finally released her, he took her chin in his right hand, lifted it up, and then gazed deeply into her eyes.

Ben

He remembered her silence, her distance. All of that seemed to have melted.

She was quiet, but a tear stung her eyes and rolled down her cheek. She said, "You know, I felt like I'd killed a part of me, of us. The only thing left was work. Paula told me you'd forgiven me. Do you mean that?"

He looked at the woman sitting next to him, and he knew she was not asking him to say the words, but to think about what it was she had done. They had five months of separation and their own child to grieve. This would not be easy for either of them. But as far as forgiving Chelsea went, there was only one thing he could do. He wiped her tears away and gathered her into his arms.

Ben noticed Jake was nervous—a little beyond grieving—when he and Chelsea entered the hospital room. But when Nan and Jake sat down with Chelsea to begin work on the obituary for Marj, Jake warmed to her immediately, as though her presence were enough to bring comfort in itself. She asked him things Ben knew would never appear in the paper, but answering the questions she posed was cathartic, both for Jake and for Nan. They also formed a buffer for the hard questions that had to be asked.

Debra popped in and out of the lounge to check on things, and several times when she did, Ben caught Jake's eye. The unspoken language between them was, "We've got to talk."

And when Chelsea finally got up to leave, saying she had to get back to the newsroom, everyone stood. Ben excused himself, but not before assuring Jake he'd be back in a minute; he just wanted to walk his wife to her car. After a long, lingering kiss in the Taurus, Ben secured a promise from her that he'd see her when she got off work, and then he returned to the waiting room.

Debra was there. "So you're *the* Ben, eh?"

He colored a little. "Guilty. Chelsea told you about me?"

Debra looked around the room at Jake, then Nan, and then Ben and decided it would be a good time. They'd understand. It might even cheer them. "Did she tell you she accepted Christ?"

A grin spread from ear to ear on Ben's face, and he closed his eyes in a prayer of gratitude. Debra caught his shoulders and pulled them down for a bear hug. Jake came over to join the two. He managed to smile and draw them both into his arms. That's when Debra's tears came. She whispered, "Jake, I'm so sorry about your wife. She was the most beautiful woman!"

Nan allowed herself to cry again.

Ben told her not to worry, he'd cover for her at work, and then he excused himself.

Seventeen

Chelsea

Chelsea had not told her coworkers that she'd changed her name. She decided she would continue to use Chelsea Andressen as a pen-name anyway, so why stir the pot now? She hadn't yet explained the whole story to them. She'd told them only that her husband had been away, and now he was back. The real story wasn't something she could toss out over coffee on a deadline day.

Ben understood. In fact, he seemed to enjoy the "sweethearts'" game they played when he showed up at the newsroom to wait for her.

She smiled. He would be there soon.

Lou was watching her. "Gee, girl. I don't have to ask what you're smiling about. You and Ben are like Siamese twins, Chelsea. Don't you think you should go on an extended honeymoon or something? Give the rest of us a break." Lou lounged in the chair behind Chelsea's desk, buffing her nails. It was Wednesday, and the newsroom was slow.

"This has been a good lesson for us menfolk here," James added. "It was the flowers, wasn't it?"

Lou nodded in encouragement. "You remember that, Ace. Works every time."

Chelsea smiled, looking fondly at her roses, which were now tied in a ribbon and turned upside down to dry at the window. "They do have a way of getting to a girl."

Ben had shown up at the newsroom at exactly twenty-five minutes after 5 p.m. yesterday, which meant that his office was only that far from hers. Sweet! He had stayed in the recliner the writers used for their breaks, just behind Chelsea's desk, reading last week's issue, and throwing (James told her later) as many glances at his wife as he could get away with. John persisted in calling him the stalker now, saying he had good reason to after watching Ben in action for a while.

It was nearing 11 a.m.; Chelsea's calendar showed AHO lunch on the 11 a.m. line, and two interviews following her real lunch hour. She was looking forward to seeing Ben there; he was volunteering today. She gathered her things, told John where she'd be, and headed for the Taurus.

The church was only around the corner and a couple of blocks away. As she pulled into the parking lot, Chelsea noticed several people in line at the door to the dining hall. It was a ragtag group this time. She remembered what Paula had said about the soup kitchen reaching out to the people who would not qualify for the overnight shelter. It was a contrast, for sure, not just from the type of individuals she'd met at her overnight stay. It was a much larger group than she'd expected. When Paula had first invited her to the kitchen six months ago there had been a smattering of takers. Food had been sent home with anyone who would take it, because word hadn't gotten around at that point, and only five or six people had come in for the meal. This time she wondered whether there would be enough for those who came in, much less leftovers.

In the corner, outside the door, there were picnic tables set up on a patch of lawn. She guessed these would accommodate the overflow. Right now they gave place to an intense conversation going on between Paula and someone Chelsea didn't recognize.

"Oh! Who is that?" Hands covered her eyes from behind. "Ben, you scared me!"

"Want company?"

Ben wrapped his arm around her waist, pulling her tight to himself while they walked to the line. As they drew nearer to Paula, Chelsea was surprised her friend did not hail her, like she usually did. Paula continued talking to the man across the picnic table. Chelsea wondered whether she'd remembered they had an interview scheduled. Looking back at the line, she decided this might not be the best day for it, anyway. It would be tight quarters inside, and that meant she'd have to rely on her note taking. A tape recorder would never sort out the overplay.

Ben took his leave, explaining he needed to get set up for clients.

"Okay—I'll see you after." She watched him make his way inside, passing several men and women on his way. One man, Chelsea noticed, sneered as Ben walked by. *Strange*. She turned her attention back to Paula, who was still in conversation. When she looked up, Chelsea caught her eye.

Paula looked relieved. "Chelsea! So glad you're here. Come and meet someone."

Chelsea walked quickly over to the picnic table, glad to be called out of the line.

"Chelsea, this is Mr. Peterson. He lives next door."

"Mr. Peterson, good to meet you."

The man did not offer his hand but dipped his head slightly and returned his gaze to Paula, continuing to talk, becoming more agitated. "This is a decent neighborhood, Ms. Frean. You can see that. There has got to be another location you can use for this—this zoo here."

Paula took a deep breath and exhaled slowly before she said, "Mr. Peterson, I understand your concern. We take every precaution, though, and I wish you'd come inside and talk with our social worker. He'll explain their procedures to you. These people you see here today—" she lowered her voice—"these clients have come only for the noon meal and to pick up provisions to get them through the rest of the day and tomorrow morning. Our overnight clients have been thoroughly screened by a licensed social worker."

"Lady," he said, "take 'em to your own neighborhood, why don't you? See you at the council meeting." Peterson stuffed a pen he'd been pointing at Paula back inside his shirt pocket and got up to leave.

Chelsea had never seen Paula as upset, or near as weary as she looked now. She said, "Forgive me, dear. I just—I forgot—in all this I forgot exactly why we're meeting today."

Chelsea nodded past Paula to Peterson's receding shape. "How long has this been going on?"

"Do you mean the hassle from neighbors or this man's rant?"

"Both."

She checked her watch. "Fifteen minutes, and six or seven months."

"We were, uh—following up on the investigation. The bullet, remember?"

"Oh." Paula let out a long breath. "Let's see…I have one client who lives down in the riverbed—who I can trust—at least one I *know* I can trust. Peter. I haven't seen him yet today, but he was supposed to let me know what he found out."

"So you don't know any more yet?"

"I'm working on it. It's just—these neighbors! We are going to have to round-robin this thing very soon. I hope to have the Foursquare facility set up by Friday. We can't afford for this man to make a fuss at the council meeting next week. Maybe if we're out of his back yard by then, he'll drop it."

"You look tired."

"I'm discouraged, Chelsea. We have money—in our hand *right now*—for a new facility. It's ours! The problem is location. Pastor Trukee and his people have given us a half acre—right here—to build on. That was what the prerequisite to getting the grant we were after. We've got it! All I can do is perhaps find another location for the kitchen, and build just for the overnight clients. But if *The Examiner* doesn't stop its harangue, we'll lose that."

"What can I do, Paula?"

She smiled and patted Chelsea's hand with hers, lifting the other one to support her forehead. "I don't know."

Chetty

"Did you see the lovey-birds, Sam?" Chetty pulled a cigarette out of his pocket and lit it. The line was long. "Cute little blond over there chattin' up the old lady—she an' the big guy—did ya see 'em? Don't think they're here for no hand-out, that's for sure."

"Prob'ly not. Why you s'pose they *are* here?"

"Ah, who knows. Churchies, or—ya know, I seen that girl before."

"Where?"

"Don't r'member. It'll come to me. I don't forget somethin' like *that* too quick. For sure I don't. Yassir. She's a real cutie."

Catch

Catch Hodges liked Ms. Paula, called her the "Rabble-Rouser Gal." That's why when she called him to ask if he'd meet her at the kitchen today, he made sure he got there. But why she'd asked him not to "be too conspicuous this time," he didn't know. She was about the only person he'd do that much for, so today he'd tried. He covered up the tattoos on his arm with a light-weight blazer he found at the thrift store. Why invest much in something he had no intention of wearing again—if he could help it? He pulled a baseball cap over his bowling-ball-shaped head, even took the biker rings off and wore tennis shoes instead of leather boots.

His Harley was another thing—but the Gal had said to believe her, there was a good reason she was asking—so he'd even left that off and borrowed an Escort from his neighbor.

"No problem," Arlene told him when he asked for the keys. She was good people.

When he drove into the church parking lot, his disguise had the right effect, sure enough. No turned heads like he was used to. He noticed that right away. Good. He guessed he'd done it right, then. Maybe even the Gal wouldn't recognize him. Now, that would be fun. Maybe he'd play it a while, just for a laugh.

It wasn't hard to meld into the line. Except for his huge frame and his height, he could be confused for a homeless man. But, were these guys for real? In front of him was an overly skinny man, probably only twenty or so, who literally shook while standing there. Catch had known addiction in a former life; this was sure a picture of it. He guessed it was a good sign the man was coming in for food, at any rate. "Hey, man!"

The addict turned to look up at the voice behind him. "Hey."

"My first time here—heard about it from a buddy o' mine." Referring to the Gal as his buddy made him smile.

The addict only nodded, and then turned around, holding his

elbows to keep them still.

God, help 'im, Catch prayed. *This guy's in bad shape.*

In front of him there was similar silence, save for a banter he could barely hear between a couple of guys about to round the corner into the building. One of them drew a long toke on a cigarette before bending down to scratch it out on the sidewalk, then tossed the nub to the bushes. That irked Catch. Hoping he wouldn't blow his cover, he walked over to the bushes and proceeded to collect butts. Apparently others had chosen this way to dispose of their trash while they stood in line for those inside to wait on them. "There's a trash can two inches away from you," he muttered, not for anyone's ears.

"Now don't that beat all, Sam. The big guy's anglin' for a janitor job here. Look see?'"

Catch eyed the wiry man with the attitude, smiled, and tipped the bill of his hat. "Yes, and your occupation would be?"

But by then the client had sniffed off the comment and was inside the building, closer to food. Paula chose that moment to brush by— barely nudging Catch's arm on her way. No one else saw her wink, Catch was sure. So much for surprising the Gal. Catch noticed the slim blond next to Paula. Both women excused themselves to those at the entrance and slipped inside ahead of the line.

Chelsea

It was surprisingly quiet inside for a while, Chelsea noticed. The atmosphere was polite, but she felt uncomfortable somehow. She guessed it was just being there and obviously not needing to be there that made her feel squeamish. Paula offered her food, but she said no, she was going to eat lunch later.

But then her host said, "Please, you do need to have a little something." And she filled two plates with salad, gathered plastic cutlery, and steered Chelsea to a table not far from Ben and his spread of files and forms.

Chelsea watched him.

Paula noticed and drew her down into a chair. "You've talked to Ben?"

"Yes, a lot has happened since we had lunch."

"Why didn't I know this?"

"You don't know because I haven't told anyone, hardly. We just got back together yesterday. I meant to call you and tell you all about it."

"Well, we can do that now, because I'm afraid I have nothing more to tell *you.* Except—don't look—but one of my main men has just entered the building. *No.* Don't look. You can't miss him when you do see him, though. He's about six-five."

"Okay—what's this about?"

"Catch may look like a biker—well, a homeless man today—but he is the genuine article. I need someone who can cross over. I think I told you."

"You mentioned a Peter, I think."

"Peter's from the river, but I haven't seen him here yet today. I was hoping he'd mix with Catch—oh! Good. There he is, at the door."

Chelsea tried not to stare, but Paula's choice of decoys or plants, whatever she called them, were not easy to ignore. Peter walked with an obvious limp. He was skinny and tattered, but he had something the others lacked, a twinkle in his eye. It was completely out of place, camouflaged by beard and jagged-cut hair the color of a crow. If eyes were the window to the soul, as they said, this man was one happy individual, a total enigma. Judging by his clothing and his thin, somewhat dirty frame, Peter, by all the world's standards, was a bum.

Paula watched Catch until she caught his eye, then nodded to the doorway, where Peter stood, grinning affably at the young woman and child in front of him.

Chelsea followed Paula's gaze back to Catch, who was about to harness a fistful of plastic cutlery and a napkin. His plate was full. She couldn't miss the height, but he didn't look at all like a biker, not in a baseball hat, dirty tennis shoes, and a Dickie's blazer. "He doesn't look…"

"He did that for me—good job, too. You wouldn't recognize him today, that's for sure a relief, too."

"Why?"

"He's my spy, Chelsea. You'll see."

"For the river bottom, like you told me?"

Paula nodded. She'd already lowered her voice. As she gathered a forkful of lettuce, she said, "He'll be here for a little while, make a contact or two, and then show up down at the river pretending he needs a place to stay."

"I hear it's dangerous down there."

"These fellas don't care, they really don't. If his background isn't enough, and his size, as you see, then his faith is. I've never seen a stronger faith. Say, have you had time to read that book I gave you?"

"*Words to Love By?* Yes, I have. 'The fruit of quiet is prayer, and the fruit of prayer is faith. Love comes from faith, and service comes from love.'"

"You memorized it?"

"Paraphrased, but yes. It's beautiful. And, by the way—thank you for your prayers. They've done their magic."

Paula beamed, her former stress visibly dropping away as though it had never been there. "Welcome home, dear. That is just the news I needed today. When my prayers are answered like that, it builds my faith."

Noise grew like popcorn in a microwave, until there was quite a clatter of voices to be heard in the room. Chelsea glanced over at Ben. He was interviewing now. She noticed a line forming at his table.

Ben

Ben would never understand the diversity, and yet the sameness of the people he interviewed. At his office, he talked to people who were serious about bettering themselves. Here he would simply try to match those he interviewed with some kind of marginal work in the community. Some already had jobs, and he was there to see what he could do about getting them into something that would actually pay the bills. Today's group, for the most part, already had employment. For the rest, getting an employer to hire one of them would be a trick in itself; getting them to want to work was the larger challenge. He was of the opinion that a lot of his clients were their own worst enemy. The epitome of that sentiment sat in front of him now.

Men like this Chetty were the reason he chose to stay at the river in Paso Robles rather than Atascadero most weekdays. He'd be blowing his cover, and this type would be the first to slam him for it. They wore a crust on their hearts that outweighed the one on their clothing, and it hardened each time they found another reason to hate. His pretending to be homeless in order to understand them would be one more chip for their shoulder, he knew; one more reason to hate; one more lesion caused by broken pride that would have to heal before they would ever receive real help.

Ben wondered why the man had bothered to sit down. His manner was more of a challenge than a petition for a job. "You can find me somethin' that'll buy me better than this swill I'm havin' to eat here?"

Ben looked hard into the disfigured, knotty face that was talking to him, and understood how it got that way. This attitude earned stripes in prison. Bony hands gripped a plastic fork oiled in red sauce from the enchilada casserole the man had just devoured. The knuckles were numbered, and the man's sleeves had been cut off at the shoulders to show off a faded indigo swastika.

"What are your skills, sir?"

"Hmm...skills. Let's see. Sammy, this man wants to know my skills," he hollered over to a man sitting at the next table.

The man, Sammy, shrugged. "I guess you're a good for—let's see—nothin'?"

The man cackled. "You got a job where's I kin do nothin', man? My friend there knows me well—yes, indeed."

"Sir, with all respect, I have only a short time here, and there are people I really want to help. Please join your friend. If you think of something you can do, I'd be happy to see what I can do for you."

"Oh, see here what you kin do...I know one thing I'm *real* good at. You bring that purty little yellow-haired bird you came here with over here, and I'll give you a dee-mone-stra-shun. I shore will."

What Ben did next couldn't be helped. He wanted nothing more than to add to the tracks on this gentleman's face, but instead he upset the table—and his neatly stacked files.

Paula

Paula was in front of Ben before he could get any further. Seeing trouble at Ben's table, she'd left Chelsea with an order to get out her cell and dial 911.

"Is there a problem here?" Paula hardened her eyes to steel.

"Not 'nless this 'ere coun-se-lour makes one, there isn't," Chetty spat.

Paula looked down at Ben's scrawled information sheet and saw that it had a name listed. "You will have an escort home, Mr. Armstrong, along in about one minute here, unless you leave now. You are no longer welcome at the kitchen. I am sorry."

Chetty shot up out of his seat, tossing his plate and utensils onto the floor in the process. The last thing he said to Ben was, "Think I hit a nerve there. Yeah, I did. A little yella nerve."

Then he was gone.

Sam

Sam whistled under his breath. Best stay where he was. No tellin' what his pal had up his sleeve to do next.

Catch and Peter

Catch and Peter stood at the door together. Both men watched hard after the evicted diner, who disappeared into the clutch of cars in the parking lot just in time to avoid the arrival of a black and white.

Ben

Ben gathered his things into the carry-all he'd brought with him, looked at his watch, and held it up to catch Chelsea's attention. She was still talking to the officer. Ben thought to take the form over that the man had half filled out a few minutes before, then decided against it. This guy had threatened his wife. The police harassing him would only rile his feathers more.

He hoped he could gather Chelsea and go for lunch soon. What else could be done? "Honey, we need to go."

The officer looked confused. "Can I get a better description first? Sir, what did the man say?"

Then Chelsea interrupted. "Officer, the digital I took ought to suffice, really. I'll e-mail it to your office after lunch. And—here." She held up the screen for him to see. Ben tried to oblige but couldn't think of what to say in front of his wife.

Catch was nearby. "Officer, I heard the whole conversation. So'd my friend here." He motioned to Peter, who walked over as well. "These kids need to get to work. We'll fill ya in." Catch's expression told the man he thought it would be better if the lady weren't present when he did.

Evidently the policeman caught the logic. "Yes. Sir, ma'am," he said to Ben and to Chelsea in dismissal.

The couple left for their cars.

Ben opened both front windows in his car on the way to Chelsea's apartment. Evidently he'd forgotten a bag of leftover fast food somewhere. After lunch he'd clean the car out. He could use a good workout, anyway, to vent this anger. He knew he shouldn't have let the man—obviously crazy—get to him. He wouldn't have, either, had it not been for his saying those things about his wife. It wasn't far to her apartment. He hoped he could get some peace before he got there. He switched on the CD player and listened to *Amazing Grace*. It helped.

Only a couple of minutes later, he was there. He left the windows down to catch more air. He'd clean up whatever it was he smelled later on. Chelsea's Taurus was already in the driveway, but she was not in it.

Chelsea

She had heard the phone ringing just as she'd pulled into the driveway and hurried to the door to unlock it, get in, and answer. It was Debra calling to say she'd be working another late shift tonight. Chelsea told her that she and Ben would be staying at his place, anyway.

Debra

Debra was tired. She'd worked late on Tuesday, so she'd asked to come in a little late again, and then to be put on swing shift until her weekend. She'd come to work at noon, and this worked well in another way, too. She had been there in the afternoon when Nan and Jake came by to pack up Marj's room. The rest of the staff gave her leave to help them. It was good to be with them, she thought. It wasn't often the staff was given time at work to grieve like they needed to.

Marj's funeral was scheduled for Saturday. Debra knew it was healing at a time like this to ask questions about the loved one, and she was curious anyway. Her time with Jake so far had been spent in this way. To Debra's frustration, there had been no mention of Annie. She considered that perhaps so much time had passed that Jake felt it unnecessary to go into the subject. And Herb's insistence on severing the past in this situation had probably been passed on to Jake. Debra felt that to break down that wall of silence would take quite a discussion, something Jake was not up to right now.

She turned her attention elsewhere and noticed that Nan seemed unusually quiet. When she went to her car to get something, Debra decided to ask about the girl. "Jake, how is Nan taking this? Has she talked much?"

"No. She hasn't."

"I guess she'll open up when she needs to. Can I ask you another question? Does it bother *you* when I ask about Marj?"

"No. I would tell you if it did."

"You would?"

"It helps to talk, and it's hard to talk. It's a diversion, and at some point we all have to be alone with our thoughts, but the diversion is welcome right now."

"It always helped me to talk."

"Herb?" Jake motioned to Debra to sit beside him. She did. He turned around to face her, folded his long legs up onto the bed Indian fashion, elbows on his knees, chin in his hands, studying her.

It was just this familiar, brotherly posture Debra remembered. And it was nice to call back these memories. Michael would be making up the third part of this discussion if he were here. The three of them had spent many hours talking, just like this, so long ago. And now, in this friendship at least, it was as if no time had passed at all. No ground had been lost.

"Yes. He passed several months ago, but I've lost others."

"We need to catch up, don't we? I've been so..." Jake's voice broke up.

"We will—soon—but I do need to tell you I lost Michael and our daughter in an accident ten years ago."

"Oh, Debra, I'm so sorry! I truly am!"

"Jake, I told you only because I wanted you to know that I know how it feels—at least some of your pain right now, how it hurts, physically even. So, if you want to talk—I just want you to know that I'm not just nodding here and asking questions."

Jake buried his face in his hands. "You never asked me about the baby."

"I never saw you again. I realized what Michael and I asked you to do was too much to ask. We were young, and I'm so sorry to have put that on you."

"There's no need to be sorry," Jake said.

But Debra felt awkward and changed the subject, saying, "How do you know Ben?"

"I've known him since he was a boy."

"In Louisiana?" Just then the door opened. Nan looked from Debra to her father and back. Debra had mirrored his posture, and was now facing him, Indian fashion on the bed. Their knees were almost touching. In silhouette they looked like kids.

Jake extended his knees and put his feet back on the floor to face his daughter. "Hi, Hon," he said. "And then he turned his attention back to Debra.

"I think it's time you heard the whole story, but it's long. It's complicated. Can I"—he looked over at Nan—"that is, can *we* meet you later for coffee? When are you off?"

"I get off at eleven. I really would like to know, if it isn't an imposition right now."

"We haven't been sleeping much anyway. We'll pick you up at your place, then?"

"Okay. We can talk there, I think." Debra took a long, deep breath. Twenty-five years...she guessed she could wait a few more hours. She fished in her pocket for one of Chelsea's cards, wrote the address on the back, and handed it to Jake.

He looked down at the card and realized it was Chelsea's.

Debra noticed he looked puzzled, so she said, "I moved in with Chelsea not long ago. Her address is on the card. It's pretty easy to find. I should be home by 11:15." Debra walked over to Nan, who rose to receive her hug, and then she left the room.

Chetty

Chetty Armstrong jumped out of the car a minute after Ben shut the driver-side door. He stood up and turned in the direction the car had come from, eyed the neighborhood, and spotted a mailbox perched at the curb. In a low voice he squealed, "Oh yeah! I once wuz lost-ah butt-a now I-umm fownd-a. Wuz be-lind but-a no-oow I-a seeeee. Yess-uh. I see the light. I do. And it's shining at number 207-B Pine Acre Road. Oooh, baby!"

Noticing a tall evergreen bush at the side of the building, he crouched down low and made his way to it, passing under the front window to the apartment on his way, and then he curled up in the needles and dirt underneath. He could wait.

A half hour later both cars pulled out of the driveway and Chetty found his way easily around the tree, through the gate, and onto the back patio. The slider was easy. People were really stupid, he thought, or maybe this girl wanted company. He'd see. Meanwhile, he'd just make himself at home, take a bath, and see what was in the fridge.

Debra

Debra was not tired. She was excited, but another part of her was anxious. She didn't know whether she was ready to hear what Jake had to say. As she rounded the corner to the apartment, she could see that Chelsea's car was not in the driveway. She remembered the girl would be staying with Ben tonight.

She gathered her things and climbed out of her Jeep, shut the door, and then headed inside. No lights were on, but the porch had a motion-sensor that tripped when she approached. She opened the door, drew off her parka, and hung it on the hall tree along with her purse and keys—as usual, but something seemed odd. The floodlight on the porch lit the living room, but only dimly, so she flipped on the switch inside by the entry door.

Maybe Chelsea was home after all. "Chelsea!" she called. "Is that you?"

There was no noise, but a shadow appeared as a light went on in the bedroom—her bedroom. Before she could think what to do or see who it was, a body slammed into her full force and pinned her against the door.

"Hey, purty gurl!" A man's arm closed around her neck and all but choked her. She struggled to scream, but his other hand closed over her mouth. "We're gonna take a little ride...Get your keys! Give 'em to me."

At that point, a sort of slow-motion camera began to play in Debra's mind. It was surreal; she wondered why she was this calm. Deep within, she drew from something extraordinary. It was as if she were not really there, just watching some sordid movie from outside herself. Somehow she could not find the words to even think a prayer. In fact, she couldn't find words at all. She did everything she was told.

She was jerked into the passenger side of the Jeep and left for a moment. While the man ran to the driver's side and opened the door, she had time to fasten her seatbelt. Almost as soon as the man got into the driver's seat the car popped into life, then into reverse, and was careened backward, and then forward, tires screeching and sliding.

Debra's slow-motion tape was still rolling, though. She noticed everything. Only an instant into the ride, she saw headlights pass. There were two figures in the front seat of the oncoming car, which her driver barely missed sideswiping. She hoped it was Jake and Nan. Then she noticed the headlights stop, turn, and then appear in the rear view mirror, following.

The man at the wheel was jabbering something obscene, but she didn't understand what he was getting at. It sounded like nonsense anyway. Her attention was riveted to the side-view mirror. The lights behind her car were steady and close.

"I kept my promise," Jake had told her. In the mayhem of the moment, Debra's thoughts went from slow motion to freeze. A rainbow settled itself in her spirit, and a still small voice, audible and confident, said: *I keep my promises.* Immediately she was engulfed in warmth, her mind and heart in total contradiction to the moment. She held the thought close and kept her eyes glued to the light in the mirror.

Jake

Jake tried to stay as near the car as possible, but it was hard. Whoever was driving seemed to tumble and toss between gears—not slowing for curves, so that on the straightaways, it took the length of a block to right its position on the road. He could see two heads, he thought. He'd been right to follow. The address was clear, fastened in glow-in-the-dark numbers on the mailbox, and luckily he'd seen which driveway the car had pulled out of just in time to focus on the passenger. It looked like Debra or Chelsea. He wasn't sure. The door of the apartment—he'd gotten just close enough to see—was wide open.

Something was wrong.

As soon as he was able to read them, he called out the license plate numbers to Nan. "Call 911, hon. Tell 'em it looks like they're headed to El Camino; they're out of control. Something's wrong."

Within seconds after Nan's call sirens could be heard, and they grew louder until Jake saw red lights flashing behind him just after they'd crossed the El Camino. "You'd better call back. Tell them we're right behind the car. I'm afraid to slow down and lose them, but I'll try to get out of the way."

As Debra's Jeep headed east, Jake wondered whether it would turn at the river crossing. It did, but the front right fender caught a guardrail several yards from the corner and sent the vehicle careening end over end, down toward the riverbed. Jake froze, watching headlights disappear and come back until they stopped at the bottom of the embankment.

Nan was still on the line to the operator, so she shouted, "Send an ambulance to the river bed at the Traffic Way Bridge. Hurry!"

Jake pulled to the side of the road, tore his door open, and leaped out of the car. Nan was right behind him. Two officers flew down the hill, but they stopped at the torn body of a man lying limp and bloody, thrown out onto an outcropping of brush near the sand shelf above where the Jeep sat.

Jake shouted, "There's a woman still inside! Help me here!"

The car had somehow landed with all tires down, and when he got to it, Jake noticed Debra's seatbelt was in place. Her head was frozen against the side passenger window, and her arms lay at her side, bloody and motionless.

"Jesus," he cried. "Please, Jesus!"

Nan pulled her father aside in order to allow the officers to work.

He sat down helplessly on the sand, with one thought on his mind. *Debra has to live.* He didn't know now whether he was crying out of pent-up grief for his wife or concern for his friend.

Nan nestled into her father's embrace. He held her so tight she couldn't move. "Daddy, she'll be okay. I know she will."

Eighteen

Catch

Catch had hoped to find that Chetty guy at the riverbed after lunch. He wanted to watch him. Something was up with that pop-off. Peter had told him to be sure to first look *him* up when he got there, though, and so Catch looked for signs of a hidden camp under the bridge, just like he'd been told about. These people sure could hide. Peter's camp was camouflaged against a cement pier with brush covering all vision of it from any angle. If he hadn't known to look for a hanging Coke can on a lower branch of brush, he wouldn't have been able to tell one pier from another. It made him wonder who was hidden under the several other piers that held up the bridge.

He rattled the can, and peeked under the branch it was on. Sure enough, Peter sat inside a hollowed-out circle, probably ten-by-ten, cross-legged and smiling. "Welcome to my humble abode!" he invited.

"Peter Cottontail, I presume!"

"Catch-as-catch-can...is that you?"

"The same. At your service, sir!" Catch felt like a ten-year-old. This could be fun. First things first, though. "Paula tells me to look for a Vietnam vet named Connor Boggs. Know him?"

"No one, but no one, uses their real name here, and the vet thing could apply to most of us, you know. Any other clues? Sit down, by the way, sit down and make yourself at home, Catch!"

The big man folded himself as best he could, and sat down across from Peter. "Couldn't we just ask, since we have the name and all?"

"Um. They get paranoid. Can't do that. I do know one thing, though. You said the cops got his name because a bullet was traced to a gun. Now, that means he doesn't have the gun anymore, right?"

"Right."

"So, we look for a ticked-off cowboy, soured on poker, drunk. No one loses a gun here unless they're comatose or duped into it."

Now Catch understood why Paula had chosen Peter for this chore. "When can we start?"

"After dark. Make yourself comfortable. I'll start a fire."

"That Chetty guy. Do you know him?"

"Sure. Hasn't been here long—just got out of the State Hospital."

"I guess that figures."

Peter nodded. "Lotta them down here."

"What's your story, Peter? Just curious."

Peter looked up and grinned. Sizing the big guy up with his dancing blue eyes, he decided this was one he could trust. "Peter McNabb, Father Peter McNabb, that is."

"What?" Before Catch could adjust his thoughts the man in front of him had pulled off a straggled wig to reveal a close-cropped curly head —clean—and unbuttoned his threadbare flannel shirt to reveal a turned, very white, collar. The biker's mouth dropped open. "Huh? You're not foolin', are you? You're really a priest."

The loud guffaw could be heard down the river both ways for a good long stretch. Catch wondered whether they shouldn't be quiet and he said as much, but Father McNabb didn't seem concerned.

"Your face! Oh my, I love it!"

"Is this a joke? You're foolin' with me, right?"

"No. No. But do you know how silly you look in those tennis shoes and baseball cap?"

Catch was a little offended at that, and his face said so.

"Ohhh, sorry, friend. Listen, you look like you belong down here, that's all I meant. And Paula's people are hard to spot. That's what makes it so much fun."

"Paula's people?"

"You, me, and someone I may introduce you to. I've only been down here for this little chore of hers so far, that's all. But it *has* been fun, and you're gonna get a kick out of it too. I can tell. Are you game for spending a little time here?"

It was Catch's turn to laugh. The Gal—she was really something. Yeah, she was. "How much time are you talkin' about?"

"You're having fun, aren't you? Admit it, because I don't really know how long this will take."

"Well, it *is* different."

"I knew it." Fr. McNabb pulled his wig back on and buttoned his flannel. He found two tin cups and poured hot coffee into them from the kettle on the coals. "Drink up, then I'm gonna put you through a short course. By the way, don't worry—no one says much about their past here, and no one asks unless you've been around awhile. Your real name isn't Catch, is it?"

"No."

"Explain?"

"Charles Atlas, The Christian Hulk. And I didn't make it up myself. Real name's Charles Atleberry. I like Catch."

Peter liked to laugh, Catch noticed. A lot.

Peter

The two men had been mingling with the rest most of the evening, but had not seen Chetty. Sam—the man Peter said was his sidekick—said he hadn't seen him, and who knew where he was, and who cared.

They had watched the nightly poker game, even played a couple of hands. Things were being exchanged, not money. These ranged from food to booze to bags of dog food. Some of the residents had pets. Cats hung out around the fire pits here and there. Some of those were claimed, but most were about as unattached as the other residents of the river bottom.

Finally, with what Catch was afraid was nothing accomplished, Peter got up, stretched, and said he was going to call it a night now. Catch followed him back to the piers, which were some distance south of the poker game.

Peter had cautioned Catch to hide his watch earlier. He found it now in his jeans pocket and read the time. It was almost a half hour shy of midnight.

In the distance sirens could be heard, not uncommon so near town, but Peter looked up, concerned. He crossed himself. "I always pray at sirens. Habit."

"Then you pray a lot, I guess."

"I pray a lot. Yes."

"Wait a minute. Hear that?"

"That ain't uncommon, either, when you live under a bridge, friend. Cars."

"Listen." The sound coming from the road high up was erratic. The sirens grew strong—then stopped, it seemed, right on top of them. "Get down!"

Both pseudo bums shot under the bridge and buried themselves low, but Peter reached for Catch, telling him he'd better get into the camp, and behind the pier. They made it just in time to hear a loud metal-on-metal crunch. Then they saw lights turning. When they stopped, Catch jerked up, ready to run toward the open riverbed where he saw a car land.

"*No!*" cried Peter. "There's help right there. Just watch. Keep out of sight. I'm going to go peek, though."

It took a long time for the cops to clear out. After the ambulance left, they stuck around taking pictures, and then they spent some time putting articles that had scattered during the fall into bags. "They know there are scavengers out here," Peter explained. He'd returned to camp soon after the ambulance left.

"I wonder who they were—the people in the car, I mean."

Peter said nothing.

"Can we get a fire going? We didn't accomplish much tonight. I guess I'm staying."

"You don't have to stay, son. That was Chetty. He's dead."

"But we still..."

"No. I figure tomorrow tongues will wag all day, and they're not gonna be as loose if a stranger's here. Besides, I'm pretty sure it was him that had possession of that gun. I just have to get Sam to talk. Now that Chetty's gone, he will."

"How're you gonna prove it?"

"Well, that's where you come in."

"I don't understand."

"You tell the cops Chetty's their man, and Connor Boggs is 'Hagan' down here. I figured that out at the games—he was mad as smoke that Chetty wasn't here—said 'I want that piece back. Where's the nut-case?' Remember?"

"Guess I didn't catch that."

"It takes time. Listen, I can't blow my cover. This is a ministry, you know. This way the guys will just think an undercover cop was here—that'd be you—and duped me into takin' him around, and that you heard Hagan squealin' about his gun. Now, you really need to go home. Don't wear that get-up again, and you might want to call Paula and take her with you to the station. They know her."

Nineteen

Meg

The hospital room was quiet; only whispers could be heard. Paula sat close to the bed, periodically dabbing Debra's forehead with a cool cloth. Chelsea had been in twice in the time I'd been there, but had gone back to work. Jake sat in a chair with his laptop open, working on a sermon. Debra lay motionless. Both her eyes were bruised, but almost healed. An IV line ran from the back of her hand where it was inserted, to a pole above her head. I watched as the drip, drip, drip of fluid counted the time. It stood still in that room, stubbornly refusing to move forward. And it held us all in a circle of silence, hovering, like eagles over a friend.

When an eagle is sick, others come together, nurture it, and then they wait until it recovers in body, or only in spirit. Over time, there is no eagle nor is there a believer who has not known grief. But I believe there is no grief given up to God that does not eventually make a believer soar just like an eagle.

I opened my laptop, turned it on, and settled in to read the diary I'd scanned into it. I was still looking for that conclusion that eluded me in my novel. Maybe I'd missed something.

2003
Debra wrote:

Dear Annie,
I woke up from a harsh dream to find that I had thrashed around so much that I'd unearthed this journal. There are quite a few pages left to fill, and my heart sinks because of it. I had hoped you would be reading this by now, and that I would not need to share news of the more recent years of my life with you. But my dream

was about you. I think that finding this book right now is more than a coincidence.

For so long I have thought that you will need to find me, not the other way around. I will not intrude on your life. I'll wait to be invited. But this dream troubles me. It reminds me that there is still someone who needs me. By now you are twenty-five years old. You should not need me now, but I feel that you do.

In my present circumstance, all I can do is pray.

I am living in my car. It's very early, but still the part of autumn that is warm. At night I park in the lot at the convalescent hospital, where I work. It's safe here and convenient. I wake up early to go in and shower. My first blessing, then, is that I can stay clean. I don't pay for the water or the heating of it, but I get to enjoy it. For a small fee I can take my meals here, too. Most days I do that. In this world I live in now, the library is my lounge and my study. The park is my yard and my garden. The grocery store is my pantry. On Sundays my church is my parlor, where I can invite my friends over for fellowship. So, I simply have a very large house. I have a gardener, a cook, and a housekeeper.

People have become my treasures. The elderly here struggle with physical pain, but losing their independence and their sense of purpose is their most difficult struggle. It's like childbirth in reverse.

We had an elderly lady in here for about a year before she passed away in the company of her daughter, her granddaughter, and her great-granddaughter. Four generations were in one room. Her daughter sat by, making sure she was fed small bits of crushed ice to wet her tongue. Her granddaughter read aloud from the Psalms, and her great-granddaughter held her hand and brushed her forehead with a cool, wet cloth.

Pamela's body had been thrashing around, as they sometimes do when they are about to die. When it finally stilled, the room seemed to burst with excitement. I saw all three faces that were left behind light up in wonder, so I knew I was not the only one feeling it. Pamela's spirit seemed to be racing back and forth along the ceiling shouting for joy. It was more like witnessing a birth than a death. I felt exactly like I had just attended a graduation and needed to celebrate this triumph in the worst way.

The Church Triumphant is what they're called, those who have gone on ahead. And we are *The Church Militant.* We are not to be comfortable. We are to be diligent.

Annie, if you're reading this, please know I don't consider my circumstances a hardship. I consider them a privilege. Please don't pity me. Remember, the wisdom of this world is like foolishness to God.

Well, it's time for work.

I love you, little one,
Mom

I looked around the room. Paula was asleep next to Debra's bed. Jake was reading the Bible, speaking close to Debra's ear on the window side of her bed. Nan came in and quietly took a seat near mine. It was at that moment that Debra moaned and her eyelids began to flicker wildly.

Paula pushed Debra's button, and Nan went to retrieve a nurse. When she came, there were the usual checks, vital signs, readings...but no change lasted. Debra did continue to move, but only a little. Still, there was a dramatic change in the inert posture her body had held for days now. Periodically she moaned and turned a little in the bed, as if she were seeking a way back out of her slumber. When Chelsea and Ben arrived in the afternoon, Jake told them he thought she was going to wake up soon.

Gradually her moaning became more coherent, and her movements more controlled. And then she opened her eyes. They were wide with fear. Jake leaned down to calm her, and she whispered something, which he apparently heard. He said, "Debra, it's okay. Shh..."

Her voice became stronger, so that we could all hear what she said next. "I want...to...see her."

Jake rang the buzzer, and the nurse came in again. She was relieved to see her patient had come to but worried that Debra was so agitated. "I am going to have to give her something if her vitals don't even out soon. But I'd rather not. Can you calm her down? Did someone say something that might upset her—even when she was still asleep?"

We looked at each other, trying to remember who had said what, or if anyone had said anything unusual. All we remembered was Jake saying she was going to wake up, and certainly that couldn't have upset her. She continued to beseech Jake to tell her where Annie was, until he said, "All right, Debra. But I'll need to talk to Ben first."

He took a long look at Chelsea, silently asking her to stay with Debra while he and Ben left the room. The young woman was laughing and then crying, stroking Debra's hand, trying to calm her down.

I followed the men into the hallway. Jake said, "I can't tell her, Ben. What are we going to do?"

The silence that followed maddened me. I said, "What are you talking about? You can't tell her where Annie is?"

"I can't tell her that Annie's dead, Meg."

"Oh, no, she's not!"

"I received the death certificate in the mail shortly after the Wallaces adopted her."

It was Ben's turn. "Jake, what do you mean? She's in there with Debra right now. That's our Annie. You know that's Annie, don't you? They told you she died? Oh, no. How could they do that to you?"

"They told Marj they'd given birth to Chelsea, that Gail had been carrying her when she found out Debra was pregnant, and that's why it took so long for them to decide to adopt her." Jake pulled a folded, aged piece of paper out of his pocket. "I've been carrying this around, trying to decide how to tell Debra." The document looked legitimate. It was yellowed and worn, but it was a death certificate.

"Wait a minute," I said. "Is this the first time you two have put your heads together in—what—over twenty years?"

Ben turned pale, and he covered his face with his hands. "That's why they told me never to call her Annie again. It was so long ago, I hadn't thought about it in years. I had no idea there was a connection with Debra until this sister thing popped up. But it made sense to me, because the story I was told was that Jake had kept her at first because Gail was sick, but that she was Gail's daughter. I was little. I just accepted it. And they were angry he'd called her Annie because they'd named her Chelsea."

I was amazed. "So you two didn't keep in touch? I don't understand."

Jake said, "It was best to let them go. I didn't want them running back to me, maybe causing trouble with their new parents."

"I looked Jake up just before I came out here," Ben explained. "I thought certainly he knew Chelsea was Annie. But now I can understand why he didn't. We didn't make the time to talk like we should have, I guess."

Part of me was getting a little bit excited about telling the girls. The other part was almost afraid to. "Ben," I said, "do you have the Wallaces' number? I'm going to call them if you don't." He handed me his cell phone after pushing in their number, saying he'd rather I did because he was afraid of what he might say.

Gail Wallace answered.

"Ms. Wallace," I said, "this is Meg O'Malley. I'm a friend of Debra's, and of Chelsea's. Debra has just awakened from a coma....Yes. I thought you might know. They're together, and they think they are sisters...No. You need to know that Debra is upset, and it's giving her doctor fits right now. She's upset because she thinks there is something wrong with Annie. We're going to tell her the truth, Ms. Wallace...No. That isn't the truth...No. I'm not crazy. I'm here with Jake Highland, Ms. Wallace, and with Ben Mitchell. We're going to tell her the truth...Yes. He's right here." I handed the phone to Ben.

By then Gail's voice was shaking, and out of control. Jake and I could hear her from two feet away. She was in hysterics, saying Ben could tell Debra if he wanted to, and yes, it was the truth, and she was sorry. Could they please get the girls to Hawaii just as soon as Debra was well? The tickets would be sent out.

Ben closed his phone. "Well, what do you say we go in there, see how Debra's holding up, and then assure her she will meet her daughter in Hawaii as soon as she's well?"

Jake scratched his head. "You can't be serious."

"It might be just the thing to get her up and about. Besides, she'll put two and two together about the Hawaii thing. The girls already think there is something fishy about their both 'winning' trips there at the same time, from an anonymous source."

"How's Chelsea going to react?"

"It won't be easy for her, either. I'll have to tell her everything, and then let her decide how to tell Debra, and when. It's her call. The problem is, she'll need time to digest all of this, and I don't think it's necessary to tell Debra about the death certificate, do you? Not now, at least."

I agreed, and so did Jake.

The hospital chapel was empty, and I was glad. The little vibration in my ear had come on so slowly, and I was so used to it by now that until it had become loud and almost obnoxious, I paid no attention to it. As I neared the cloistered room, it calmed, and as I entered, I heard that giggle.

It was peace to my soul. The pent-up fear and dread of the past several days had taken their toll on my nerves. But I'd learned that when Omni giggled, I could look forward to good things.

I knelt before the altar, allowing myself to be drenched in the silence. After a while I looked around. Symbols were everywhere, telling stories of pain, grief, and joy. Some accuse the church of idolatry because of these statues and carvings, but to me they are an invitation to meditate. After all, symbols are all around us; these I trust.

I lifted my head, and closed my eyes, breathing in the stillness of the cool, waiting air around me. A faint scent of incense, the wax of several burning candles, and the iconic color and light offered relief from the endless sterility of Debra's room. So grateful were my body and soul for the respite, and for the promise of the vigil's end, that I allowed Omni's giggle to infect me, and I laughed.

To the left of the central raised crucifix stood a statue of a blue-cloaked Mary, a teenage mother of courage, holding the baby Jesus in outstretched arms, as though offering him up to the world as her gift of love.

God's plan, and her agreement.

I thought of the decisions so many make to end the plans God has for them, and for the world. Millions of good plans, and yet these same people complain that he has not intervened on the world's behalf. How heinous to blame him for our discomfort. I looked up at the figure of agony carved on the cross, and then back at the virgin. Her eyes were love itself, but they were not focused on the child she held. They looked straight at me. I shifted my gaze to the infant, and that giggle assaulted my ear again; I saw a twinkle in his eye.

Twenty

Hawaii
2004
Debra and Annie

"Annie, I can't believe we're on our way!" Debra cried, squeezing her daughter's hand and relishing the experience.

"I know. I'm excited. Can't wait to feel that ocean air and walk barefoot in the warm sand. At the same time I don't want to see the folks."

"I do want to see them, but I'm afraid of what the years have done to them."

"They're rigorous folks. I doubt they've changed much. You know, there were always new things to do, new places to see, and the old was left in the closet, never to face again—if possible. And then there was work. It never stopped."

Debra gazed across the narrow seat at her daughter, memorizing the lines of her profile, the way she crinkled her nose when she smiled, and how she smiled more now.

Annie—the name she insisted on using now—rested her head on Debra's shoulder and sighed. She massaged her swelling abdomen softly, in a circular motion with her right hand. Debra's eyes teared suddenly. Forgiving her parents would be a process, and probably a painful one. Thank God they were together. She pulled her daughter close.

She had so many questions. Why had they adopted her daughter, and why had they kept her from Annie for so long? Were their hearts that hardened to her, or were they trying to make amends for their rejection of her? Only God knew the secrets of the heart. Debra had trouble knowing her own, and it was that fact that made her uneasy.

She prayed: *Dear God, You've carried me all these years. Carry me now.*

A metallic crackle could be heard then, and the intercom jumped to life with a tinny male voice reciting a script of welcome, and announcing their arrival at Kona Airport. The two women gathered their purses and watched the window as the plane descended slowly to the runway below. Outside they could see the slate black ribbons of lava, which the electronic voice said flowed not long ago down to Kailua from Mt. Mauna Kea east of the city. This lent an otherworldly dimension to the view, in stark contrast to the sky-blue sea beside it.

When the engines quieted, Annie flipped her phone open to retrieve a message from Ben and relay it to Debra. "They're headed down to Meg's house," she said after listening for a minute. Then, "I guess they figured it would be a good time to reminisce. Meg's working on the sequel to her book, and they want to make a trip to the old village. Guess we're all dealing with old business." Annie closed the phone and sighed. "You know, I don't remember a thing about those years with Jake. I wonder if Ben isn't going through some old pain of his own, or he will be."

"You'll have a lot to talk about next time you're together."

Annie smiled. "For now, there is enough to deal with, right?"

Debra gazed into her daughter's blue eyes. "Honey, I am sure there will be. Let's go meet the folks."

Annie rose and gathered her carry-ons from the overhead compartment and quickly found an opening in the queue headed to the hatch. Thinking Debra was right behind her, of course, she paced herself to the crowd and made her way onto the tarmac. A minute later she was in the terminal. It was not hard to recognize her parents, who stood there, front and center waiting for her, so that she had no time to check whether Debra was at her side.

Gail Wallace stood stock straight next to her husband, and they appeared, as always, to be of the same height, because the woman wore two-inch heels.

Confusion struck Annie as she wrestled with her mind in order to remember they were really her grandparents. Her mother was a faded but well-preserved image of herself, so she had never doubted they were her parents. She had wondered, all of her life, why they'd waited so long for children, and why she was an only child. She had assumed it was their lifestyle that caused them to delay a family, and had even gone so far as to imagine they had not really wanted her, since they had not stopped their hectic pace once during her childhood.

When she'd had occasion to ask these questions she received only one answer. It was that she had Ben and Pia right next door. They had never considered she would need more. On that score, she had early on thought of the Mitchells' home as her own, and Ben and Pia her family, much more so than Gail and Ron Wallace.

Because of this the Wallaces bonding as a family had come late, but it had come. The time she had spent helping them at the pharmacy during her high school and college years had been good. After all, that was where they were at home, not in the sparsely furnished lake house where they slept. The pharmacy was also where she caught the notion to become a journalist.

Unlike her parents, Annie had shown an interest in everyone who entered the shop. In fact, they had told her that business had picked up considerably from the moment she began working there. Annie particularly loved chatting with the elderly customers, learning their various stories. Because of her interest, they often rattled off details of interconnected relationships within the community that her parents had not dreamed existed. In fact Gail Wallace had once admitted she often found herself eavesdropping on conversations her daughter was involved in, transfixed by her interest in so many trivial details, and sometimes fascinated by them despite herself.

One day she threw up her hands and said, "Chelsea, you will never make a pharmacist, but you certainly have the nose of a reporter. Ever consider journalism?"

She never had before, and she still didn't consider it her real career. She preferred to write fiction, but if journalism pleased her parents, well, it was a way out of the family business. She'd take it!

And there they stood, probably wondering only about her feelings. They had seen to it they knew the details of her life otherwise. It was the intrusion of various private detectives into her life over the past year that had caused her to close down any communication between herself and her parents. After all, she told herself, her feelings were the last thing they were interested in, and they knew everything else. What was there to communicate?

A hard lump rose from her heart to her throat, making it impossible for her to speak. She supposed that by now they even knew she was pregnant again. Anger and fear mingled with resolve in her soul. She stood still, looking from one to the other of her grandparents, and thinking only of Debra and how they had hurt her. She could not move.

Dear God, she prayed, *what is it you expect of me here? What would Ben do? What would Debra do? But it is not Ben, and it is not Debra here…not Debra. Gosh. Where is she?*

Annie had never felt so alone.

Debra could not move quickly yet. Her injuries would take time to heal. She often forgot that fact until something like this occurred. She watched as Annie blithely left the plane, and she eventually composed herself by looking out the window while the line in the aisle thickened and finally began to move, flowing slowly out toward the hatch. For the moment she was alone, and it was a familiar feeling. She needed the familiar just now, badly. She hoped Annie would notice her absence and wait for her. She breathed in and out, counting to ten each time she did, until the air around her grew less close, until the voices and the footfalls grew thin and then nonexistent save a faint, last *bye-bye* from the front of the plane.

Only the clearing activity of the steward brought her head around, but he was not insisting she leave, so she hesitated, took another deep breath, and thought what she should do next. She didn't remind others that it was hard for her to order her movements to her thoughts. The doctors had said it would take time, but her coordination would eventually return. She needed rest and easy exercise, physical therapy. They'd told her walking in the sand would be a good thing. Jake had been the only one present to hear these advisories, and Debra had not mentioned them to Annie.

Lord, stay close. Please. This was all she could manage of a prayer. She took a moment to rehearse her movements before she stood and retrieved her things from the overhead compartment and walked away from her seat.

After she rounded the corner and looked out into the sea of people, Annie's narrow, still back was the first thing she saw. In front of her stood a couple, scared statues together, holding each other up. They looked older, tired, but most of all, scared.

What had she been afraid of all these years? She'd had Herb right beside her for many of them, as tall, straight, stubborn, and loving as a rock. These people had abandoned her, she realized, all in an instant, because of their fear. *Their* fear!

Dear Lord, what about her fear? But then it occurred to her that a few months of it was all she'd had to face, and even then she'd held the hand of her strong mentor until he placed it into God's own. Would she have ever met God had it not been for her parents' actions? How else, in the spiritual vacuum they'd raised her in, could she possibly have met him? She drew a deep, long breath, the truth assaulting her like a spear but quenched quickly by the shield of Herb's everlasting shadow—his, and now her own, faith.

Selfishness. All of those years, in every disguise imaginable, it was only selfishness that had motivated them and finally bred such fear. And why not? They had rejected God. Who else was left to sit on the throne of their hearts but themselves? Was it really that simple? But something in that strong, tall presence of Herb's she felt now, coupled with a still, small voice said it was.

And now she knew what to do.

"Annie!" she called. When her daughter turned to face her, there were tears streaming down her face, and Debra crossed the distance between them as quickly as she could, and drew Annie into a long hug. After a while she pulled herself away from Annie and faced her parents. She smiled and said, "Mom, Dad, don't be afraid. We love you, and we forgive you."

In a moment the four, a family, were engaged in a long-overdue embrace.

Twenty-one

Hawaii
Debra

The ice had been broken, but after a not-good-enough night's rest, the first day of their visit passed in a flurry of activity, which frustrated Debra, taxing her energy reserve to the max. She'd managed to hold her peace through a grand tour of the island, no expense spared, and an ostentatious luau at a large hotel, which had rendered her too tired to think, much less talk.

When she fell into bed, there was one prayer on her mind. Forgiveness had been offered, and now it needed stillness to be accepted. She wanted the air cleared. She wanted love, not this frigid fear and stilted conversation, skirting every subject that would dare come near honesty. They needed to face the truth and each other.

But to her chagrin, the following day was no different. She finally decided to accept things the way they were. At least it gave plenty of time to talk with Annie, and by the end of the second day, she realized it was all right. Time was in their favor, after all. Still, she prayed things would come closer to a real reconciliation soon.

On the morning of the third day in Hawaii, Debra woke slowly to the keening of water birds from the bay below. She was still in that in-between state after leaving the daily routine of physical therapy at the hospital, and then traveling and sleeping, where she could not get it quite into her head that she was not in her own room. With muddy eyes she looked around. Nothing came into focus, save the huge expanse of window facing Captain Cook Bay, which could barely be seen for the lush green overgrowth screening it. It looked like a jungle prison. Adding insult to injury, she was fairly drowning in chintz and finally screamed in protest, falling in the process of jumping clear of the entanglement.

The door opened. It was Gail, wondering what in the world was wrong.

"Oh, Mama." Debra pulled on her slippers and reached for her robe. "Sorry. I'm not used to all this luxury." Then she began to laugh because she could not get her legs to obey her so she could get herself up from the floor. She hadn't yet explained to her mother that her motor skills were a long way from normal just now.

Gail just stood there with a disappointed look. "I am sorry," she said crisply.

Did she think her daughter was drunk? Debra rubbed her eyes and took a deep breath before she purposefully pushed herself up and walked over toward the door, holding her mother's gaze for a time before she said, "Mom, I'm still recovering. It's an effort to walk first thing in the morning. I forgot myself and jumped out of bed. I just haven't got my senses yet."

The woman softened, but Debra could tell this only by looking closely at her eyes. In another time she would have given up. Now she was determined not to.

"Mama, let's have coffee."

"Annie's still sleeping."

"She needs to sleep as long as she can. And that's good, because you and I need to catch up, I think."

Gail's eyes clouded then, and she turned away, but Debra reached over and gently turned her mother's face back to her own. She smiled. "Mama, I missed you, and I didn't like it, and I want to spend time with you now."

The elegant kitchen was immaculate, but the coffee pot was engaged. Debra could smell the strong Kona beans brewing as she walked into it. "May I?" she asked, while she drew a mug from the counter.

At her mother's nod, she took up the carafe and poured a full portion, then handed it to Gail. Then she filled another cup and made her way to the table. She sipped once, then drank a little more before she looked up. Gail was watching her closely, with an expression either condescending or crestfallen. Debra could not decide which.

She tried to think of things she could say, but decided it was best to hold her tongue. The atmosphere was too familiar, even after their long separation. It was best, she thought, to wait for Gail to initiate the conversation. *Your serve, Mama*, she thought, and waited for the first volley.

It was a harsh one. "I suppose you thought you were waking up in your car again?"

Debra choked. It was all she could do to get the mug back onto the table. She took a deep breath before she said, "No. I've been in the hospital so long, I think I was expecting a nurse to check on me, and my bed to be a little sparse."

"Yes. I know. Your tangle with that homeless person, that madman."

Debra stayed quiet.

Gail coughed uncomfortably and took a long drink herself.

Debra decided to change the subject. The conversation was going right into a ditch. She scanned the sunny breakfast nook. It was professionally decorated in the island motif she'd expected—bamboo, windows everywhere, pleasant but almost too perfect, and a little uncomfortable because of it. "You have questions, Mama. Don't be afraid to ask them. Do you know much about what happened after you moved away?"

"To you, you mean?"

"Yes. I understand you were in touch with Annie all along, so you pretty much know her story."

Gail's face became stone. She again reached for her mug. "Nerves."

Debra laughed. "Yeah. I know. Me too."

For the first time their eyes met in a frost-free gaze, and Gail teared first. She choked, and then in a hoarse whisper said, "I'm sorry."

"After you and Daddy left, I was a wreck, but only for a little while. Michael's grandpa took me in, and I was able to finish school, and then to work after Annie was born. Michael finished school, and we were married."

"Wait. Where did you work?"

"I, uh, I trained as a nurse's aide, and I worked in a nursing home while I took art classes. When Michael finished school, we were married. We lived in a small cabin in the mountains, and we had Caroline. Did you know any of this?"

"No, Debra. We didn't. We did find out early on, of course, that you planned to adopt Annie out."

Debra couldn't stop her words this time. "And you didn't approve?"

Gail winced, and Debra did not trust herself to talk again. She waited.

It was a long time before her mother spoke. She was crying, and got up to find a box of tissues before she continued. "We missed you."

Every emotion imaginable assaulted Debra then. They could have written, or they could have called. They knew where she was. "I didn't know where you were, or I would have called." She had not realized there was anything left of the bitter sorrow she'd gone through so many years ago, but it had surfaced in the tone of her voice, she knew. "I thought I was past all that, Mama. I'm truly sorry." Debra reached for a tissue from the box Gail had placed on the table.

She had so many questions. Were they punishing her all those years? Were they—just what were they? They *missed her?* She gathered her emotions and tried to replay the epiphany she'd come to the day before clearly in her mind. She would never have met the Lord if they'd taken her back. She probably would not have married Michael or had Caroline, or known Herb as her family. *Quiet*, she told herself. *Be still.* But she wept.

Gail found her voice first. While Debra cried she explained, "When Annie was born we decided, no, we knew you would regret giving her up. We looked everywhere for a solution. We thought we might find her a home, people willing to keep in touch somehow. We couldn't. So we arranged to raise her as our own. At that point, we could not get in touch with you. It was too awkward. And it would have been too hard for you, and for Annie. We missed you, Debra. We really did!"

Gail got up from the table and made her way to her daughter but hesitated to touch her until Debra looked up and literally jumped into her arms.

After a long time Gail said, "Tell me about Caroline. How old is she?"

Debra could not stop crying. She simply held onto her mother, hoping that information could be part of another conversation, another day, but she did manage to say, "She died. Michael's gone, too."

Fresh tears ran down Gail's cheeks. "Tell me about her, Debra."

Debra sat down, pulled another tissue from the box, and blew her nose. She waited for Gail to sit down, but this time her mother retrieved her mug from the other side of the table and sat down next to her. Debra finally managed to talk. "Michael and Caroline were on their way to town. He was going to drop her off at school, and then go to work." She was talking slowly, deliberately, trying not to work her way into another emotional pool. She drew a deep breath and continued. "They liked to sing when they were together, and the radio was up too loud, I guess. They didn't hear the train coming, and they were hit."

"How old was she?"

"Ten. And I have to tell you something. If we'd kept Annie, she would have been in that car, too. Some things just happen for the better."

"Did you wish you'd kept her?"

"Yes. But it's true. She would have been gone, too, just like Caroline."

Debra's tears continued, and Gail clutched her shoulders. "I want to know all about her, Debra, everything. Let's talk about Caroline, okay?"

Debra smiled, and then chuckled, remembering her daughter's little face. "She was so—um—elf-like. She was a little red-haired, freckled faced Scot, green eyes, skinny. Oh, I want to see pictures of Annie. I'll bet they were so much alike. Do you have pictures of Annie when she was little?"

Gail rose, smiling. "We could not have told you two apart, Debra. Honestly, I had a devil of a time sorting through them if I didn't label them right away. And I didn't have time to do that, so now I just try to figure out which is more aged and go by that. I've taken the time to put them into books, and I hope they're right. You can tell me, maybe."

Both women were relieved at the concept of doing something besides crying. The boxes were nearby.

Gail

Gail had hoped her daughters would want to look through them, so she'd brought the albums to Hawaii with her. In all honesty, she envied Debra. It sounded like she'd had time to enjoy Caroline. And she would have regretted it if she had not.

Gail knew. For all their efforts, in the end Annie had spent more time with the neighbors than with her grandparents. And Debra? They'd poured their lifeblood into Debra. She'd won every prize she'd gone after in school. The disappointment when she turned up pregnant had sent them into paroxysms of anger. They considered it the worst ingratitude. They'd moved away in order to teach her a lesson, hoping she'd finally decide to abort the child, or if she did not, she would keep the child and learn just how hard it was to raise it.

Either way, they had no intention of abandoning her beyond the few months it would take Michael to face his responsibilities and Debra to appreciate their decision. They'd planned, of course, to have her come back to their home, which would be far away from the boy, and then get her back on track and established in college.

When they learned she'd decided to adopt Annie out, they recoiled. And their decision to adopt the child themselves made it impossible to reunite with Debra. The pain went both ways, and it was a hard pain. What cut most was the knowledge that Debra had to feel she was totally abandoned. They had consoled themselves with the fact that she would not have a child to care for, at least, and she was smart. She'd make it.

When Chelsea was growing up, they'd thought often about contacting Debra, but they had been afraid of the fallout, first because

Chelsea had not been told about her mother, and second, could Debra ever forgive them? Would she want her daughter back? And what would Chelsea's life be like in that case? Did Debra have the means to care for a child? Would she be too proud to receive help from them if she didn't? Shortly after they adopted the two-year-old, they decided to cut the last line of contact, and they told Jake Highland the child was dead.

Over time they'd come to believe what they'd done was unforgivable. They'd just have to live with things as they were. But when Chelsea left and refused to contact them, they were heartbroken and worried. So they had decided it was high time Debra knew who Chelsea was, and besides that, in their retirement, a reunion was something they could no longer avoid. The girls were their heirs. Perhaps the money they'd be given would soften the pain a little. In any case, it had to be done. They were intent on this, especially after finding out recently that Debra had turned up homeless some months ago. It was unconscionable. And that was not to happen again, not to their daughter.

Gail studied Debra as her hands moved lovingly over the pages in one of the scrapbooks. At one point she looked up with that radiant smile she had. The room fairly lit up all around her.

"Mama, thank you for loving her so much! I know you did, didn't you? And you loved me, too." Debra was taken by the fact that her baby pictures were installed on the left of every page, and Annie's on the right. A healing was taking place in her heart that she had not expected, had not even known was needed until now. "Boy, do we have time to make up for, you and I!"

It was Gail who needed the tissue box this time. She was thinking of Annie. Gail smoothed her hand over the right-hand page of the open scrapbook on the table and traced the image of the tiny face of the three-year-old with her index finger.

"I'll talk to her, Mamma. But remember, she's vulnerable right now. It may take time. I've had more time, and more comfort than you know."

"In your faith?"

"Yes, and in the people God's put in my life."

"I wish I had faith."

"Well, we can start with this, and it is something that all this time has proven true. There is a Scripture verse that says all things work together for good for those who love the Lord, and are called according to his purpose. Mama, if this whole thing hadn't happened…"

Debra

Debra did not know how her mother would react to what she was about to tell her, so she hesitated.

"I wish I could believe that," her mother said.

"Well, I do, and that's why it's so easy to let go of the past. If this whole thing had not happened, I might never have accepted the gift of faith."

Her mother stiffened, but she asked, "How so?"

Debra fought for an answer that would not hurt her mother, but she could not find one. The longer she remained quiet, though, the more eloquent the silence became. She decided to tell the truth, as gently as she could.

"You were always so sure of what I should do, and what was next. Until I was faced with the reality of either taking a life or giving it, I thought I was, too. But I realized what I believed and did had always simply lined up with what you and Daddy thought I should believe and do. When you left I had to start learning those things for myself, and because I was so hurt, I had the courage—or the anger, I guess—to lay aside all those things that hindered me from giving faith a chance. I guess it is really that simple on my part, but pretty miraculous in another way."

Her mother looked puzzled, but Debra continued, hoping she would understand, praying she would.

"Things just began to line up, both to push me further toward realizing my own helplessness, and to confront me with God's availability—his reality." She could see her mama was open, more relaxed. In any case, she had to go on. "First, of course, the pregnancy moved along. I was sick at first, helpless, scared. But when you left, Michael's grandfather took me in. I was safe, and I was comfortable. He let me help him with things around the house and in the garden, and he seemed so glad I was there. His wife had passed away, and he was lonely.

"I wanted my baby to have a mother and a father, and even if by some miracle Michael and I stayed together, the statistics were against it lasting. I wanted her to have a solid home, and I could not offer it to her."

"So, how did faith come into the picture?"

"I couldn't do it, Mom. I knew I should give her up, but I also knew there was no way I'd have the strength in myself to do it. I needed God, and then Jake Highland showed up..."

"Jake Highland?"

"Yes. He introduced me to God."

Her mother remained quiet for a while, and thoughtful, until she said, "You know, Debra, we did have some dealings with him through the agencies. He's a stubborn man."

Debra's heart sank. She knew all too well her parents' attitude toward clergy, but she had not heard their side of the story. "Tell me."

"Well." Her mother hesitated. "We had a hard time raising Chelsea the way we felt was best, because of him. However, it did turn out well, after all, except for..."

"Except for Ben?"

"Well, yes. The boy was...because Ben was always there, Chel—I mean, Annie—didn't have a chance to meet anyone else, you know."

Debra tried to understand, realizing her mother had an entirely different perspective than her own. "You wanted Annie to have a chance to travel, and to grow, and become her own woman before she settled down. I know, Mother. And I know you felt she'd settled down too early. I know about the abortion, and the separation."

"Oh, it wasn't our intention for Annie to leave Ben, not really."

"Why did she?"

"She changed. She became moody and depressed. She left without telling us, and we were worried sick. We had our friend from KSLO e-mail her an offer, and then we hired detectives to make sure she found you; we hoped you could help her."

"The private eye?"

"Yes. You'd changed your name and we didn't know where you were. We were worried, Debra. She never wrote or called. We learned too late that this sort of trauma happens often after an abortion. We had to keep tabs on her. We were having a hard time living with ourselves, for sure."

"I know. She still mourns for the child she lost. You need to know that."

"What's done is done, as far as that goes."

"No. What's done cannot be changed at this point, but it is being healed because she has learned to give things to God. And she's back with her husband, which has been healing, especially since she's been able to be honest with him. And now they share a faith, so all that time apart can be forgiven. But it doesn't make it right."

"And you think it is our fault."

"No. But I do think it would be good for your sake and for Annie's if you would accept your part in it all. The truth is hard to face, but once you do, the road beyond is hopeful. Everyone can move on together. Otherwise..."

"Otherwise?"

"Otherwise, it's sort of like losing yourself in a forest and walking in circles forever. Senseless, scary, and lonesome."

"And that is what you think we've been doing?"

"You know, Mother, I'm not that smart. I don't know why wars happen or why people lie or cheat or steal. I don't know why children go hungry on one side of the world and are spoiled rotten on the other. I do know, though, that if I can pick myself up past a mistake and then do the right thing, it will cause a ripple of good to spread out from my little life, and I know I'm responsible for that.

"Right now I want healing, and if we choose to face this thing together as a family, we can enjoy the love we've all missed. It's there, right on the other side of all that fear, and I want it. I want it so badly. You don't know how much I've missed you!"

A sniffle could be heard in the kitchen. Both women looked up to see Annie wrapped in her robe.

Their mother spoke first. "How long have you been there, honey?"

"Let's see…since it wasn't your intention for me to leave Ben."

The air between them stilled, as though the atmosphere was holding its breath. Debra stood up, gesturing Annie to come to the table, but Annie shook her head and said in a barely controlled voice, "I know the truth, and that's enough. I love you both, and nothing will ever, ever, ever change that. But right now I can't take it all in, so let's just concentrate on the love part of all this."

Twenty-two

Santa Barbara
Meg

The fog had cleared in the late morning, and I decided a walk on the beach would clear my head. I'd abandoned the notion that today would be spent at work on my second book, but I was hopeful Jake and Ben could help me round out my project when they came. The guesthouse was ready for them, and Jake had been almost sure they'd be there. But was I putting off work simply because I did not want to be alone in the house?

I laughed. Where Jake Highland was, there was the Lord. My putting off facing things did not matter, and certainly did not warrant worry. Besides, in the back of my mind, I was thinking that maybe their presence in the house would alter its sameness. Jake and Ben's visit would put new memories into the place. It would be good.

The gentle, persistent sound of waves spilling onto sand, overlapping one another, was always a comfort. The vastness of the sea and the timeless character of this beach was soothing. It was a grand picture of life. It continued as life continued, relentlessly, and without remorse. The lush roar of tide quieted my thoughts, reminding me that somewhere deep inside there was life, life that would grow strong on its own and help me meet today. Just like the waves were compelled to meet the sand, the one who was greater than me would continue to carry me out to meet the world.

It did more than calm my spirit; it beckoned me to tune into the moment. Who could think of other things or worry or fret when color and movement and sound and life chorused in such abundance here? It would be absurd, like attending a concert with Mozart at the piano and trying to write a shopping list while listening.

One by one small things drew attention to themselves. Seagulls called out their intentions as if to say, "Watch this! Red ball in the right corner pocket," and fled the throng to glide over the waters, diving purposefully, expertly, after food.

I could not see the jellyfish, the crabs, the seals, or the fish in every size, shape and color imaginable that filled these waters. Still, I knew they were teeming there. Often I had explored the tide pools at low tide. I never tired of it. Life was everywhere, and it was always surprising. What looked like a rock was not always a rock, and the hermit crabs came in so many sizes. The tiniest ones caused me to laugh every time I saw them. To see such a minute shell inhabited by a creature that scurried along busily on legs almost invisible to the eye was enough to strike my funny bone. It delighted me every time I ventured to the puddles between rocks, no matter how sad I'd been before.

I sat down on dry sand, close enough to the lapping waves to touch the foam. I could almost hear Patrick say, "I have blessings to count, for sure, my lady! And if I could count the grains of sand on this beach, their number would not rival the goodness in my life."

They had enjoyed a good life together.

Patrick was a teacher before he became a writer. I had been one of his students, fifteen years his junior, in fact. I had become his assistant, and when he began to write, his secretary. When his first book hit the market and was well received, he found himself called to travel.

"I've given it a lot of thought," he told me. I was twenty-nine, and he was forty-four. "If I ask you to be my wife, I am asking too much of you. I am not young enough to start a family, and you are. If I ask you to continue as my secretary, we will be traveling together."

"Do you love me?" I had asked him.

"Too much to let you go, and too much to ask you to give up a family."

"Did you ask me whether I wanted children?"

"It is a moot point, Meg. Do you want children?"

"I want you."

"Well then, I will do my level best to remain childlike at all costs. Will that do?"

There were times now when I wished sincerely that I had

children to enjoy, especially since Patrick was gone. But something Jake Highland said reminded me that it did not matter at this point in time. He said, "There are still people to love." And he was right.

Smiling, I drew my sweater around my shoulders against a sudden breeze. The ocean seemed to engulf me, surround me, and fill me at that moment. *There is God to love*, I thought. *There is still God to love, too, and that is forever. It is enough.*

I returned to my desk to find an e-mail from Jake. They were coming, and in fact, they were on their way. *Tonight?*

I bowed my head. *"Thank you*, Lord!"

Oh my, the guesthouse! I made my way to the back yard. The O'Malley guesthouse had seen many visitors in the past, but since Patrick's death, very few. It was a small, U-shaped building, with two bedroom suites, one on each end of the U. In between the rooms was a shared bathroom, which connected the wings. On the inside of the U, so that both bedroom sliding glass doors opened onto it, was an atrium area. This small garden was often used for barbecues. It was a wonderful way to share company time, and still give guests their privacy and peace. Patrick had insisted on making the library in the main house accessible to guests by building a door from it that led out into the atrium. It was unlocked when guests were there. Many had enjoyed quiet hours reading, reclining near the sunny west window overlooking the ocean.

My first chore was to clean the waterfall, fill it, and plug in the cord. Patrick had built it himself with rocks and shells he'd collected over the years of beachcombing we'd enjoyed. It cascaded in a spiral from the center wall of the guesthouse, so that it could be seen from my kitchen window as well as the guest bedroom windows. The sound of water spilling gently over stone and shell always made me smile.

I assessed what else needed to be done, and in a hurry. Collecting the sheets that covered the furniture, I put them in the wash. The building was tight. It would not need more than a little airing. I opened the windows one by one to admit the gentle ocean breeze that now blew in from below. The beds, I knew, had clean sheets on them. All that remained was to stock the kitchenette and hang clean towels in the bathroom.

When that chore was done, I went to the front yard, collecting clippers and two vases on my way. Whether they liked it or not, the men would have a bright bouquet of fragrant flowers on their dressers. I wanted them to feel welcome. It was nice to look forward to guests again. I'd missed that!

San Luis Obispo
Jake

Jake sat on his front porch waiting for Ben to show up. They would take Jake's car from there to Santa Barbara. It was a beautiful drive, with coastline opening up on the west only a few miles down the highway. If they timed it right, they would catch the sunset on the ocean near Santa Barbara.

He hoped Meg didn't mind them hustling down there in the evening, but knowing Meg, she'd be thrilled. He knew she enjoyed people, especially if she knew them well. Their weeks of prayer and care together for Debra while she was in the hospital had virtually made them family. Jake was pretty sure Meg was happy as a clam to have them, and the sooner the better.

Ben pulled into the driveway at six-thirty, rolled down his window, and held up a bag full of McDonald's burgers. "Dinner!"

"Good," Jake shouted, reaching for his suitcase. "We won't waste any time that way."

"Yeah. I figured you'd be ready. I miss her, too."

Ben thought fondly that Meg O'Malley knew how to liven things up. She thought like a writer, always burrowing into situations with questions and insights. She knew when to listen, and even when she got a little too feisty (usually in defense of Debra or Annie), it was refreshing. Once Ben had held his tongue after hearing a doctor's abrupt assessment of Debra's "hopeless" situation, only to hear Meg declare, "She'll come out of it. You watch! And I'll thank you to never, ever say that in front of her again."

Jake closed the door of Ben's car behind him after the younger man had climbed out. He gave Ben a bear hug and slapped him on the back. "With Annie gone, you'll need a little distraction. Am I right?"

Ben could not suppress a grin. Meg was more than a distraction. She was a dear friend. But she could be distracting, for sure. And he did need one. He had become used to fending for himself in the months he and Annie had been separated, but he had never gotten used to her absence. And with only three weeks to kill, he couldn't very well go out and get a second job. This was perfect. "You're right," he said as he climbed out of the car. "What's your plan?"

Jake invited Ben to put his suitcase into the trunk of his car first, and then placed his own next to it. "Well, we could drive up to Ta-te, stay at the mission, I hope, and then drive to the airport and fly into Dallas or Shreveport, rent a car and stay with your parents in Natchitoches. If they're available, that is. Otherwise, I believe I can scare up a place on the river. It is the off season right now, and I know people who own a vacation rental there."

"So, we have some phone calls to make tonight."

"Sure do. And I figure it's good we're going down to Meg's early, because we can make our plans together while we're there. It'll be easier that way."

"You're right." One more night he did not have to spend alone sounded good to Ben. He knew Jake felt the same way, but he could only project how difficult it was for someone who was struggling into widower-hood. Jake had not had time to think much after Marj died. Now, time must be weighing heavily on him.

Within a minute Jake's car was pulling onto the 101 off-ramp heading south, toward Santa Barbara.

The two men were pleased with the accommodations at O'Malley's B&B. Though small, the buildings were bright, cheerful, and homey.

From their rooms the murmur of waves falling on shore could be perceived, even though the air had turned chill and Meg had long since closed the windows in the guest house and turned the thermostat up. It was perfect.

"Wow, Meg!" Jake cried when he opened the small refrigerator in his room. "You've thought of everything." The shelves were well stocked with yogurt, cheese, lunchmeats, juice, and fruits. On further inspection, Jake found the modest cupboard equipped with paper plates, bowls, cups on the bottom shelf, and comfort food on the top one. "You really don't want your guests to go home, do you?"

"That *is* the whole idea. You're perceptive."

"I'm not going to want to travel any time soon, but we'd better talk this adventure through. We only have three weeks."

"We will. I've already done some research online. Ta-te is a fair drive from here."

"Right. That's what I was thinking."

"So, if we went there first, we could spend as much time as we wanted to, as long as we have a place to stay, and as long as we allow ourselves plenty of time in Natchitoches, and then time to fly home and get you two back before the girls show up looking for a ride home from the airport. Have you heard from them, by the way?"

Ben's eyes lit up. "They made it there fine, and the folks are showing them off around Big Island. That reminds me, I need to plug in my laptop. We'll check our e-mail. And, Meg, I may have to spend most of my time here at this desk. I had to bring some files with me in order to break away from work."

"Well, you party pooper! Jake had better not tell me he brought a sermon to write up!" She set her fists on her waist, and scowled at the both of them. "Well?"

"No, ma'am!" Jake assured her. "I'm officially on vacation."

"I'll see to that, you know. Trust me!"

Meg showed Ben where to plug in and set up for the Internet. The O'Malley's friends were, for the most part, in the literary world. The place was wired for convenience, so they could stay and work if they needed to.

Meg and Jake left Ben to his computer and took a tour of the house.

Jake was feeling at home, and he was not sure whether it was Meg's company, her hospitality, or the anticipation of being able to talk with good friends long into the night and enjoy the ocean. He did hope she wouldn't turn out to be an early-to-bed type. He tried to remember if Debra had said anything to that effect, but he couldn't, so he asked.

"Meg, are you a morning person or a night person?"

"Jake, I can't sleep most nights, at least until it's late. I watch a movie or read a book. If the book's good, I don't sleep at all. You?"

"I was trying to think of a polite way of asking you whether we could sit outside and talk for a while. It's already getting late."

"Lonely?"

"Very."

"Me too, or at least I was until you two showed up. Now I'm just grateful."

Jake smiled. "Let's see how grateful you are after Ben and I get through botching up your beautiful guest house, eating all your food, and talking your ear off tonight."

Meg grinned. "You'd sure better eat that food! That's what it's for. Listen, can you stand a hot bowl of soup, or would you like hot tea? What did you two eat for supper?"

"McDonald's hamburgers."

"No vegetables. You're tryin' to kill yourself? Here, come with me." Meg motioned Jake into the kitchen, dished up two steaming bowlfuls of soup out of the crockpot, and handed one to him. "Let's go outside."

A star or two twinkled occasionally through the evening mist, and it was cool enough for both Jake and Meg to go back in after jackets as soon as they set their bowls down on the picnic table. Meg retrieved a few candles for light while she was in the house, and then set a match to the wood and kindling she'd prepared in the fire pit. After a few minutes, it was almost as comfortable as sitting inside.

Jake made short work of finishing his soup, to the last drop. Meg, he noticed, was only half finished.

"Would you like more?" she asked.

"I'm fine. I wasn't that hungry, but it was so good I couldn't stop."

"Doesn't take much to please you, Rev, does it? You make an easy guest! I'm glad you liked it."

Meg

It became quiet, so I could only hear the cadence of the waves. I missed the nearness of the ocean when I was away in Atascadero. And tonight it was okay that Patrick was not here. Tonight it would not remind me of my loneliness.

"I'm grateful you two came down, Jake."

"We want to help with the book, Meg, and it is wonderful here."

Although I was outspoken by nature, I now relished the quiet, and let it answer for me. I smiled back at Jake. For a while we watched the fire burn, alone in our thoughts. Tonight, I sensed the good reverend was overdue for a little time to reflect. I felt privileged that he would choose this place in which to do that.

Jake

Jake returned from his own thoughts, which he'd seemed to be feeding to the fire and drawing from the fire. Patrick's large presence seemed to be everywhere. And here was this woman left to herself, still younger than a widow should be. Meg had been alone for over five years, though. For him, it had been only a few months since he'd lost his wife.

He seldom asked for help. Others were usually calling him for it. He was not used to asking, but since Marj died, it had often been in his mind to talk to Meg. He hoped she wouldn't mind. A tear filled his right eye and threatened to spill over.

Meg

I saw Jake's tear glisten in the firelight. *Oh my,* I thought. *Could it be the pillar of strength, the great conduit of God's love is finally going to let himself go to his grief?*

Jake nestled his head down into his folded arms and wept.

I got up quietly and went into the house for a box of tissues. I took time to turn the teapot on low heat as I passed through the kitchen and back out to the patio. Drawing a chair nearer to the fire, I sat down a little nearer him on his left. And then I waited. Warmth, like the presence of God or of Patrick's hand upon my head, seemed to visit me. This was a special gift I'd been given on rare occasions. I bowed my head and prayed for my friend, confident my prayers would be heard.

Jake

For Jake, there was much to let go of and still so much to sort out. His first memories of his wife were evenly woven into his first heartbreaking grief, that of losing his children. It was this memory that had been hardest for him to face. Jake remembered the first time he'd seen Marjorie. Until it dawned on him who she was and what she must be there for, he was transfixed. For a while she stood on the outskirts of the village, periodically raising a camera, taking photographs, smiling. It was a lovely smile. She moved gently, as though not wanting to disturb anything, willing the scene to stay as it was without notice of her presence.

That was impossible.

He went to her and introduced himself. He'd been in correspondence with her for a long time but had never met her. So they discussed the children. Marj had struggled with him from the beginning of their correspondence, trying to persuade him to lighten his demands on the adoptions. But his life was teaching him to stand firm and watch God part waters. He would have to watch his children go, but he would not allow them to be separated from each other.

God did part the waters. The Wallaces met the Mitchells, fell in love with their home on the river, and bought one next door to it. And by the time the children had to leave, Marjorie had accepted his proposal. His comfort was in Marjorie. Jake dried his eyes with a tissue, turned back to the fire, and asked, "Do you still see him? Can you still hear him sometimes? Do you know what I mean?"

Meg smiled, and when she turned to face Jake, the happy glow on her face was his answer. She said, "Funny you should ask!"

"But are there only memories? That's what I mean."

She furrowed her brow and took a little time to think before she said, "Pretty much. They're like a treasure pouch full of things you collect greedily, not wanting to lose one word or look or experience. And for a long time you attach it to your belt so you will be sure not to lose it. You take memories out and touch them and turn them over often, especially when you're all by yourself. Then, one day you forget to wear the belt, and go outside into the world without it. That's when you realize you didn't need the pouch at all, because the treasures are still with you. And that's when you begin to wonder whether they are memories, or whether your loved one is really right there with you, to remind you of what's important. It's like that. You've sorted the memories for so long that they are in a file box, and you can reach for one whenever you need it. You know how they'd react or what they'd say in any situation. They're part of you.

"It's been hard to face the house alone, Jake. I'm glad for your company. The house needs fresh, new memories, and now I will have them. I'm hoping all of you will want to call this a second home from now on."

"It does feel like home, Meg. You know, I grew up by the beach."

"It gets into your blood, I know."

"Um-hmm. And it helps."

"It does."

It was a long time before the fire went out, and there would be two days to relax before they headed up to the village. They would be good days.

Twenty-three

Debra

Debra had once told her mother she dreamed of going to Hawaii, and now here she was. But she'd never said she'd meant a real dream, and she wouldn't tell her now that she'd seen this bay before, and these strange rocks, and many other things.

Their time together was coming to a close, and her mother sat beside her on the beach, as if they'd never been apart. Annie was up at the house catching up on things with her dad and planning dinner. They both loved to cook, and with Annie's new appetite, it was a good thing.

Her mother's voice interrupted Debra's thoughts. "Sweetheart, I want to hear more about Caroline, and about Michael. I know you loved them very much."

"Why, Mother? Why do you want to know?"

"Because it's a part of your life I missed. I know you didn't think so, but it tore me apart to lose you for so long. I think it would be good for both of us, to talk about it. I know I used to long to find someone to talk to about you.

"Your father found it difficult, so sometimes I would go over to talk to Mrs. Mitchell, and she would listen, but she didn't understand. She must have thought I wasn't a good mother to Annie. I left her with them so much, you know. But part of me—the part that was sure what a mother should do—was destroyed, and what the child had with Pia and Ben was so strong. I felt like I'd be uprooting a good plant if I didn't just encourage it, and let her grow where her roots were happy. And there was another thing...."

"What's that?"

"I had it in my mind all along that I was saving Annie for you. I know it's not the best way to raise a child..."

Debra lifted her face to the ocean breeze, gazing as far out into the blue expanse as she could, reaching with her mind and her vision into the past. Yesterday and today Jake had been on her mind. She was looking forward to seeing him again. *Jake's village, and Pia...*

She smiled. "I want to meet Pia sometime. What was she like?"

Her mother smiled broadly and tossed her own head, pushing her chin into the air for a fresh taste of the breeze. It was healing. Pia Mitchell had been just like that breeze, but putting it into words was a challenge. "Let's see. Pia was music, melody, song, dance, earth touching sky. Until I met the little thing, I hadn't believed Jake Highland's impudence in insisting a teenage girl had already bonded with Annie as her mother figure.

"The day I met Pia...well, let's see...she was holding Annie on her hip, stirring bean dip, singing, and dancing so that Annie laughed and laughed. It caught my heart, and it took my breath away all at once. When she saw me, she stopped still, but it was only like a rest in a measure of music.

"And to tell you the truth, my short visits to the Mitchells' were the highlight of life. When I'd pick Annie up at the end of the day, she'd be sleepy. Pia would have already told her a bedtime story, bathed her, and dressed her for bed. It made me feel like I hadn't taken anything away from her. And Annie never fussed. She always went right to bed. Sometimes she was asleep before we made it home. And then little Ben was there at the door first thing every morning, like clockwork. Six days a week, I didn't even feed her breakfast, just got her into her play clothes and kissed her good-bye."

Her mother's eyes were tearing, and Debra decided it was a good time to branch the conversation. "You asked about Michael and Caroline. Michael was like that, you know. He loved music. He sang or whistled or danced around, whatever he was doing. Caroline loved it! In fact, now I think it's fitting they stayed together. They were bonded like glue, those two. Maybe it was because he felt the same way I did about losing Annie, or maybe it was just the way they were. But I'm glad."

She noticed her mother was smiling again. "When you said that about Pia carrying Annie on her hip, it reminded me of a picture I took of Michael and Caroline. I'll have to show it to you sometime. But, you know, you're right. It is so good to talk to you now, to hear these things!"

Gail looked closely into her daughter's eyes. "Annie had a rich upbringing, but it sounds like it would have been just as wonderful had she stayed with you. But all in all, you are probably right. I'm glad she's here, and that she's yours again. But how did you face all that loss, Debra? How did you do it?"

"It's funny. All my life I'd had a fear of that. I'd been afraid to lose your good graces, but I did. And then I met Jake. He put my hand in God's hand, and I was left with a brand new future."

"How?"

"Well, Mamma, the more I learned about God, the more I loved him. And the more I loved him, the more I trusted him. It's like having your best friend right there with you all the time, and knowing nothing will ever change that, whatever happens. I realized that in every relationship or possession or government, or anything else we tend to trust, there is uncertainty. But where they might disappoint us or leave us, he won't.

"Giving Annie away would have been impossible without God. Going through that was like meeting wave after wave of loss, until finally I realized she was fine, and God knew where, even if I didn't. That realization was like having completed an obstacle course in a training camp. Then Caroline was born. Ten years later, only a little while before Michael and Caroline were killed, I began to feel those waves again—very strong. Later I realized it was a grace. When they were gone, I knew deep inside that Annie wasn't, and it kept me going. Herb's health took a dive after that, and I took care of him until he died. Then the waves came back, and that was shortly before I met Annie. I had dreams. I couldn't sleep sometimes. I felt she needed me."

"Did they stop when you met her?"

"No, but when we got to know each other they did. I should have connected the dots, but she told me she was definitely not adopted. She'd gotten into the habit of concealing her past. If she'd told me her maiden name sooner, I might have figured it out. As it was, I dismissed the idea as just another primrose path. I had imagined I'd seen her in a lot of girls—for years. I was good and tired of looking."

"I'm so sorry…"

Debra smiled at her mother, then pulled her into another hug and whispered, "But you're *so* forgiven!"

Debra

Debra couldn't remember when her feelings for Jake changed. Maybe, she told herself, it had only to do with the fact that they shared Annie. They had both considered her their own child, and they still did. How else, she asked herself, could one be so comfortable around a person and so unattached to them? She longed to see him now, if only to thank him for staying by her side when she was in the hospital. It took her days to gather the courage to call him. She waited till late in the day to phone him, making sure she would have some uninterrupted time alone in her room. It was the day before she and Annie would return home.

"Jake! How are you?"

"Debra…yes. I'm fine. It's been good here. I've been walking back into some old memories and putting them to rest. The village is where I first met Marjorie, you know."

"Hmm. No. I don't think I knew that." It was good to hear his voice. But why were they talking about Marjorie?

"I got some things worked through, I think," he said. "I needed to grieve." And then he changed the subject to ask, "How are you? How did the reunion go?"

"Oh, real well. I keep seeing you here, though. I guess I got used to talking to you every day. I miss that."

"That is probably because I've had moments here when I wanted to be there *so* badly!"

What did he mean? Oh. She laughed. "I'll bet you did. Meg told me how hot it was in the village—and hot *and* muggy in Louisiana. I want to hear the whole story, but yours will take longer to tell than mine, and mine's too long for the telephone."

"I know. I'm looking forward to seeing you tomorrow."

"Me too!"

There was a long pause before he said, "We'll be back in Atascadero around the same time. Maybe we can spend some time together."

"Let's do, Jake." Why couldn't she think of a question to ask? So much had happened. "Can you talk now, for a little while, I mean?" She did not want to hang up.

"Are you on the beach?"

"No. I'm in my room. It's quiet here. Where are you?"

"In the library. Are you holding up physically? Walking better?"

"Yes, better by the day. It's not a chore to walk here. And time with my parents has been good."

"Your parents don't think much of me, you know."

"They will."

"They'll think I'm crazy."

"Well, you are."

"And so, that's what you like about me?"

"Among other things."

Jake

Meg could have told Jake word for word what he told her that night at dinner.

She said, "I wish I'd written this all down so I could prove to you that I knew exactly what you were going to tell me tonight, Jake! The two of you are as transparent as water. Ah, but maybe it's just the writin' blood in me, tyin' things up all over the place that might not have any business being tied at all."

"Are you talking about Debra and me now, or something else?" Meg had a faraway look in her eyes, the one she got when she was deep into constructing one of her scenes. Jake imagined her fingers moving for a keyboard mirage on the table. "You've been writing again!"

"Guilty. But yes, you're right. It is something else I have on my mind now. It's Ben. He'd make a fine vicar in that little village, don't ya know."

Jake laughed, and then cocked his head. When he thought about it he could almost see it. Of course. Ben had been taking seminary courses. "Meg, you might be right. You're tying things up a little too quickly. How about we wait for Ben to bring the subject up himself, then we can tell him we knew all along."

Meg raised her water glass into the air. "Here's to that good idea, Friend Jake. Now, what's all this about Debra?"

"I thought you said *you* could tell *me.*"

"Okay then, I will. You've come to chat with me about the grieving process and how discombobulated you are regarding your feelings for Debra. That right?"

"Am I that transparent, as you say?"

Meg laughed. "No, Jake. Only to me, and probably to Annie, I'm guessing. Tell me, was it good, the little time you had at Ta-te? Have you thought about Marj lately?"

"Yes. I have memories of the village, and I relived them. I guess you could say I 'saw' her there. It was like putting the past away and rejoicing in it at the same time."

"That's a good way to look at it. I like that."

"But it's only been months, not even a year."

"How long did you know you were losing Marjorie, Jake?"

"It's been about three years, I guess."

"Well, for me it's been five, but mine was a shock, very sudden. I don't think there is a rule. I think there is just God, don't you?"

Meg

I noticed Ben was quieter than usual.

"We'll be leaving tomorrow," I said, trying to cheer him a little. "And the girls will be there to meet us. What's on your mind, Ben?"

"Annie, of course. But there's something else."

"Is it Ta-te?"

He shrugged. "They're my family."

I knew that Pia and her husband, Mark, had decided to transfer their orphanage ministry to the village. I remembered Pia's words: *"This is home. We will still travel, but I have always wished to come back. This is my family."*

I bit my tongue regarding my own notions of Ben returning. But I did allow myself to say, "Annie will help you make the right decision, Ben. With Pia there, they will be fine for a while. There will be another orphanage in Ta-te, and the music is back."

Ben smiled. He told me he was thinking of the colorful costumes and children's antics, kicking up dust and sand in the street. He told me he was thinking of Martin, his brother.

"He is a fine man, isn't he?" I said.

"He is the village. Their common blood has always been a spiritual blood. It's a special place."

"Makes you wonder, doesn't it, Ben?"

"You're editorializing again, Meg, aren't you?"

"I'm about to. In my experience, what the Lord redeems, He uses mightily."

The faraway look returned to Ben's face. "I've often thought I'd go back there, but I could never imagine it without Annie."

"We need to think about getting some sleep tonight. I'm sure you're anxious to get back to her, but try not to stay up till all hours."

"Thanks, Meg. I won't."

Ben

Ben's next thought caught him off guard. He wanted the village for his son and for Annie. Annie had been taken away too early. She needed the village now. So did he.

A sure knowledge settled in his soul, and he could not wait to e-mail his wife.

San Luis Obispo
Jake

Jake had a good view of the tarmac from his, Ben's, and Meg's perch on the outdoor airport balcony. From below he could see Annie and Debra waving to them. The women were both dressed in gaudy Hawaiian dresses and were jumping up and down in excitement. Meg said they looked like two little dolls, the kind you set on a shelf dressed in costumes from another land.

Jake drew in his breath, growing solemn as he watched their hair blowing freely in the breeze, their arms encircling each other. They looked carefree now; he hoped that meant Annie was finally at peace with her parents. Debra had told him as much, and it appeared it was true.

Debra was walking well now, it seemed, but the doctors had insisted she take at least a year off work. At a distance there did not appear to be any problem with her gait. She seemed to be moving quickly and easily. But what caused him pause was Debra's youthful appearance. This woman was more than fifteen years his junior, he realized. What was he doing, thinking about a future with her? She deserved more than the prospect of looking after an old man for the rest of her life.

They met at the baggage round, and Annie flew into Ben's waiting arms. Debra approached and met Meg in a grand hug. After that there was a general struggle after suitcases and bags, Jake's excuse to avoid Debra's eyes. It was Meg who solved the issue by saying, "We're on our way. I'll ride with the lovebirds over there. Jake, you take the RV. I'll have Ben drop me at your house. I don't know where it is. Is that all right?"

Jake was about to protest when Debra stepped in and said, "We'll see you there, then!" She grabbed Jake's hand and guided him to the parking lot before he had a chance to say anything. And they were in the RV and on the road before he did.

"You look wonderful, Deb. And you seem to be walking well now. Hawaii was good for you."

"Thanks! Long walks on the beach *were* good for me, I think."

"What will you do now, I mean, for work?"

"The folks were kind, Jake. They wanted Annie and me to take part of our inheritance now. I'll be able to go back to Bumpy Junket. I'm buying it."

"Where's that?"

"It's what we called our cabin. It's in the mountains north of Paso. Michael and I used to live there. It burned down, but I got in touch with the owners, and they said they rebuilt it. I'll go back there to live."

"You own the property?"

"I've made an offer. The owners live out of state, and they've been wanting to sell it. I'm just a little apprehensive about going back there alone. I know I want to. It's very clear that I'm supposed to. But it's remote. I'm hoping there are neighbors by now."

"Did Herb go there a lot?"

"He did. It was his getaway, I guess, before we moved there."

"I've been there."

"Really? It's beautiful, isn't it?"

"It's more than that. It's a place where you can clear your head and think. I almost hope there aren't any neighbors out there yet."

"Go with me! We'll find out."

Jake was quiet. But she took his hand then, and he looked at her. Before he could stop himself he said, "You're so young, Debra, and I'm confused." It was awkward. He did not want to release her hand, but at the same time he felt he had no right to hold it.

As though she read his thoughts, she squeezed his hand, lifted it for a kiss, and then released it. She whispered, "I know, Jake."

He had invited Meg and Debra to stay at his house. Nan would be there after work and they could all catch up. He decided talking about today's plans was a good way to change the subject. "We'll, uh, have a little time to visit before Nan gets home from work."

Debra said, "Good, because I want to hear all about your trip. Tomorrow Meg and I are driving the RV up to the cabin. Please come, Jake. We'll stay the night. There will be plenty of room. The cabin should be in order. What do you say?"

"I'd like to go back."

Debra

Hidden Valley Ranch, or Bumpy Junket as Debra called it, was almost entirely the same as Jake said he remembered it from when he'd first seen it with Herb over twenty-five years before. Time spun backward as they scaled the curves and tangles of the dirt road that cut deep into clay and shale mountains, and finally down into a quiet green valley.

When they arrived at the little cabin at the top of a hill, Jake was anxious to look down into the creek bed. It was running, but barely. He smiled and stretched, drinking in the quiet. It was still there, just as peace-giving and prophetic as it had been all those years before, and it rushed into his senses like an old, happy friend. "Glory!" he shouted, and the proclamation shot into the wide sky, splitting the silence for an instant until it echoed back and dissolved into the cool earth.

Debra smiled, drawing on memories beyond the hurdle of grief, but for her the feelings elicited by this remote place were more complex than Jake's, bittersweet even in the abrupt silence and solitude that at once soothed and invigorated the senses. She gazed out over the ridge toward the mountain where Michael and Caroline last hunted together. She had left so much of herself here. She'd not returned to see the place in rubble after the fire, and now she wondered whether she'd waited long enough. Was she ready for this?

The owners told her they'd tried to rebuild it just as it had been before the fire, and it looked as if they'd succeeded, disconcertingly so. It was the same, and that fact made her more than a little grateful to have her friends with her now. It would be easier to face this place with them.

In Hawaii buying the property had seemed the most natural thing to do next. But now that she was here, she did not want to be alone, and she knew she never would want to live here alone. Instinctively she walked into Jake's arms, giving him no choice but to close them around her. It seemed the most natural thing in the world, to be in his arms, and for a moment she felt courage settle in and calm her misgivings.

Meg

I caught a glimpse of the light embrace as I climbed out of the RV, so I ducked back inside, deciding to read for just a little while.

I knew Jack had seen me out of the corner of his eye, though, so after a minute had gone by, he called me out, saying, "We need you, Meg. Debra's got a hard thing to do, and she needs both of us now."

I exited the vehicle and locked arms with my two friends. We made our way to the cabin, opened the door, and looked inside....

Jake

Jake was first to speak, and he could not contain his surprise. "Debra! Are these yours? Is this your work?" All around—on tables, attached to the walls, and even on the floor, were sculptures. They included wildlife, people, and some simple designs that were pleasing, though not identifiable as any given thing at first glance.

Debra took a look around. "I guess they are. I'd left them in the shed. The owners must have gotten them out."

"I don't blame them," said Meg. "You don't hide a light under a rock, you know. These are something, Debra. They're really something."

"Meg, you've seen one, haven't you?"

"Yes, but I didn't know it had babies!"

Jake was laughing. The tiny cabin looked more like a gallery than a dwelling. It was amazing, like going into a room in Debra's heart he had not known existed. It was—as Meg intimated—like a room full of babies. Very precious babies, in various stages of development.

By then Debra had gone over to one of the sculptures and was running her finger along the lines, obviously deep in thought. Meg and Jake looked at each other, not knowing what to say. It was a long time before Debra looked up at them. She said, "Meg, Jake, here are Michael and Caroline."

On a corner table in front of Debra stood a three-foot rendering of a small girl sitting on top of her father's shoulders, reaching into heaven.

"Oh dear!" Meg gasped. "I've seen the miniature of this, haven't I?"

"Debra, you're ready to work again, aren't you?" said Jake. "This was awfully important to you, wasn't it?" He was only just now fully understanding.

"Oh yes, Jake. I'm ready, and yes. It's important to me. But I won't come back here alone. I'm not ready for that. I know that now. I feel a little foolish."

Jake thought of the stars and the quiet of a night many years before this, in this very place. He'd come here with Herb to decide whether he should make a promise to Debra and Michael. He had, and he'd kept it. It was a life-changing, almost life-long promise that seemed to have melded their hearts together. If only she were not so young....

"So, then," Meg said. "You can share my guest house with Charlie if you like. She's moving in with me. I told her I hated living alone, and there is no sense both of us suffering through such a thing. There is plenty of room for you to work there, and you can stay as long as you like."

"Thank you, Meg. I feel so foolish and wasteful, though. I thought I could live here, but alone, I don't think so." Debra was visibly distracted, her eyes still traveling through the scene of her past that stood around her in that room, each sculpture representing hours and hours of thoughts and feelings, most of which she'd all but forgotten about.

Suddenly her hands shot up to her face. "Oh my gosh!" She walked over to what looked like a wildlife statue set under a window in a corner, picked it up to get a closer look, and then carried it back to Meg, but in the process her hands trembled so that she stopped for a second to make sure her grip was steady before she handed it off to her friend. Meg accepted it, and saw that in this piece a tiny duckling was half hidden under the feathers of a swan, but it was blurry and almost imperceptible until she stared at it for a minute, just like Debra had been doing. Then it became very clearly what it was.

As Debra drew Meg's attention to the lines of the duckling by tracing them, she said, "I'd forgotten this one. It was meant to be something very different, one I never was able to complete. When I'd finished I was actually disgusted with myself because it didn't turn out as I'd wanted it to. But the fire must have changed it, I'm guessing. I was so frustrated, but I didn't destroy it that day because it was the day I quit trying."

She handed Meg the statue, saying, "Do you remember when we first met on the plane, Meg? The birds, the stories you told about the birds?"

"I do." Meg took the statue reverently in her hands and turned it around. It took a little while to focus and pick out the objects as a swan and a duck, but they were there, plain as day. "And I remember thinking Annie was the ugly duckling that was really a swan."

Jake was scratching his head. He'd stared at the statue long enough to see the swan and the duck. "But what is that they're standing on?"

"What do you mean?" asked Debra, and then she looked again. "Of course. I had been trying to make—well, the sculpture you see there." She pointed at the statue of Michael and Caroline. "But I'd been doing it at the wheel, so it would keep turning. The swan was going to be Annie on top of God's shoulders. It was my prayer, so those would be God's shoulders."

"So you didn't design it this way—that they're sitting on an eagle? You didn't mean to do that?"

"No. It's never me, not even when I work them still. It's never me. Don't you know that feeling, when you just make a beginning and you have a thought in mind, but you cannot even put it into words? It's like faith. You just pray, and when the knowing comes over you, you step out."

Meg nodded. "And you're always surprised."

"Yes, that's it. Only this one took almost twenty years to recognize."

Jake looked at Meg and then back at Debra, and then their eyes locked together. His heart pounded like drums inside his chest, but he managed to speak. "And faith is like marriage," he said slowly. "When you're sure that you know something, you pray and step out …together. And years later, if you continue to trust God, you look back and see that it really wasn't you, but God that made you one."

Meg excused herself quietly, saying she had to get something down in writing, and then she was going to take a quick nap or something.

Debra remained at the table, her hand tracing the eagle and the swan. She said, "When did you know, Jake?"

He took a deep breath before speaking, drinking in the reality of her gentle, near but almost ethereal frame, completely guileless and expectant. The bare truth of what she had just revealed reinforced his courage, even as his mind drew an image from the past. It was an image of an eagle, a lone herald on the edge of nowhere, holding his gaze steadily in reassurance—at the very moment before he left his past and fully accepted his future without doubt.

"When I saw the eagle," he answered her. "I was not absolutely sure until I saw the eagle." And then he reached across to accept her hand as she offered it to him.

Epilogue

Rebuilding from the Inside Out:
The Rev. Ben Mitchell installed as Ta-te's vicar
By Chelsea Andressen

Benito Mitchell never expected to return as vicar to the village he'd left at the age of seven, but last night he was installed as the Rev. Ben Mitchell, vicar of Ta-te, by the regional bishop, the Rt. Rev. John P. Sedgwick. He will replace the interim priest, Fr. William Proust.

Over two years ago, Mitchell revisited his childhood home with his friend, the Rev. Jakob Highland, who had been the mission's vicar for twenty-two years before transferring to San Luis Obispo. It was that visit that convinced Mitchell to finish his seminary studies and return to the village.

At the time Mitchell was employed as a social worker in San Luis Obispo. He had begun seminary courses, but had not decided whether he would go into full-time ministry. "We don't know what the Lord has in store for us," said Mitchell. "Most of us just keep putting one foot in front of the other, looking toward the light. I have to say that in this case, God's surprise was well thought out, and a delight. When my friends and I returned to the village last year it compelled me. It was then I decided to apply for the vicar's position here."

Mitchell recently completed his seminary studies, internship, and deaconate under the Rev. Jake Highland. "I know that I stand on the shoulders of giants," he said. "Jake is one of them. He has been my mentor, father, and friend, and he is the one who encouraged me to ask for this position."

Highland served a two-year term as vicar of the Ta-te mission over two decades ago. Villagers still affectionately call him "Da."

Fr. Mitchell and his wife, Anne, also a former resident of the village, will reside in the rectory with their son, Michael.

Author's Note

The idea for *Jakob's Promise* was born because I seemed to be collecting women friends who were finding their lost daughters after twenty to forty years of estrangement, due to their decision to give up their babies for adoption.

The concept intrigued me, and I began to notice my friends had several things in common. They remembered the birthdays, the time, and every tiny detail left to them, because they could keep this child only in their hearts. Even in our cast-it-off society, the effect of everything they'd gone through or relationship they had acquired since giving up their infant to adoption paled in comparison to their desire to know their child was okay. My intuition told me they longed for even more. They longed for relationship with their daughters.

The women I knew waited until their daughters contacted them, and after they did I noticed a joy and excitement that broke into these birth mothers' lives like summer on snow. Even so, it seemed to take the same courage they'd mustered at childbirth to meet their daughters as adults.

That discovery piqued my curiosity in the extreme.

Writers are told to write what they know, and I did not know firsthand what it felt like to bridge such a chasm as these women were called to bridge. So I asked them questions, and their answers transformed them in my mind back into young girls whose courage had to be taxed to the limit. Although I knew them in the natural as older women, I then saw them as children called to an unnatural task. It was as though I was allowed to see them lying in pieces on the floor, and to watch them carefully and slowly build themselves back into a shell of flesh until they were made to walk and talk and learn how to live all over again. Being a mother myself, I knew that is what they must have had to do.

As a reporter I had also done extensive work with a pro-life organization concerned with providing grief counseling to post-abortion women. The question surfaced in my mind: if it is so difficult to give a child up for adoption, how much more difficult to give it up to death? What if I contrasted the two? As a Christian, I knew that with Christ it was possible for these women to heal, and that is what I wanted to explore and then explain.

Pundits say what writers write is autobiographical, so I will admit here that I have experienced being pulled out of death into life after discouragement threatened to destroy me, and I know firsthand that the world's definition of life and the abundant life found in Christ are two very different things. Before Christ I thought I was alive. Afterward, I knew it.

To give the pundits their due, I did pull my characters together from bits and pieces of people I'd known or interviewed. After a while Debra, Annie, Ben, and Jake became my good friends, as they did Meg's. But fiction is fiction, and Meg is Meg, not me. And that's the fun and the fury of it all, because she could go places and do things I could not.

Writing *Jakob's Promise* reminded me of the experience of raising my children. Having poured my life into the effort for what at times seemed like an eternity, I finally sat back to see what they would become, because I had nothing more to give them save my prayers and hopes that the world would somehow be better because of their presence.

About the Author

SANDRA LUND grew up on the Central Coast of California and now lives in a small town in Idaho. She is a former newspaper reporter and columnist who still writes occasional stories and columns for her local paper. She and her husband, Tom, are the proud parents of three children and four (almost five) grandchildren. *Jakob's Promise* is her first novel.

You may write the author at jakobspromise@gmail.com.

www.oaktara.com

Breinigsville, PA USA
25 August 2010
244209BV00001B/65/P